Help Yourself

· * ¢ Ψ ? †

CASPAR ADDYMAN

Copyleft 2013 Caspar Addyman

This work is licensed under a Creative Commons Attribution-ShareAlike 3.0 Unported License.
http://creativecommons.org/licenses/by-sa/3.0/

In other words, help yourself.

Except those bits copyright the philosophers © 2003

ISBN: 1475199465
ISBN-13: 978-1475199468

This book will change your life. But only in subtle and insidious ways that you may never notice.

~

With a guide to the meaning of life, the universe and everything, thrown in at no extra cost.

For Ailsa, who wrote the bit about the horse.

PROLOGUE
THE FOOL ON THE HILL

•

A man stood on a hill. He looked up at the stars and tried to remember what on earth he was doing here. Why had he climbed this hill? Such memory lapses happened to him all the time when going from the living room to the kitchen, but this was the first time one had happened at the top of a big hill. It was a big hill. He was out of breath. Perhaps, he reflected, this was not the first time it had happened. After all, his memory was evidently less than reliable.

There was no fridge at the top of the hill, so he did not think he had come to get something out of it. There was no kettle to put on and nothing on which to put it. There were none of the makings of a cheese salad sandwich. It seemed increasingly unlikely that applying the insights of his previous kitchen-based amnesia was going to help here. Although, now that he thought about it, he could do with a nice cup of tea. And maybe some toast.

The man thought he had better sit down and think things through. There was a seat - the plastic bench at the bus stop where he had finally stopped walking. His kitchen would have been much better but he sat down anyway because he was tired. He had just walked several miles. Several miles in the rain and mostly uphill. He sat for a long time.

He soon forgot about his forgetfulness. He was not thinking of very much instead. Mostly he just sat there. Sometimes he prayed, sometimes he looked up at the stars, but mostly he just sat there. However, by the time he stood up he had come to a conclusion. It was time to stop taking his medication.

Moments later, a bus arrived at the bus stop and stopped to let two passengers off. The man got on it. He liked buses. Buses were good.

CHAPTER ONE
DEATH

XXXVIII.
One Moment in Annihilation's Waste,
One moment, of the Well of Life to taste--
The Stars are setting, and the Caravan
Starts for the dawn of Nothing--Oh, make haste!
– Edward Fitzgerald, The Rubaiyat of Omar Khayyam, 1859

* ¢

John Smith was dying again. It happens to even the truly greatest comedians. John Smith was not great. Truly, he was not even good. He wasn't terrible. There is something memorable and remarkable about a dreadful comedian. John Smith was forgettable, anyone who had to sit squirming through his obvious observations, over-contrived anecdotes and featherweight punchlines wanted to forget the experience. Occasionally he would get a few mercy laughs or the momentum of the previous performer would carry the audience laughing into his act. But tonight he killed them; he reduced the whole room to a deathly silence. Yet this would be the second best performance of his life.

The fantastic acoustics of the Covent Garden Comedy Club only enhanced the unpleasantness. Tombstones of silence marked the death of every gasped-out joke. Everyone in the room could hear everything with crystal clarity. They clearly wished they couldn't but no one was intervening to put John Smith out of their collective misery. Instead one hundred and thirty seven people squirmed uncomfortably in their seats, checking their watches or looking longingly toward the exit. In the darkness of back rows, friends exchanged pained looks while the people in the front rows, illuminated by the footlights were finding their shoes very interesting, desperate not to make eye contact with the condemned man before them.

The compere stood, sadistically impassive in the shadows, indulging his long-standing dislike of Smith; a largely irrational, highly visceral antipathy borne out of personal loathing and professional derision. Davie Wales had been on the stand-up circuit seventeen years; he had toiled through the apprenticeship and was now acknowledged by his peers as a senior member of their establishment. He was usually a generous mentor to struggling newcomers. Assuming there was some talent to nurture. He really hated mediocre no-hopers who did not know when to quit. He was a professional jester but he didn't suffer fools. Fools like Smith. He could not stand nor understand them. They must know that they were not funny. Being at the centre of a horror-show like this, stared down by nearly three hundred despising eyes ought to work its way into the mind of even the most self-obsessed egotists. After all, didn't they claim to be good at observation?

Attending your own funeral was an unusual thing to do voluntarily. It might be a thrilling experience, just once to dig your own grave and deliver your own death sentence in front of dozens of stony-faced mourners. Mourners whose only wish is to bury you quickly and piss on the grave. But why put yourself through repeatedly and why should everyone else suffer too? Why spend ten minutes every Saturday night making strangers hate you? Normally losers like Smith were only inflicted on small groups in tiny basement clubs or the upstairs rooms of pubs. Tonight, for some inexplicable reason, he was being allowed to make over a hundred new enemies all at once.

Davie could step in at any point and win the crowd back at the drop of a hat. If he wanted, he could do it at the expense of Smith and having the whole room laughing with him before he had even said a word. All he would have to do would be to walk onto the stage at a dead march. The tension would be burst as everyone felt the relief of release. He had done it many times before and it never failed. Tonight he was going to let the corpse swing a little longer before he cut it down.

He was not typically malicious but something about Smith got up his nose. Nothing in particular distinguished John Smith from any number of other unfunny wannabe comedians but Davie had taken an instant dislike to Smith when they had first met a few years ago. Perhaps it was the slight air of superiority and awkwardness with which Smith failed to fit in with the other comedians waiting to perform. Or perhaps it was that he was wearing on of those pathetic, supposedly amusing t-shirts. Davie could not remember but thought that this was exactly the sort of thing Smith might do. When Smith turned out to be as crap at telling jokes as he was wearing them, it had only cemented the hatred. Two years later and if anything, Smith was a shitter comedian but with a thicker skin that kept him coming back. Still, this was his biggest gig and this was the biggest fuck-up Davie could remember, maybe this would penetrate.

So he let Smith struggle on with some pathetic sequence of jokes about replacing the pieces in chess with different types of dinosaurs to make the game more interesting. Chess? For fuck's sake! Nobody would blame Davie if he went and broke a chair over the man's head. In fact, why hadn't anyone in the audience thrown anything yet? Or shouted him down?

The Saturday night crowd at the Covent Garden was comedy's bear-pit; multi-millionaire stars of American sitcoms had come off this stage in tears. Tears that were often mercifully hidden by the beer dripping down their perfect features. Yet tonight the audience sat in ominous silence. He hoped that this was not the calm before the storm, because if it blew up they might lose their entertainment licence. Westminster Council would be unlikely to let them continue trading after a lynching. But if silent treatment was enough to stop Smith from ever performing again, Davie was going to let the audience suffer a little longer. The rest of humanity would thank them in the long run. This first three minutes had been uncomfortably long enough for most.

Eric Hayle was more uncomfortable than most. Twenty minutes ago he had done a line of coke as long as his cock and it was starting to work its South American magic. Or it would be, if it wasn't for this fucker on the stage spoiling his buzz. He was tempted to leave. But gave up on the idea when he realised how much hassle it would be to try and explain to his party that they were leaving. He doubted that this Thai prostitute spoke much more than massage parlour English, and while Raoul, his favourite Brazilian rent-boy, was a very talented linguist, he was very petulant and would not leave without a scene. So Eric gave up and resigned himself to being trapped in a darkened basement, folded into a highly unergonomic chair. The Viagra he had popped was starting to make it's presence felt too. He tried distracting himself by texting Hans to see if the party was still on for later. When a Berlin fetish night comes to London you can never be entirely sure what might go down. And this was tolerably interesting in its own way. He had seen and done things a lot more unpleasant in his long life. As Mih or Liu or whatever her name was would probably find out later. His night was young. Eric Hayle was ninety-one years old.

Despite Davie's doubts, John Smith was not enjoying his evening much either, and to Davie's potential glee he was seriously considering his future. And he seemed to have a lot of time to do this in the gaps between the jokes. Gaps that in his interminable rehearsal he had left for laughs. Having practised so much for what was the largest showcase for his talent, he was unable to deviate from this timing. This was of course his problem. One of them. Poor timing was one thing, lack of decent material did not help, but having no discernible talent to showcase was the real iceberg to his Titanic comic pretensions.

Though his perpetual failure was more in the style of King Henry VIII's hopeless vanity, the Mary Rose. Never once had he got out of the comedy harbour before sinking under the weight of his over-preparation, his archaic jokes top-heavy with his intellectual arrogance. In real life, Smith had a dry sarcastic wit, he had the ability to make his friends laugh with arch and accurate dissection of the preoccupations of their small circle. This convinced him he was funny, and he was, though in a particular wordy and unworldly way. Sadly it was a brand of humour that did not sell well to the customers of the comedy store. Right now it was selling like hot cowpats.

He noticed the word 'OFF' on the handle of his microphone. At first he saw it just for what it was, a tiny white stencilled word on a black background. At the same time, he really 'saw' it, his vision focused down to a narrow beam, momentarily unaware of anything else in the room or anything else in his mind. And then as suddenly as it had arrived this fleeting moment of intense conscious experience was lost. He became aware of the room again and of all the people in it and of how they felt about him. He had lost track of where he was in his script. It was completely gone. He could not remember a single one of his jokes. (This was a good thing, though he had not yet realised it.) He became aware of a panic like none he had ever experienced before. His bowels had turned to ice water and his intestines were rearranging themselves to escape the cold. In the process they bustled uncomfortably against his stomach and pancreas, releasing acid and bile that rose alarmingly in his throat. His adrenal glands became aware of the commotion and flooded his body with adrenalin. It was this that saved him. And made him famous.

The audience had noticed that John had not said anything for nine seconds and a second is a long time in comedy. For the first three seconds they had assumed this to be an over-long pause. For the second three seconds they struggled to work out if this was some joke that they were failing to get. After sitting through the last three minutes, it was a feeling they were becoming accustomed to but they recognised this as something new. In the final three seconds they divided evenly between two camps. Those who thought and prayed this was the end and those who had registered the panic spreading across Smith's face. The second camp split into a faction who were feeling dreadful, stomachs knotted in sympathy with the poor performer and a faction of those who were starting to get excited in anticipation of an on-stage breakdown. Davie Wales and Eric Hayle were both in this last category but they would be disappointed and delighted respectively.

"Whoa!" Smith broke the silence but not the tension.

"A few moments ago I was wishing I was dead. I would have given my life to be anywhere but here, but now I am not so sure. I can feel my heart racing, like I have just escaped a race with a leopard. I feel great. I feel alive and I like it. I had a scare and I survived. But this is what I am wondering; Why is it that this is what it takes?" John knew that he had not quite worked out what he was trying to say so he went slowly. He saw it clearly in his head but had to untangle the thread to lead himself logically through it.

"Why is it that this is what it takes to make me wake up?" he continued. "To make me stop and look? To really look. I want to be clear here. I want to try and tell you what I mean because it has amazed me. Amazed me that I have never noticed this and I want to know if you are the same."

The uncertainty in the room indicated that, by and large they had absolutely no idea what he was talking about. It is unlikely that Smith had noticed this and it was even more unlikely that it would have mattered to him if he did. He was at this point mainly talking to himself. He carried on regardless, picking up the pace and pacing the stage.

"I have awoken to the moment. In my plodding life from past to future, I had never noticed 'now' before. Not before now, not properly. I had always gone along reflecting on what was going on or reacting to whatever had happened. But when you are reflecting or reacting you are attached to the past. Your attention is engaged with events that have already occurred. You might be getting something right, but you are lost to the world as it unfurls around you." Smith did not know exactly where he was heading but he had found his feet and was starting to warm to his theme.

"If I was not looking back, I was preparing to act. Planning for the future, which might be ten minutes from now, it might be next week or a couple of years. You are laying down waiting for the world to wash over you. Between the past and the future there is a tiny sliver in which we live. Except we do not use it to live, the present does not get a look in. We stand here, arranging the remains of the past into what we would like for our futures." He looked around the room. One usually could not see much beyond the stage lights and John could not see the people looking at him. But he knew from the silence that everyone was attending to his every action. It made him even more aware of himself, of what he was doing right at that moment. Everything was beyond real. Exactly the same but different, as if he had been seeing the world in black and white and the colour had switched on.

"I have just woken up to the present, I had always been absent from it because I was not paying attention to myself. Nor to the world. And it took the visceral shock of this death by comedy to make me spot it. I am not talking about living your dreams. That is trite American trash. Your dreams will always be implausible and distant.

Or else I was frozen in the amber of experience. You are either observing the world or looking inwards. It seems very hard to do both simultaneously. Yes, we have times when we are living 'for the moment', but these are the times we are most likely to be lost to ourselves. We are so wrapped up in our enjoyment of whatever intense pleasure it is that is pleasing us to reflect on the self that is experiencing this buzz. We do not pause on the dance-floor to take stock of our mental state; we do not become contemplative in the middle of the plunge of a bungee.

Or just now, as you were sitting there in the audience enjoying some comedy. Or you were originally back then before I messed it up. But after that, after it stopped being a performance. Then we've had to do something new and that has woken us up.

To put it another way. What is like to be you, sitting there right now, staring out of your eyes, thinking your thoughts? I cannot know, but most of the time you don't know either.

Because most of the time, it is not like anything. You just are. But you are unaware of who you are. You do not look inwards because the world is rushing past so fast on the outside that you are caught up in the experience of things rather than the experience of experience itself.

Do you know of anyone who has had cancer and has not had their life changed by it? Tragic isn't it, that it takes the face of death to wake people up to life. It would be more remarkable to find someone whose outlook on life wasn't changed by cancer. Who took it in their stride because they knew they were liable to die anyway."

John Smith was starting to enjoy himself. He was getting a reaction. He was figuring things out and able to explain them to the people in the audience. He took the luxury of looking round the room, becoming aware of his surroundings. He saw the 'OFF' switch again and stopped. It was turning back into a performance.

"No! Stop! Look, you are all getting comfy in your seats again. I am getting relaxed into telling you this shit. We are back to the beginning where you're the audience and I am the performer." He looked around. "Just a few moments ago we were all uncomfortable. It was not 'nice' but at least it made us think. Even if all you thought was 'I wish this idiot would quit it.'

"The rest of the time we are not really here to think. We prefer to play mental games. The comedians make you laugh and some of it may stick with you but mostly it's just a way to fill an evening. To take your mind off things. Well, it's a waste. But I am not saying it is the opposite either.

"I am not saying we should be alert and questioning at all times, going though life thinking about every little detail. It would be exhausting, impossible.

"Just as there is more to it than material goods, than power, status or even spiritual enlightenment. There is also more to it than that rational sense of purpose and need for explanations. There is something simpler; there is a need to be alive right now. To live for the moment, in the moment, of the moment.

"It is unrelenting and, as a consequence, we get tired, we get lazy. Lying in bed all day is one kind of laziness, but lying to yourself is far worse. We get swept up in the humdrum, the comprehensible and the everyday and our lives slide by without is even realising we are alive.

"That is all I have to say. All I should need to say."

The audience did not know how to respond, the whole event was unlike any performance they had ever attended. Their repertoire of ways to act in social situations did not provide a script that fitted what they had just witnessed. It was certainly not comedy and nor was it theatre so they did not think they should be clapping. And though it had something of a sermon about it, it was too impassioned to be left with respectful silence as they reflected on what they had been told. Likewise, it wasn't rabble rousing. This was more complex than something you'd get from a showboating politician deliberately inviting audience appreciation. So they dithered, they looked uncertainly about to see if anyone else would take the lead. For a few seconds nothing happened, and then one member of the audience started clapping. This was joined by someone else clapping faster and more enthusiastically.

Eric's companion Liu had not understood a single word of what had just occurred and consequentially was a good deal less confused than almost everyone else in the room. There was a lot she did not know about British culture. She had arrived here a year ago from Thailand on a student visa but never studied. Even before she arrived she had known that was sham; six months working in a Thai brothel teaches you to be realistic. Equally, she was pleased to have come, virtual slavery in England was far much preferable to virtual slavery in Thailand. When Eric had started to clap, she understood this must be the end of the show they had just seen and so joined in with the ostensible enthusiasm of someone whose profession is to please others.

Davie Wales did not really know what to do either. As the clapping died out, he went onto the stage, but arriving at the mic, his mind went blank. He could not think of anything more to say. There was one more act, the headliner, but during the clapping he had been signalling frantically to Davie that he did not want to go on. Davie could see his point; there was no joke that felt appropriate to the moment. In any case, some people had already decided that this was the end of the night and were getting up from their seats, manoeuvring themselves into their coats.

"That's it, thanks folks. See you next time," he said and left the stage.

Eric, tall, skinny but far from frail, elbowed his way through the crowds who were milling around the stage finishing their drinks. He approached the curtained doorway to the backstage area where John Smith, still in a daze, had not quite made it off the platform.

"Mr Smith, I have one very important question and I want you to answer me truthfully. Was that performance rehearsed or for real?"

"It was.. I.. well no, it just sort of happened, I guess. I said what I saw as I was seeing it."

Eric fixed him with a bright penetrating eye as he considered Smith's answer. He had been surrounded by ingratiating liars and yes-men for his whole life and he knew their sort. At times his own life had depended on being able to tell who to believe and who to trust. This lifetime of experience told him that this hapless buffoon was telling the truth. He was not some amazingly talented actor working from a dazzlingly original script. He really was a hapless buffoon who had in a moment of deep crisis stumbled across a profound personal insight and had the intelligence to express and communicate his experience. He was the genuine article, and that could be very marketable.

"Excellent, excellent! That is what I had hoped. I will be in touch, Mr Smith." And with that, the conversation was over. Eric's own highly developed sense of the preciousness of time had him impatient to get on to Hans' London Extravorgasma.

"Raoul, tell that dumb bitch we are leaving."

Smith was left standing even more bewildered than he had been thirty seconds previously.

"You don't know who that was, do you?" asked Davie Wales, who had been hovering nearby.

"No"

"Eric Hayle."

"Fuck me."

"Yes, he probably would."

•

The man had spent Saturday night laughing. He was rediscovering the world. He had forgotten what a wonderful place it was. What a funny place. Earlier in the day he had been to the supermarket. He had been there six hours and had a wonderful time looking at all the super things they were trying to sell him.

In fact, he had spent his afternoon in two different supermarkets. After a couple of hours they had thrown him out of the first one. Even though he had shown them his loyalty card. He wondered if, with that sort of treatment, he would remain loyal after all.

When he had first arrived at his regular supermarket it was almost overwhelming. How had he not noticed this before? It was so colourful and had so many different things. Or they had seemed different. He wanted to buy some toothpaste, but with so many choices he wondered how anyone ever made up their mind which kind they liked. He watched other shoppers for a while, but there was no brand that was universally acclaimed. People would hurry along the toiletries aisle, scan for the one they were looking for and hurry on. They were extremely sure of themselves. It would be a shame, he thought, if all your life you had stuck to using one particular toothpaste and never discovered another that you might have liked more. So he tried a few. This was when they had thrown him out.

Upset that they could treat a loyal customer in this way, he went to a rival of his normal supermarket to see how he would be received. The second supermarket was even bigger and no one noticed as he had spent four hours roaming its aisles. Here, he had chosen to try something new and take a trolley. It had been a revelation. He had spent the first hour just learning to drive it; gliding up and down the aisles, sliding it round corners, spinning it on the spot. You could not do any of this with a hand-basket.

The trolley solved the problem he had at the first place. The choice was overwhelming him. So many brands, so many variations within a brand. Would he prefer his toilet to smell of pine forests or of lavender? Would he prefer his Ribena to be reduced in sugar or with added vitamins? He even had difficulty with the vegetables. Each red pepper was individual and unique. Each aubergine bulged in subtly different directions. (Although they all had that pleasing bouncing baby texture and soothing hollow wobble as you tapped it.) He knew he would never get away if he was forced to choose. But with the trolley he could at least sample some of the vast range the world had to offer. He could take one jar of kosher peanut butter, one jar of diabetic peanut butter and one tub of organic satay and he would be able to compare them at home. Spreading them on rye bread, seven grain granary baps or poppy seed and loganberry bagels. One day his toilet could be lavender whilst his air was a refreshing pine, the next it could be the other way round. He man was carried away by the new opportunities and yes there were still choices to be made, even more of them in fact, but none had to be final. For every satsuma he selected, he was not forced to deny himself a pomegranate, as he might have done back in his basket days. He could have tinned peas and frozen peas. He could even have fresh peas but he did not like fresh peas. He was happy and four hours of the afternoon flew by as he granted himself all his wishes.

His trolley completely full, it was only as he stood in the queue to the checkout that he thought about the cost. Looking in his purse, he saw that he had seven pounds and a little change. He realised that this selection would cost more than that but fortunately he had his plastic. Unfortunately the shop did not accept any of the cards he tried to give them. It seemed that this chain would not accept any of the credit cards he tried to use. In fact they had kept quite a few of them, saying that the credit card companies had cancelled them. The man could not understand this because he never normally used any of these and so they should be as good as new. He filled in any form that got sent to him and had received five or six credit cards as a result but he never needed to use them. Normally he just got money out of the building society with his bankcard but the store wouldn't accept this either, apparently it could only get him money directly from his account. His House of Fraser store-cards weren't any good in this store either, which was a shame because he'd never found anywhere to use it. He had been signed up for it by a salesperson in some department store but he had forgotten which one and since that time he had never seen any Houses of Fraser. By this point the highly aggravated check out assistant had called her supervisor and shortly thereafter another security guard threw him out of his second supermarket of the day. Then it was quite late and the man, tired and distressed by his experience, had to be content with stopping at the late-night garage on the way home. Here he had bought a loaf of bread (sliced white being the only option), Rice Crispies and a pint of milk.

Now it was late evening and all the disappointments of earlier were forgotten and the man was happy again. For the last hour he had been sitting at his kitchen table crushing Rice Crispies. There was something so pleasing about picking up a single Crispie with your fingertips, something endlessly fascinating about bringing it up really close to your face and rolling it gently back and forth between your finger and thumb, studying at its uneven surface; where had it puffed up the most? Which end was bigger? Which was the biggest bubble? Some of the bubbles were so delicate that you could see through them into the middle of the Crispie and if you were not careful they could break. Of course, some of them had broken already in the bag; sometimes it would only be half a Crispie. There was not a lot you could do about that. That is just the way the world is.

He liked looking at the little Crispies, but even better than that he liked to get one of the good ones and squeezing and squeezing it until it collapsed in on itself in a cloud of Crispie dust. He liked the dust. Sometimes if he thought a particular Crispie was going to be a good one, he would put it on the kitchen table and press down with his thumb. Now when it burst he would not lose any dust and he could look to see what was left behind. Crispies are a pale yellow colour, when you crushed them you got Crispie crumbs and some white dust, but if you looked at the dust in the bottom of the bag it was all yellow. He spent a long time wondering about this. A lot of Crispies were crushed as he tried to figure out the secret of the dust.

Each Crispie was crushed individually. Each was a separate entity. For each he constructed its history, its Crispie biography. This turned boring very quickly as all the Crispies had a similar tale to tell. Born in a paddy field far, far away, living the simple rice life for a season before being harvested and transported overseas to a Rice Crispie factory. Where they were fortified with seven vitamins and iron, and baked in an oven till they bubbled and popped. Packed into bags and transported to the shop, some settling occurred in transit but it was an unremarkable part of their trans-continental life stories. The whole thing was, no doubt about it, a great adventure for an individual Crispie, but it was wearying to hear it so repetitively.

And yet they all popped so differently and he did not know why, they all lead similar lives and yet they bubbled up with great individuality. It was another Crispie mystery and many more Crispies were crushed as he tried to spot the patterns behind their variety.

He hit upon the idea of pretending they were little Crispie people. He had even tried drawing faces on the individual grains but this was not a success. He satisfied himself naming the ones that he thought would crush especially well. He gave them names of people who he would especially like to crush, the names of his enemies, names from The List. The List was his liturgy, he repeated it to calm himself down and because it had power. The List had begun a long time ago and the start of it was worn into his memory from thousands of repetitions and not even his more vibrant mind could confuse him on this but it was always getting longer. There were a lot of these people, too many to remember especially at times like now when he would get easily confused. But that's why he had his notebooks. He gave the Crispies names off The List and then he crushed them. There were a lot of Crispies but luckily, there were a lot of names on The List and it was being added to all the time.

He knew it wasn't really his place to smite them but he just *playing* God not *Playing God*.

*

John had spent much of Sunday staring at the ceiling of his bedroom. After his rousing call to action and experience the previous night, he felt dazed and unable to face much more of the world than the crumbling and discoloured plaster of his rented roof.

Partly he was exhausted by the bombshell of the previous evening but also by the need to attempt to watch the workings of his own mind. To try and reconnect with the immediacy he had felt on stage. The intense and singular sense of being himself right at that moment. He concentrated but every time he thought he had captured that feeling, it evaporated and he had to begin again.

In other cultures, his introspective sloth might have been called meditation and respected as a valuable tool for self-analysis. Brought up with the protestant work ethic, John merely felt guilt about his sojourn. He gave up chasing after a perfect crystalline appreciation of the present moment and let his mind wander more slothfully through his past. He wondered how he had ended up where he was now. Lying in a single bed that hadn't been changed all month, in a rented two room basement flat in a less pleasant part of Brixton.

John had always been differently motivated. Not exactly lazy, he was conscientious but unambitious. To him the phrase 'being driven' conjures up chauffeured limos rather than psychotic over-achieving. (Often, of course, the two go together.)

His childhood had been a happy one. If he stopped to think about it, this was a bit suspicious. It did not fit in with how his friends claimed they felt. The older they all got, the more dissatisfied they were about their childhoods. Which was another mystery. Surely the problems of an unhappy childhood should grow smaller as one moved further away from it in time?

Like a river flowing down from the mountains, he had always taken what appeared to be the path of least resistance, heedless of the rocky path and sudden falls this would lead to. He had often wondered at university and in his first years of work quite why it was that some of his contemporaries strove so very hard when there really was no immediate need. It was not until half a dozen years down the line when they were four levels above him in their careers that he realised that there really is no alternative to hard work. The trouble was that by the time he realised this, it would have taken even more hard work to have any chance of catching up with them. So until he had decided to try to turn himself into a stand up comedian, he had drifted moderately successfully through the world of offices.

A vocation was a weird and wondrous thing that in his mind was only possessed by priests. Even the word sounded ecclesiastical. There was, he always thought, something of the kindly parish priest about the earnest medics, vets and engineers who came to university having known for years what career they wanted and who happily shuffled towards it. Then there were others among his university contemporaries who were pathologically ambitious and had a definite air of zealotry about them as they chased after their perfect careers.

John was definitely more a career agnostic than a career atheist. He was put off applying for the investment banks, the management consultancies and the advertising agencies not by any strong political principles more by a dread of the company he would keep. A career with any of these large firms was the ultimate prize of a group of people whom John despised; the shiny-eyed capitalistas and proto-politicos who knew where they were going and so screw you. The law school had the lion's share of them but every course and subject had a couple of scarily serious careerists who always wore 'business casual', sat at the front in lectures and who by now, a decade out of college, probably sat on top of the world. Or, at the very least, they were firmly establishing their base camps, sucking up to and supporting the lofty careers of the rulers of the world.

At the time, he consoled himself that by resisting the bland attractions of accountancy, he would not gradually get drawn into this world and its way of thinking. But with the lack of any well-defined alternative he had in the end, with his fingers crossed behind his back, filled in a few application forms. It was only going to be temporary so it did not count. His first and only full time job after leaving university was with a medium sized global mega-corporation. An empire that sold groceries as if it were a military operation. Albeit with better technology and far more impressive logistics.

John had put on a grey suit and began life as a faceless drone toiling away in the trenches of 'the retail sector'. A foot soldier in the supermarket wars, doing his bit to help Sir Harold McIntyre and his band of bloated pinstriped sociopaths in their campaign to control the wallets and shopping baskets of the nation. He got the opportunity to travel to far away new towns and meet dull people. He had attended meetings with them. Long, dull meetings. John contributed to the dullness too; it was what was expected of him, what you were supposed to do. He did not think he was a dull person but that was the role he was expected to play. Occasionally, he thought he was being unfair to assume that his colleagues were no less bored and out of place than he. But stilted conversations in the gaps between meetings proved this to be untrue.

The job was easy but everyone he worked with had a very inflated sense of their own importance. John found it very difficult to build this false consciousness. Primarily, this was because his work compiling statistics on people grocery shopping habits was a continual reminder of the pointlessness and repetitiveness of mundane, everyday life. Each week he would produce another report on the regional whims of consumers. He would combine sales figures from across the regions into colourful pie charts that purported to explain why fish-pies were not selling in Cardiff, proposing patterns in the popularity of Rice Crispies or presenting figures showing which was the nation's favourite toothpaste. As one-off exercises these analyses were fairly meaningless snapshots of random local fluctuations. But to his managers they represented windows into the minds of their customers. Each week's figures were treated like holy scriptures and were analysed for their gnostic significance.

One day someone might come along and extract a lot of comedy from the office environment but John was not that person. Having lived through it, he felt that it was no laughing matter and besides as, he proved beyond question in the last two years, he was not a comedian.

Now, as of the night before, he was not even going to do unfunny impressions of one. Having failed at these diametrically opposed career paths. John did not know what he was going to do next but he did know that it would not involve travelling up and down the country trying to make people either laugh or yawn.

CHAPTER TWO
TRAINS

Rail Haiku

Light showers leave pools.
Laughing ducks paddle past us.
How I love the spring!

Sunshine bakes the rails.
Stuck! Seat heaters still heating.
How I love summer!

A single leaf falls
and we pause to admire it.
How I love autumn!

These snowflakes look wrong
and they frighten my iron horse.
How I love winter!

– Caspar Addyman

Ψ

Some people hate travelling by train. They see it as an unreliable, uncomfortable, and slow way to get from A to B. They are not without reason. Train companies do a lot to encourage this view; they continue to use forty year old trains that break down in the platform at station A, they leave rubbish aboard from the previous journey from station B to station A, once under way they go out of service at some station C which you had never heard of but at which you will spend the next hour waiting on the platform while they find a coach to take you the rest of the way, the coach will be unheated and the driver will have been specially instructed to drive slowly, taking the scenic route to try to make everyone feel better. Or, if by some happy accident it appears that your train may arrive on time, it will stop mysteriously for an impassive red light, just four hundred yards outside station B until the requisite two-thirds majority of passengers are crimson with fury.

Of course, there is absolutely nothing a traveller can do except console himself with exorbitantly overpriced cans of Tennent's Extra or start meticulously plotting the kidnap and torture of the fat controllers who run the railways. Those rich and doughy men who come on television to lie about 'every effort being made' and 'continual programmes of improvement'. Before being driven away in their chauffeured Jaguars to supervise the swimming pool installation people involved in the very real continual programmes of improvements to their country homes, paid for out of the fat productivity bonuses they made every effort to award themselves. And that portion of the travelling public that lets itself get madder and madder.

Having just picked his way through previous passengers detritus, David Gardner was in this category before he had even left station A (which in his case was London.) He had been down to the capital on business and had already today suffered one travelling incarceration at the hands of this rail company on his much delayed journey down. Then a day of hostile jostling in the energy-sapping metropolis had kept his anger and resentment alive and now he faced the prospect of returning slowly home on an antiquated train that had not been cleaned since the age of steam. He took the empty crisp packets off his chair, saw that there was no way to fit them in the minuscule inter-seat bin and so reluctantly threw them under his seat. He flopped down fuming.

There are other passengers who are more sanguine; they view each journey as an adventure, each setback and breakdown as an added amount of excitement and the long unexplained waits as an opportunity to bond with their fellow travellers. They love the uncertainty of an hour outside Stevenage with no information on the tannoy (sometimes because it is broken, but mostly because the crew have not got a clue either.) If these happy-go-lucky types are forced to get off the train at some place they have never heard of, they let the other two hundred passengers attempt huddle into the two replacement buses with seats for fifty, while they happily spend three pounds on a cup of tea and a digestive biscuit at the improbably named Ye Merrie Wayfarer station café. Then they attempt to engage in conversation the bored teenager who has just served their tea half in the cup, half in the saucer. Quizzing the resentful and monosyllabic teen, ever keen to find out all about the local area. At least this is better than having them sat next you on the train, their gleeful bonhomie throwing your own seething rage into sharp contrast and making everything ten times worse.

But as the perpetual optimists would be the first to point out, whenever these two types of traveller meet, it is always 'interesting'. Hazel Cole was one of this band of merry wayfarers and she had just sat down next to David.

"Wasn't that lucky? I was running late and I needn't have hurried anyway because they had cancelled my train," she offered.

"Me too but I was here on time," he threw back.

"There is probably a very good reason why they are having problems."

"If there is they are not sharing it with us, there have been no announcements whatsoever." David said with an unfriendly finality that he hoped would end this annoying conversation. There was indeed a silence from the grey haired old lady next to him as she started rummaging in her huge handbag. But that was not the last of her conversational gambits by any means.

"Need a light?" Hazel asked.

If this had been any other carriage on the train, such a mark would have met with righteous indignation and any other opening gambit with feigned deafness. In the smoking carriage the rules are different. One is allowed to smoke (obviously) and by some other unwritten rule, one is allowed to talk. Which is to say that, for whatever reason, people in smoking carriages are more chatty (and coughy and wheezy.) And although David was in absolutely no mood to be civil to anyone, something about the convivial atmosphere of smoke filled rooms and his need to let off some steam got his chin wagging. That and the fact that Hazel Cole was an utterly unthreatening looking old lady who happened to be able to get a conversation out the corpse at a Trappist funeral.

"I shouldn't have come by train, I knew it would break down. It only makes me mad, bloody useless."

"Ulcers?"

"Yes, as it happens."

"Ah, so you are an executive monkey"

"What?"

"Do you have ulcers?"

"Yes"

"Well there you are then!"

"I don't see how that makes me a monkey."

"In 1958, a man called Brady performed a very infamous experiment, where he had two groups of monkeys, Workers and Executives They lived in adjoining cages and every so often they would get an electric shock. The executives had a button in their cage to make it stop. That stopped it for the workers too. Both groups got exactly same number of shocks but it was the hectic executives that developed ulcers."

"You are saying I work too hard."

"Not quite. A man called Weiss performed another more subtle version of the experiment on rats. He divided them into several groups. Some getting inescapable shocks, some not, some could control their destiny and others were there as a 'control'. Their job was to do absolutely nothing and get no shocks and report how they felt at the end. These lucky rats probably thought they had died and gone to rat heaven. But chances are someone used these ones for some cortical dissection experiment where they see how well the rats function without large lumps of their brains. At which point they really would have died and gone to rat heaven. You wouldn't believe how many rats it takes to tell something that is kind of obvious with hindsight. In this case, they learnt that a combination of unpredictable stress and the illusion that you could do anything about them that had the worst effect."

"Like travelling by train?" David concluded, at last realising why this sweet if hectoring little old lady was telling such a gruesome story.

"Yes, And?"

"And so go by car?" he said, proving that he had not completely grasped her point just yet.

"That is along the right lines but that is not what I was thinking," she offered encouragingly, "What happens if you hit a traffic jam?"

"True! True! Well maybe I am screwed whatever I do?" David ended uncertainly, worrying if he should say 'screw' in front of this woman, who was clearly a schoolteacher, headmistress or something.

"Yes, maybe. But what you got right was that the way to deal with things you cannot control is to change your behaviour. There is nothing you can do about the state of the trains."

"Well, not much" David interrupted, his head filled with images of him kidnapping and torturing the rail executives responsible for this mess.

"So you have to change how you view of the problem. You change your behaviour in this situation."

"You are telling me I should not get mad? I can't help that! They do this every God-Damned time I travel." David snapped, starting to get mad again and not even caring if this headmistress slapped his wrists. In fact, maybe he would quite like it if she did. She was not so old as he had first thought; she had grey hair but it was still shiny and full-bodied and she had a lively face with bright hazel eyes, a clear complexion and what wrinkles she had, were more likes lines from smiling. She paused, watching him as his anger dissipated somewhat.

"But yes, if it is always like this I should be used to it by now."

Once David had let his guard down the rest was easy. Between London and Stevenage, Hazel had shown him that his real unhappiness came from his feeling that he was not in control of his own time. The demands of his job and his family made him feel that he had no choice about anything he did and so when things went slightly wrong and in ways beyond his control, like today with trains, it was too much. He snapped, he stressed and, as he now saw, he wasted even more energy railing against something implacable. Trying to rush in situations where it simply was not possible.

Now that he saw it in this light, he saw the same pattern in other low points in his life. Supplier delays that set his contracts behind schedule, clients who changed their minds, drivers who were moments too slow to pull off at traffic lights. He even realised he was furious about the rain delays at Wimbledon. He was unsure if he would quite follow this headmistress's advice about taking each delay as a little holiday for himself, but he conceded that his own fury was not helping him. It was amazing how, now that she had pointed it out, it was all so simple. He wondered why he never stopped to question what he was doing before. He supposed he had been in too much of a rush. But now thanks to Hazel, he was starting to realise that his life was not in fact a sequence of cruel tricks and it was mostly only his treating it as such which had made it such a trial. Taking a step back to include himself in the picture, he saw quite how much he contributed to his own unhappiness and in turn saw the opportunity to improve his own state of mind. As he thought some more, he got a little dizzy. It was simple to lay out in objective terms but as he switched from examining a situation to examining his reaction to it, he felt like his mind was getting tangled. It was like trying to see the back of you own head when standing between two parallel mirrors. It ought to be easy but every time you look round to one side, your own reflection gets in the way.

"You know, this has been a revelation to me. I had never thought about my life in these terms before. You know what you should do you should write a book about all this stuff."

"I have. It is being published this week."

Ψ

When Dr. Cole held the first copy of her book in her hands she allowed herself to feel proud. Throughout her career she had been published many times but only ever in academic journals and tomes. When she retired two years previously she had decided to write something more accessible.

She shuddered at the thought that is would be mistaken for a self-help book. She shuddered more that this is exactly what it was. It did not help her that she had lost the battle with the publisher and against her every wish they had called it 'Help Yourself'.

It attempted to demythologise the whole genre. To remove the cult of the personality from personality profiling. She did not want people to do what she told them because she had all the answers (which she did not) or because she had three degrees and two doctorates (which she did) nor because she was a self made millionaire with perfect teeth (which she wasn't - she wore dentures and had a clinical psychologist's pension). She wanted people to stop expecting to be given simple answers, to realize that the world is actually an extremely complicated place and that no expert could possibly know them better than they knew themselves. She hoped her readers would realise this and thank her when she told them that her book did not have the answers either and she was not going to solve their problems. That was the main problem with her book: it ultimately removed its own foundations. She hoped that she would succeed in being supportive enough that it would convince people that they could indeed support themselves but not so forthright that they dismiss her advice as an exercise in circular argument.

Though of course all these problems would only be problems if anyone actually buys the book.

~

And buy it they do, in their thousands. A goodly legion of others are more literal minded and steal it. Though she does not know this yet because it has not happened in her subjective time-line. I can tell you because we are floating above this book and you could have guessed anyway that a character would not appear here unless there was not some point to their existence from the point of view of plot development. Obviously this nice old woman is a counterpoint to that strange young man you met in the last chapter. Heck, it probably even tells you this on the fly-cover. (If it does, I lost my battle with my publisher.) So it is not as if I am giving away any surprises. If on the other hand, I told you that at the climax of the book he pushes her off a tall building then that would spoil things, so I will not do that. I cannot really tell you much about the man who pops up from time to time slightly unbalanced and confused by things. It would only confuse and unbalance you. However, do pay close attention to the duck in chapter five.

A note to the reader:

You are still with me this far in, for that I thank you. Especially now that I am trying your patience with these little asides. I am afraid there will be more interludes in the pages that follow. I did try to avoid it but in the end I was not clever enough to write it in such a way that everything flowed happily along from one phrase to the next. Therefore, all too often I shall interrupt myself and break my stride with trivia and digression that I have been too stupid to work into the body of the text. When you encounter a discontinuity such as this, I beg your indulgence and your pity. I hope that you will forgive my failings as an author and acknowledge that while he may not be the sharpest pencil in the case, at least your author is trying his feeble best. I hope also that you are able to follow the thread that I keep laying aside.

$$\Psi$$

If she was honest with herself, Hazel welcomed the opportunity to get out of the house. Since she retired two years previously she had nothing to do. One day she was visiting lecturer at two local universities and a clinical consultant in the mental health sector. Now she was talking to her plants and going half crazy. Writing a book about how to stay sane had been her way of staying sane.

Writing it had been hard. At first she had been too highbrow. She was oblivious to her own academic jargon. It seemed obvious to refer to hypotheses, experimental paradigms, neurotransmitter modulation, cognitive dissociation, existential self-actualisation and social constructivism. Fine for textbooks and journals but it would have been utterly discombobulating for the audience it was intended for. It needed a more popular tone.

She started again. This time she dictated it, imagining she was talking to someone like the man on the Great North Eastern Railway. She was all chatting to her fellow passengers and her book needed a more chatty tone. So she had imagined she was explaining her subject to him, or someone like him. Random imaginary train passengers seemed like the ideal test population. But this still didn't quite work.

A journey by train tends to be slow and seems to set the mind on train tracks too. Like David on her journey to York, doctor Cole's imaginary audience threw up a lot of objections to her helpful advice. Which she answered, at length. Her second draft had been far too long-winded. She needed another imaginary reader.

It would not have got through to the man on the proverbial Clapham Omnibus. Nor any other hassled commuter hurrying to work. He would not have time to listen as she attempted to patiently expostulate a complex but accessible story of how the world around us makes our minds out of the material of our brains. Before she even got beyond even a simple introduction, the man on the Clapham Omnibus would have leapt off the back of the still moving omnibus as it slowed somewhere along a busy high street, heading to work in a job he hates muttering about how one always gets the seat next to nutters on buses.

True enough, buses and nutters go together like horse and carriage. But there aren't nearly as many certified crazies amongst them as we think. It is just that types of normal than we are used to. Although, with the end of comprehensive mental health care, there are plenty of card-carrying service users out on the streets. And they do seem to share the impulse to hop on and off the buses whenever they can, entertaining the rest of us.

Her third draft was her last. Again, she had dictated it. Her breakthrough had come when she had visualised as her audience an archetypal television weatherman (or weatherwoman or weatherperson or whatever they were calling them these days).

She had never met one but had a clear image in her head. An amiable, slightly camp individual, a little too keen on clouds and knitwear, or at least able to fake enthusiasm for cumuli nimbi and hand-worsted merino for professional reasons.

Her everyweatherman, her man for all seasons was imagined as an intelligent person who could handle the ideas of interacting cycles of cause and effect, who understood that a certain level of unpredictability was inescapable but who needed the technical explanations in warm, reassuring sound bites.

He would be curious about the world around him but with only limited time and attention to give her because he needed to keep his eye on the sky, excited about a building storm. Fortunately, at its heart, Hazel's message was short and simple: You are the best person to help yourself.

As she saw it, everyone was a psychologist of sorts and an expert on their own condition. Even her most troubled patients knew themselves better then she ever would. Sadly that familiarity breeds contempt. The tricky bit was always persuading people that they could help themselves.

Weathermen were optimistic by temperament, it is an essential talent if you are to keep doing a job where every day your duty was to disappoint the British Public with the same depressing message; that they live on a wet and windy island in the North Atlantic that only gets two weeks of summer and one day of snow. That their island's weather is about as dull and depressing as you will get, absent of all extremes of summer heart and winter cold, no hurricane wind nor monsoon deluge, every day just another wet miserable Tuesday afternoon.

The message in a book about the human brain was essentially the same. Although great extremes of genius and retardation occurred, mostly we were average. Although we were capable on occasion of rare acts of compassion or aggression, mostly we were more temperate. Although we may be visited by extremes of sadness or joy, mostly we were slightly miserable.

The forecast in her book was not one of outright depression but it could be a disappointing one for someone who presumed to find the islands of their minds located in the Caribbean of existence. Likewise anyone hoping that a mere book might provide easy solutions was as out of their mind as someone who hoped to tow Britain south in a pedaloe. Help Yourself was a dose of reality and anyone who had understood it would probably come away with more questions than they started with.

So when Hazel rewrote her book for the third and final time, the long winding yarns of version two were trimmed down to size and her potentially depressing message was delivered in the cheery tones of Michael Fish or John Kettley.

INTERMISSION
TRAINSPOTTING

Trainspotting is not a lifestyle choice. You do not wake up one morning and decide that it would be cool to start spotting trains. It is something you feel from the very beginning. You are not interested in girls, you like trains.

It is not a phase, a rebellion or a form of mental illness. It is just a simple fact of nature. There are those people who like to watch trains and those who do not. As it happens, the trainspotters are in a minority and like all minorities they are victims of unwarranted prejudice. What the majority do determines what is 'normal', but 'abnormal' is not the same as wrong. Albert Einstein was abnormally good at sums and his sums were right. Isambard Kingdom Brunel was abnormally good at building bridges, viaducts and railway stations but no one ever laughed at him.

For a long time society has frowned on spotting. It is ridiculed and abhorred. Spotters are verbally and physically abused. All the social pressures are anti-spotting. People point and jeer. And yet still they spot. People laugh and novelists make cheap jokes about the anoraks and stereotypes. And yet still they spot.

Even among children the prejudice exists. It is an insult thrown around the playground. There are endless jokes and taunting accusations. A child who knows he is a trainspotter keeps quiet about it. Known or suspected spotters are always a target for bullying.

Parents are not much better. They can be highly unsympathetic. It is the last thing they want to hear, their son telling them that he is a spotter. They will angrily deny it or denounce their own flesh and blood. Or they may be more calm and outwardly supportive, but it still remains a family secret. And often the boy knows that deep down they hold onto the hope that it is just a phase. One day their son will meet a girl and his days of spotting will be forgotten. Just a youthful experimentation.

But if you are a trainspotter you know it is not like that. You know your love of rolling stock comes from deep within you. You see the numbers on that extra car in the Pullman's service and it excites you. You just cannot help yourself. You know a truth that other people cannot understand. Will not understand. They try to imagine what it must be like but the idea just disgusts them. You are not like them. Except you are just like them but for one simple fact; that you see something in the serial numbers of trains that they never will. This makes you an outsider.

One does not get seduced into the spotting lifestyle by its glamour, by the clothes or the accessories. Older boys do not pressure their younger peers into joining them down the end of the platform. It is not the allure of the large and shiny locomotives or the atmosphere of the station platform, though with time these become the things you love. The memories and associations they hold. But originally you go there because you cannot help yourself. You need it. You want it. You spot and it feels right. That number was what you needed.

Trainspotting is in the blood. It is biological but you will never find a 'spotting gene'. Spotting is a complex behaviour. And it does not define the spotter; it is just one facet of his character.

The stereotypes are just stereotypes. They will not all be wearing the same clothes, sporting the same haircuts. Two spotters are no more alike than two supporters of the same football team. They go to the same places at the same times, dressing somewhat alike and drawn by a common love but when they leave the stadium or the station they go in their different directions. Spotters are just you and I, but with different feelings about trains. You might be sitting next to one right now and you would never know.

There is nothing 'unnatural' about spotting. It is not a mental illness that can be cured, or a sin to be resisted. What could be sinful about it? It hurts no one; it does not frighten the iron horses. Why do non-spotters get so worked up about it anyway? What these people get up to in the obscurity of their station platforms is not affecting you. They are not waving it in your face or forcing it down your throat. They are not making you and your children join them in their unusual pastime. Trainspotters are just different and diversity is to be celebrated.

If you pass laws against it, you will not stop them. They might go Underground but still they will spot.

Yes, mature trainspotters will welcome and encourage youngsters. It is good that they do. They have lived it from the inside. They know what it is like. They know how difficult it is to be different from society's accepted norms. To have no one to turn to, in whom to confide your feelings, your fears. Or to ask those troubling questions about the transition from narrow to wide gauge tracks.

We need more spotterdarity. It is a tragedy that through the prejudices of others, people should become ashamed of who they really are. That they must hide themselves, remain closet spotters. Or act shy and furtive. You can spot them; anorak hoods raised and zipped right up to obscure their faces, they loiter only two thirds of the way down the platform, pathetically pretending that they are waiting for their train. How much more wonderful the out and proud spotter; his parka flapping open in the wind, pockets bulging with notebooks and Thermos flasks, he stands proudly at the very end of the platform a video camera in one hand, his huge Pentax resting majestically on its tripod.

CHAPTER THREE
MAGAZINES

Mephistopheles

My worthy Sir, you view affairs
Like other people, I'm afraid;
But we, more cunning in our cares,
Must take our joys before they fade.
– Goethe, *Faust I*

* ¢

John Smith had never been in a chauffeur driven limousine before. After yesterday's phone call from Eric Hayle's people, he had been expecting a car to collect him but it was something of a surprise when he answered the door to a uniformed driver. Looking past the driver, he saw the elegantly elongated Mercedes Benz parked in the road, its darkened glass making it look very glamorous. He followed the driver down the stairs and exultantly let him open the rear door for him. He hoped his neighbours could see him. He climbed in and made himself comfortable.

From the moment the door closed behind him it was obvious that this was Eric Hayle's personal limo. The floor of limousine was luxuriously carpeted in magazines. Thousands of them, strewn everywhere to such an extent that John could not see the carpet itself. It appeared that all the titles in Eric's stables were here from women's weekly gossip sheets to brash and flashy lad's mags. Pushing through them with his foot, John estimated that the carpet was four or five editions deep.

Among the more eye-catching were a fair number of more lurid fare from Eric's adult empire. And with a little digging John discovered a variety to these, from fairly tame tits and ass to things which (once he had looked close enough) John was sure were not legal in England and even some which did not seem anatomically possible.

This didn't seem out of line with what John knew about Eric Hayle and his business interests. He was most famous as a pornographer who could make the devil blush. Eric had originally built his fortune on the sort of filth John's feet were now resting on. Starting out as smut peddler in pre-war Soho and gradually extending his influence out from under these grimy counters into the more legal realms of the top shelves. From here he had built a more respectable career as the publisher of numerous other lower shelf magazines and for the last forty years he had also been the owner and proprietor of a national newspaper. A sleazy tabloid called The Clarion. As might have been expected it was a sensationalist and scurrilous scandal sheet.

Its stock in trade was the lurid sex and/or drugs scandal. But unlike its competitors it did not cover them with furtive and prurient mock-outrage. Preferring instead to condemn the lies and excuses more than the actual transgressions, which would be a little hypocritical given the Bacchanalian appetites of Eric himself. For that reason Eric went much more after politicians and media personalities than pop stars and footballers but he did not discriminate. Anyone who was newsworthy was newsworthy, and just as often Eric used it to pursue personal vendettas and persecute anyone who he felt deserved persecution. Nonetheless, The Clarion was very liberal politically, had been opposed to racism and sexism longer than any other paper on Fleet Street. (Which annoyed the feminist anti-pornography campaigners no end.)

He did not like religion and he did not like hypocrisy. It was rumoured that he had thrown one employee off the top of a tall building for printing an obsequious obituary of the fascist-appeasing Pope Pius XII. Like most rumours, it was the sort of scurrilous story put about by ones enemies that has just enough credibility to make people think twice. It was slightly more believable than the embellishment that he had first hit the poor man three times on the head with a golden hammer. Certainly, his editor at the time had fallen from a tall building and while not many people really believed Eric had pushed him, they all agreed that he had a very hands-on management style.

The man himself was fabled to be indestructible; more impervious to drugs than Keith Richards, more thirsty than Oliver Reed and with a bigger libido than an Italian football team. It was rumoured, that, in World War II, he had been some sort of double or triple agent. No one knew for certain not least because Eric had started most of the rumours himself. It was agreed that he had made enemies fairly evenly on all sides. But he had somehow managed to survive them all.

Survival came naturally to Eric. Currently into his tenth decade of life, he showed no signs of slowing down. He still kept a very firm grip on his business interests and partied just as hard as always. Nor was he getting left behind the times. Seven years previously he had been quick to adapt to the Internet age, moving a large part of his adult empire online and in the process becoming the world's oldest dot com millionaire.

John was impressed that Hayle had sent his own personal car and driver. There was enough space to seat at lest eight people, and you could accommodate a baker's dozen if a few were prepared to sit in each others laps. (Given who owned this car, it was not outside the realm of possibility, John reflected.) At the driver's end, the partition was built from a wall of LCD screens. They were all glowing brightly. Pulsing and flashing as the images continually changed. There was news, cartoons, scrolling stock prices, at least two separate computer screens and a soft-core porn channel. Leaning forward from his seat, John realised that the most boring programme was actually footage of him leaning forward from his seat. Looking about, he saw the camera in the upper left corner. There was another on the right and there were also a couple of mini-flood lights. These were not turned on at the moment, but he felt he could make a fairly good guess as to what they were there for.

It was only eleven in the morning but it was a day that he thought might go better with a stiff drink for breakfast. He located the inevitable mini-bar and poured himself a very large whiskey. He was pleased and impressed to find there was ice in the icebox. He leaned back in the plush seat and enjoyed the journey.

They pulled up outside an identi-kit corporate headquarters, or so Smith assumed because he had only ever been in one before and it had looked almost identical. He imagined they all looked like this. A brightly lit foyer with dull blue-grey carpeting, vivid green plants in large round brushed metal pots - real, but so perfect that they did a very good of convincing you they were fakes, just as the all the art along the grey walls was doing very expensive impressions of the kind of scribbles that proud parents stick to the fridge. At intervals, three or four huge black and chrome chairs congregated round low glass tables, looking superficially comfy but having been designed by some austere Scandinavian, anyone attempting to sit in one for more than a minute or two would discover they were all form and no function. Nothing gave away what the company actually did, and if it was not for the large black E H logo behind the receptionists stealth-bomber of a desk he could not have said this was even the right place. He did however wonder if our average multi-national always had such attractive receptionists.

After a few minutes of trying unsuccessfully make himself comfortable, it suddenly occurred to John that he had little idea why he was here. The phone call had said that Eric Hayle wanted to speak to him and would he come to the offices of the Clarion. Beyond that there was no explanation. John had asked but the assistant he was speaking to had pretty much indicated that she rarely knew Eric's reasons and that on the whole it was better not to ask. And it was better not to be late, therefore she had arranged to send the car. But it was only now that he was here that John tried to figure out why he was here. He did not get far before he was interrupted by a very grumpy man.

Peter Nickles was the most aggressive and obnoxious editor on Fleet Street. The editor of the Clarion, he was the second most unpleasant man in the British newspaper business and one of the poshest by far. He had the appearance of an Oofy Prosser or a Gussie Fink-Nottle (I always forget which is which.) One of those frog-like faces with protruding eyes, a big flabby neck and no discernible chin, his skin has the unappealing pallor of the undead. Add to that the fact that he had black brilliantine hair, looking like a nylon wig, its springy volume combed into a left-parted helmet and that his pear-shaped frame, was contained in a black three piece chalk-stripe suit with a red silk tie. It was as if he was a caricature of himself.

For the editor of a national newspaper to be sent to collect a visitor that no one had heard of was unheard of. So Peter Nickles was not a happy man and he did nothing to hide this from John. Gruffly indicating that Smith should follow him, he turned back around and without saying a single word.

John followed in silence as they took the lift to the main newsroom floor. It was noisier and messier than John had imagined but also in contrast to the offices he had worked in, there did seem to be a great deal of work going on. Almost everyone they saw was busy with something; hurrying about with piles of paper, talking on phones or typing furiously. They approached the middle of the newsroom floor. Hayle did not have an office in this building. Whenever he came to work here, he would pick a place he fancied sitting and throw its occupier out. Any complaints were always met with the same refrain.

"You are a journalist, aren't you? Go out and get me a fucking story."

They approached the desk that the tall, white-haired proprietor of Eric Hayle Publishing had chosen today. Nickles stood silently behind Hayle. John chose to do the same. He saw that Hayle was engrossed in some computer game; looking closer it appeared to involve shooting Nazis. Eric was enjoying it immensely.

Thanks to his perpetual dissembling and unrelenting refusal to take himself seriously, it was unclear what exactly Eric had done in the war. Every time he was asked about it he gave a different answer, all of them vague, implausible, impossible or immoral. Any given answer was usually a combination of at least three of these. What was known was that for the first few years he continued to produce pornography and did very well out of the black market but that shortly after the battle of Britain he was 'recruited' by Gordon Fowles, head of the war office counter intelligence and propaganda unit.

Fowles himself was usually described a 'bit of a character':

unorthodox, unpredictable and amazingly good at this job, running a department the main activities of which were lying, cheating, stealing and occasionally killing. He had an intense dislike of military men, politicians and civil servants. Every day people like this pestered him, so every day he had something to be angry about. That he was ultimately answerable to them made him even more angry. That he was undeniably one of them made him permanently apoplectic. Though even his closest friends speculated that he would still be angry, even absolved of all responsibility and rewarded with eternity in a heavenly paradise, though they wasted no time speculating how likely that was.

As much as possible, Fowles tried to staff his department with people as far removed from the traditional military or governmental types. And since they were in the middle of a war on nobody minded much because they had enough problems of their own. He recruited some of his best forgers, safecrackers and housebreakers from His Majesty's Prisons rather than His Army, His Navy or His Civil Service.

Although Eric had never been to prison, he certainly operated on the wrong side of the law. Eric, as the author and publisher of some of the most depraved and debased pornography a man could hope to buy, was just the sort of chap Fowles liked to hire. Since being a Soho porn baron was also one of the most profitable lines a gangster could be in, it was often, quite literally, a cut-throat business. Given the fierce competition and the dubious nature of their work, successful smut peddlers go to great lengths to keep their identities hidden. Up until then, Eric was one of most successful, so when he turned up to the print-shop with all set to run off five hundred copies of his latest offence against decency, a charming tale of an extremely well-proportioned and disciplinarian head-master of a girls boarding school, he was rather surprised to see a tall scowling man sitting on the press.

Fowles made Eric an offer that Eric was wise enough not to refuse. And he had spent the rest of the war in even murkier waters than he managed as a black marketeer. Eric enjoyed himself immensely and increased his wealth in the process. Whether he helped the war effort of any of the countries that employed him to do so is one of those hypothetical questions so beloved of historians that are in reality almost impossible to answer.

John Smith and Peter Nickles had stood behind Eric for ten seconds but there was no indication that he knew they were there. John watched, in fascination, as the famously aggressive editor of the Clarion stood meekly waiting for his boss to finish playing computer games.

"Eric?" Nickles eventually said with some trepidation in his voice. John decided to be even more afraid than he was a few minutes ago but congratulated himself on having had a drink on the way here.

Hayle ignored Nickles.

"Eric?"

"What the fuck do you want, nob-head?" Hayle said without turning round or slowing his slaughter of Nazi's.

"John Smith is here."

Still Hayle did not look round.

"Well bring him up here then, you dozy cunt."

"He's here."

Eric Hayle glanced back and noticed Smith, standing meekly

next to the second fiercest man on Fleet Street. He returned to his game, dispatched a few more of Hitler's henchmen and pressed pause.

Eric stopped and leaned in leeringly close to John. "Have you been drinking?"

"Yes, er, I had a, er, whiskey in your car," John offered timidly back, a tiny schoolboy whose headmaster was about to thrash him.

"Oh, right, okay." Eric paused. "Come on let's go, I hate these wankers."

He swept them out of the offices, barking at a few terrified employees along the way. Back in the limousine he poured them both whiskeys, twice as large as John had awarded himself. Tennessee's finest bourbon was splashed liberally about the back seat and John's clothes as Eric added large handfuls of ice to glasses that were already essentially full.

"Wigmore Street, Dave. Chop, chop."

"I own the rights to your... *performance* last Saturday. Did you know they videoed it?" Eric threw him a gold DVD, "Here, watch it, it's good."

"I am a major shareholder in the Covent Garden Comedy Club and so I did a deal with them to acquire the broadcast rights, you obviously have legal claim as the performer but.." He paused. "But I am getting ahead of myself. As I told you, I liked what you said. I related to it. I have lived my life like that. All of it. I feel the passing of time as intensely now as I ever did."

"Did you know I've faced a firing squad? Twice? A German

one and one of our own. The first time with the Germans, I didn't believe they were going to do it. They were sophisticated, they were officious, when they sprung the firing squad set up on me, I figured it was all part of their interrogation technique and I hadn't told them anything by that stage so I expected they would wait. Nonetheless, you do have a moment of doubt, you wonder if they are serious."

"I was more scared when it was our chaps. There had been a slight misunderstanding about the nature of my work. War is a very confusing time, the left hand does not know what the right hand is doing and everyone is suspicious of everyone-else, and even more people were suspicious of me, though I can't think why. I was in the hands of the regular army; dull, unimaginative people who follow orders unquestioningly even unto their deaths. I was on several charges and they would not let me explain or get a message through to any of my friends in positions of influence. They were just sleepwalking. They did not want to think for themselves. They were sleep-marching me to my death. Turned out all right on that occasion but it got my heart racing for a while. Anyway, I am getting off the point."

"I like what you said. I thought you were very effective when you were caught up in it. I saw you get through to the people in that audience. Your message is my message and I want to spread it. I am very rich and very successful so naturally most people despise me. That doesn't bother me because I despise most people. But, maybe I am getting sentimental in my old age because I can't help but think that if these clueless morons had a little more idea about their one chance at life they might do something with it rather than wasting it and we might all fucking better off as a result."

"I hadn't really thought about it," John managed to interject.

"No, you have. And what's more you can be quite persuasive. My trouble is that no one will listen to what I say precisely because it's me saying it. But you are nobody and nobody knows you so they'll pay attention if you tell them."

"I doubt it. Like you said, I am nobody. I'm not famous. And it was only an accident that I came out with all that on Saturday anyway."

"You are not famous yet. But that can change overnight. On November 21, 1963 no-one had heard of Lee Harvey Oswald."

John spluttered through a mouthful of bourbon that went down the wrong way. "You're not suggesting I shoot someone, are you?"

Eric paused as though he might be considering it. "No, though obviously if you did, you have got to think big. How about the Queen?" For a moment Eric was lost in reverie "No, at least not yet, that would get in the way of the message. Not that Oswald was the shooter but that's beside the point. The point is that you can become famous in no time at all. Give me a month and you'll be national front-page news and not just in the Clarion. Give me two months and you'll be on the front pages in countries you've never even heard of."

"And you are sure I don't have to shoot anyone?"

"No. Just do the same as you did on Saturday and I'll make the rest happen. Although there is one thing; just don't tell any fucking jokes." With this Eric climbed out of the car.

At first, John did not realise they had arrived. Not that he knew where they were going but they had only been in the limo a few minutes. From Fleet Street they had turned up the

Kingsway and at Holborn they had turned towards Oxford Street. But rather than negotiate its buses, taxis and reckless pedestrians, the driver was double-barrelling along the back streets. They were proceeding at speed slightly to the north and mostly parallel to Oxford Street. John had just seen a street sign telling him they had passed Harley Street and was thinking that he had never known where it was before now. If he ever needed to find it again he knew it was very near to wherever Eric was taking them because seconds later they had stopped and Eric was already climbing out of the vehicle.

They had stopped about half way along Wigmore Street, your everyday central London street, the buildings showing a wide lack of variety, each nondescript office building housing the unremarkable offices of lots of unremarkable little businesses. At street level a few Italian sandwich shops sold short-order lunches to all the financial advisers, market researchers and accountants, who liked to eat quickly before rushing back to their advising, researching and counting. And to all the quacks who popped round the corner from Harley Street between lucrative appointments. A couple of pizza restaurants and basement wine bars catered for the more leisurely lunches of bosses, secretaries and those with fewer work ethics. The same wine bar provided many a measure of after work relaxation and hosted all the special office occasions; Ian from sales' leaving do, Dominic joining from the Watford office, Judith on reception's birthday (age unspecified), Simon and Aileen's engagement (Karen being notably absent).

The street was also home to a number of unlikely upmarket specialist shops; a kitchen shop that only sold Japanese sushi knives and outrageously expensive copper pans (£42.95 for a coddling pot), a shop selling bathroom lighting, a music shop that only stocked choral music and recordings of organ recitals, and most perplexing of all a chandler, a saddler and a bagpipe makers, all next door to each other.

The car had stopped about half way along the street outside a Chinese dentist. Eric had got straight out and was crossing the road toward an old building that might have been a municipal library or a registry office. John could not think why they had come here, but confusion was a state he was becoming accustomed to, so he followed Eric anyway. Crossing the street, he looked for clues as to where they had come. The building Eric was heading for was most likely a couple of hundred years old, a large stone-built structure with strong Gothic verticals but only simple ornamentation, built before the Gothic revival ran rococo out of control. The stone was blackened by soot but this added more an air of neglect than menace.

Eric was already at the top of a set of eight wide stone steps that lead up to the solid double doors. They were almost twice his height and he had to turn and lean into one to get it open.

The building was only two storeys high with another smaller floor tucked into the eaves, its attic windows peeping out over a sturdy parapet. However, such was the scale of the place that this was level with the fifth floor of the building next door. This was due in part to the raised ground floor but more because in the grand and expansive style of the building, both the first and second storeys were at least double the height of the pragmatic modern building next door. Clearly the prosperity of London two hundred years ago had something to do with this. As the centre of world commerce and the biggest beneficiary of the industrial revolution, its architects were clearly required to make everything in giant size. Doors twice as tall as people and rooms proportioned to match.

John had crossed the street and now saw beside the door Eric was holding open a mottled and tarnished brass plaque that somewhat improbably and highly worryingly declared that this was 'Saint Helena's School for Girls.'

The man had not liked school. At aged eleven he had been sent away to boarding school because his mother could not cope with both him and her alcoholism. His father could not cope with personal relationships or anything that involved people showing their emotions. So he had solved half his problem by sending the boy away to school for someone else to look after him and ignored the other half by staying late at work while his wife nursed her demons.

The teachers, the housemaster and the matron were all kind and understanding of the boy but his fellow schoolboys were evil in the unceasing but unthinking way of childlike innocence. (Whoever it was who coined that phrase was never the slightly odd new boy or girl at an English boarding school. If he or she had been, she or he might have been a little less inclined to suffer the bastards.) The man was that boy.

He was an average scholar. He was bad at playing every sport they forced him to try and was not interested in following religiously any teams of professionals doing the same thing. He was prone to daydreaming in class, which infuriated his teachers, and when reminded where he was, the boy inclined to make unusual and off the wall statements that served to remind his peers to be unkind (because he was different). He had unfashionable enthusiasms. He liked trains and buses. He preferred chess to television. He could replay in his head all the games of the Fischer-Spassky match but he could not recite a single Monty Python sketch.

He was not actively bullied in the way that is traditionally described in tales of dormitory derring-do and dastardliness. No breathless wheezes like the ultimately harmless apple-pie bed and head down the lavatory. Children are more sophisticated, insidious and damaging than that.

Yes, there were physical attacks. Times when taunted to snapping point the boy hit out and was hit back, always coming out worse. Which was of course the aim of all those dead arms, wedgies and dead legs. Beatings without bruises that left him with no option of co-opting teacher intervention and left him stranded or maddened into unilateral lashing out, landing him in more trouble than sullen, aching silence.

But that was just boys being boys, far worse is when little boys (and little girls) turn to the psychological warfare. It is not the full flush of head held in a water closet that makes them crack. It is the gentle yet unrelenting tap, tap, tap of a Chinese water torture that gets results. A whispering campaign, death by a thousand cutting remarks, the intended victim always reminded that he or she was not their friend. There is no escape and no one to turn to.

The unpopular children cannot band together because the strength in numbers always comes on the side of the strong. They will set you against each other. You could go along with it in the hope of acceptance but they will always reject you in the end. Far better for oddballs to walk alone, each taking his turn as the figure of fun, unable to understand the inhumanity meted out to those to march to the beat of a different drum.

The housemaster had noticed that the boy was unpopular but there was not a great deal he could do. Any intervention would make things worse. Whatever lecture he delivered the boy would have to live with its ignorant interpretation once he was gone from the room. He knew the others did not need another reason to dislike the boy. So for twenty-four hours a day, the boy had no privacy and no escape.

The only time he felt anything approaching happiness was in the school chapel. The one thing he could do well was sing and the one place no one could make jokes at his expense was in the serious atmosphere of a service. Once he had joined the choir, he was in chapel and in rehearsals more than almost anywhere else. The highly ostensible religious attitude that the headmaster encouraged in his school was a probably less a deeply held moral imperative and more a calculated act of brand management, designed to keep this middle ranking public school saleable in the competitive world of private education. Either way it meant that being a chorister was an official badge of recognition and the commitment of the choristers was taken very seriously. The boy was a good singer and there was nowhere else he would rather be than the safety of the choir stalls so his attendance was impeccable. His termly singing report was the only one where his praises were sung.

He settled down into a defensive existence, not fitting in but surviving. He could not have fitted in, even if he had wanted to. It was the way his brain was wired, he would always be a lone gunman. And anyway, after two years of torment, he did not want to fit in.

At the age of thirteen, the scope of his concentration widened. He still obsessed about public transport and chess, but now in class he found he could now stop daydreaming long enough to pay attention. His marks improved and his report began to talk of previously unnoticed potential. In chapel too, the boy started paying attention, he noticed the words of the hymns he was singing and then his interest awakened he finally heard the words of the interminable sermons. It was Good News. He got religion.

It did not directly help his cause with his classmates. To them, the Cross was just another stick to beat him with. But now that he had seen the Light, he had a new way of coping, his own cross to bear.

* ¢

Praying this was not what it looked like, John followed Eric through the front doors of Saint Helena's School for Girls. The entrance hall was much as he expected a posh girls' school to look. High up the walls, the hallway was hung with varnished plaques listing over fifty years of head-girls, scholars and captains of the 1st XI dating back to the 1890's. Between these a number of stern, stiff backed Old Maids peered down from dark oil paintings. Former headmistresses, he guessed. He could imagine the vaulted hallway echoing to the sound of dozens of girls giggling and clattering their hockey sticks on the black and white tiled floor as they rushed to morning service. And sure enough the steps of the curving marble staircase were worn down as if by generations of hurrying feet.

Presently, however, the hallway was empty. The lights had been off before they entered and Eric was currently disabling some alarm system. John began to suspect that this was no longer a school for girls. The last entries on the boards of head-girls and scholars were from the 1950's and on inspection closer he realised that the artistic black and white photographs hung on the lower walls were celebrating the Sapphic tradition a little too exuberantly for even a British girls' boarding school. However, the thing that clinched it was the large statue in the alcove formed by the curving staircase. While John knew these posh schools valued a classical education, he very doubted that any a girls school would have such a large and detailed marble statue of Leda and the Swan. This, it seemed, was Eric's house.

A large closed door leading off to the right was still marked as the Headmistress's office. Another to the left declared that it led to a library and it was in this direction that Eric now headed. John trailed along.

The library itself had more of Eric's personality imposed upon it. A huge, double-height room about the size of a tennis court, it was filled with a cacophony of incongruous and inappropriate items. It still retained some semblance of a library. Oak bookshelves still covered most of the walls, particularly the upper level accessed from spiral staircases in opposite corners of the room. The shelves on this level ran round all four walls and were almost all filled with books and magazines. On the lower level, however, Eric's life had taken over. This was the main room of his house. He used it as an office, a studio, a bedroom and much more besides. On most of these shelves the books competed for space with an unclassifiable range of dubious looking items; small obscene figurines, large phalluses and other sex aids both ancient and modern, macabre Victorian medical curiosities pickled in formaldehyde and a few more innocent bits of modern art.

Along one of the shorter walls, the bookcases had been ripped out and replaced with a hi-tech zoo of plasma TV's, Hi-Fis, computer screens and other expensive looking electronic gadgetry. Beside this was a fully stocked zinc-topped bar that John doubted was an original feature. The opposite end of the room was arranged like a film set. Several large floodlights stood in an arc around a brightly coloured bed on a raised platform. Off to one side were various other large props, several cameras on tripods and a small crane with a microphone boom stood idle, waiting for another chance to capture sights and sounds offensive to decency.

A spectacular fireplace dominated the middle of the longer wall. A large oil painting hung above it and around which were arranged six massive sofas. It was difficult to determine which, if any, Eric favoured, as they were all littered with discarded books, magazines and newspapers. These formed into numerous piles at the foot of each sofa but many of the piles spilled like glaciers on the Persian carpet in the middle. A further drift of paper accumulated in and around the fireplace, much of it clearly flung there in anger.

Just beside this, Eric's desk was difficult to miss. A rosewood behemoth about 12 feet across and at least 6 feet deep. It was clearly of great age because the woodwork was very dark and worn and was covered in scars. Its upper surface was inlaid with red leather, which was also very heavily worn away. The desk and Eric's leather captain's chair was arranged so that he could watch the many screens on the end wall. Two more large screens were recessed into the surface of the desk, heedless of the destruction this had caused to what must have been a priceless antique. Perhaps the most noticeable things about it were the matching bondage stockades on either end. Two short leather upholstered benches to have been bolted on top of either end of the desk, each with a very sturdy set of stocks in front of it, and various other fastenings at what looked like strategic positions around the benches. The stocks also looked out into the room. Anyone with their head and hands placed in the stocks would be able to watch Eric's many televisions. While their posteriors would be at eye level and just with in the reach of an outreached hand for anyone sitting behind the desk.

As John stood staring, Eric had wandered over to the bar and was pouring himself another large bourbon.

"Another whiskey okay for you?" He shouted over to John. John was already woozy from two triple bourbons before noon but thought this question was probably not a question. Eric handed John an even larger drink and walked around the desk to his chair. John, ever mindful of the desk's less orthodox furniture was care as he selected his own seat opposite Eric.

"Right, let's get down to business. I want to make you very rich and very famous." Eric began.

"Okay," John said happily, the whiskey warming him from inside.

"Careful, people are not usually so quick to make a deal with the devil," Eric replied and it was possible that he was joking.

"Okay, what is it going to cost me?"

"Oh, no, I don't want anything from you. I am doing this because I want to and because I can afford to. I have money to burn." Eric said.

As if to prove this, he reached into his pocket and pulled out huge wad of fifty pound notes, which he brandished in John's face. He removed one and returned the other thirty of forty to his pocket. He unfolded it that John might study it more closely. Looking at this large, clownish bright red note, John tried to remember when if at all he had ever seen one before. He did not have much chance to study it before, by some sleight of hand he did not detect; one corner of it was alight. Eric tipped it down to let the flame catch more effectively and then used the smouldering sovereign to relight his cigar.

"I will stop burning them when they take that bitch's head off," he explained, leaving it ambiguous if he favoured a change to the currency or something more Cromwellian. He dropped the still lit note in a nearby waste-paper basket, starting a small fire.

"It is one of the few reasons I am pro-Europe. Not that their monopoly money is much better.' This lecture on constitutional politics was also illustrated with visual aids. Eric had removed a handful of brightly coloured notes from another pocket. He waved them briefly under John's nose and threw them in the bin. Eric seemed unconcerned by the small but costly fire now raging in his waste-paper basket.

Fortunately the basket was not a basket but a metal bin and judging by the interlinking scorched black rings on the Persian Rug, it was a trick he done a few times before. It was a trick. The first fifty quid had been genuine but the Euros were just monopoly money. The rug was real too, from somewhere and somewhen in the seventh century Persian Empire, but it was so old that it could not have been worth all that much.

"It will not cost you anything. I do not want anything from you. But there naturally are a few small conditions. Very small in comparison to what I am offering you."

"What are you offering me, exactly?"

"In cash terms?"

"Yes."

Eric's estimate of John's earnings in the first year was so obscene that it would double John's current lifetime income within a few weeks. He then outlined some of the conditions John ought to be aware of before accepting the deal. John was not really aware of these. His head was swimming. All this alcohol was a much stronger breakfast than he had been planning and the ridiculous wealth being dangled in front of his eyes had stopped his ears from working. Eric Hayle had made him an offer so fantastic that he probably ought to refuse no but such was John's shock that it did never crossed his mind to say no.

Not paid for his stand up comedy, the only current regular work that John had at the moment was as part of a medical trial on a new male contraceptive. Four months ago he had turned up at a teaching hospital, where an earnest genitourinary consultant had asked lots of personal questions, taken lots of blood samples and prodded him in lots of uncomfortable places. Finally he had to provide a 'sample'. He was shown into an unused private room with a lock on the door. He was told there were some 'visual materials' in a filing cabinet in the corner and some hand-cream in the adjoining bathroom. He had been given a 'wide-mouthed receptacle' in which was to 'put' his sample. And when he was done, he was to hand into the receptionist. Placing it in a discrete brown jiffy bag to spare both their embarrassment. And he was, of course, to wash his hands very carefully first to spare even greater embarrassment.

As he waited for his final tests, a courier came in and collected the jiffy bag, to whisk it away to wheresoever it was that they tested that kind of stuff. It turned out that his stuff was made of the right stuff. He passed all their tests and had been invited back to take part in the trial proper. A small hormonal implant was inserted under the skin of his upper arm and once a month he was to go back to provide another sample. At one hundred pounds a pop. He was now so nonchalant about it that sometimes he even forgot to wash his hands.

Despite its great comic potential, his current professional status was not something he cared to mention to people. In a rare moment of comic insight he saw that whatever cheap shots he could get out of it, if the likes of Davie Wales got hold of it, it would confirm a lot of the things he thought they thought about him and they would milk it dry. Ironic really, though the most ironic thing of all was that in the whole time he had been on the trial he had not had sex with anyone. But if Eric was serious about the scale of John's imminent wealth then, as soon as he started trying to spend it in any appreciable amount, he would have more trouble stopping people from attempting to have sex with him.

"So what do you say?" Eric picked up a single paged document from his desk, signed it and handed it to John, indicating were he should put his own signature.

"No."

"No?" For the first time today Eric looked intrigued.

"I want twice that."

"Fuck off kid, I made you a once in a lifetime offer, if you don't accept it, nobody else is going to offer you anything. Without me pushing you there is no 'you' and anyway I own the rights to that performance and without that there is no story. So, last chance. Take it or leave it."

"Oh.. okay."

"Good for you. Wise move, kid," Eric paused. "But I tell you what, I thought you were a spineless little loser but that stunt impressed me. I am going to give you what you just asked for. I want to turn you into something bigger than a rock-star so we had better get you acting like one." He took the contract back and picked up his pen. He crossed out one very large number and wrote in one twice as large before handing it back to John.

"Er.. thank you, thank you very much." said John and hurriedly signed his name.

"*Thank you very much*" Eric mimicked back to him mockingly. "Do you get what I've been telling you? That's very fucking rock and roll that is. Where's your ego? Act like you deserve it. You're a fucking rock-star not some mincing social sciences lecturer."

"Right."

"And that reminds me, we have got to do something about your fucking dress sense. Here take this." Eric reached into his other pocket and withdrew a thick clump of (real) fifty pound notes. He threw these across the desk and slightly embarrassed to be scrabbling round on the floor for money, John got down on the ground and picked them up.

"Do you know what it is like being rich and famous?" Eric called to him over his huge desk.

"Nice?" John ventured, peering up over the screens.

"It is even better than you would ever think. It is better than sex. Well that's not true, but it does not matter because if you're rich and famous you get more and better sex than you know what to do with. Which reminds me, there is one more thing. I want a blow job."

"Sorry I don't think I'm very good at them."

"Suit yourself. Well fuck off then. I have got some work to do."

John let himself out of Saint Helena's school for girls and flung himself into the Bricklayer's Arms. He really needed the comfort of a big drink.

INTERMISSION
SATAN WANTS YOU FOR A SUNBEAM

Satanism really gets my goat. It has got to be the most stupid religion going, and that's going some, because it is up against pretty strong competition. After all, before we invented moving pictures and with it the 'job' of being a movie star, there was no better way your average charismatic egotist could pass the long dark evenings than founding his own religion. And it seems there was never any shortage of idiots to follow them either. Charlie Chaplin and Walt Disney have probably done more to right religion than a whole crusade of Richard Dawkins could ever manage. Of course, these days your average wacko is more likely to want their own daytime talk show than their own religion, although the most freaked-out ones usually end up doing both and, hell, one look at the ratings tells you there's an ocean of eyeballs out there to just soaking it up. (Jesus Christ! - who am I trying to kid? I own a Bible, a Koran, the Tao Te Ching, the Analects and even a fucking TV!)

I will give them one thing though Your average Satanist is a good deal more interesting character than the herds of empty-headed dementedly happy couch-cattle and mooning Bible bashers who keep sending the cheques that keep Billy Graham and other crooks cut from the same cloth in the fine style they have become accustomed to. Those Lear jets don't come cheap and just keeping them stocked with champagne, caviar, coke and hookers costs more than Joe Christian earns in a lifetime. They all do it, believe me - when did you ever see the pope on a bus?

Incidentally, this just shows that Elvis is above all that. My friend Chip knew this guy who'd seen the King in a K-Mart. The King is a true man of the people. Who has ever seen Gandhi dining in Denny's? Answer me that. And as for the King of the Kings, no one's seen him slumming it for two thousand years.

But I digress..

As I was saying, I grant you that the Devil does have all the best tunes and his followers throw the best parties. Just trying scoring anything the stronger Sanatogen at a Cliff Richard concert and forget about that blow-job in the car-park from some sweet young thing coming out of a Creed concert, she maybe filled with the Holy Spirit, but..(well, there's no need to get crude). Try telling me that is better than a Iron Maiden rite or a Black Sabbath Black Sabbath, where the air is chemically enhanced, people beat you up if you don't ask them for drugs and where you'll have been anally raped before you've had your first speed-ball. I still have the needle marks in my eyeballs and the bite marks on my scrotum. Oh, happy days!

But it's one thing to go to the concerts. Joining the Satan fan club offers a bum deal. Just say no.

"I'll swap you 24 years of Earthly Power for your Eternal Soul?"

"Yeah right, sign me up!"

Satanism *seems* great with its orgies, its blood rituals and those really cool black clothes, but you would think that folks would read to the bottom of the contract before signing their souls away to some swarthy dago daemon with natty dress sense and prominent eyebrows. Face it, if anyone is going to have access to good lawyers, it's going to be the Prince of

Darkness. You don't stand a chance. Remember, there are no 'good' lawyers. Hell! - to make it easier he doesn't even make a secret of being evil - you are bound to be double-crossed. (I dislike the single-crossed too - but I'm not here to diss the Christians. Not today, anyway.) So, it has been known for people to diddle the devil, and if you think you are the next Giraldus of Einsiedeln, go right ahead. All I can say is that if you think you are smarter than Satan then you are more stupid than you seem and deserve the Eternity in torment. Ironically, "the Cardinal Sin of Satanism" is stupidity! Oops! It would be a bit late to find that out once you've already paid your subscription.

There is precious little evidence that the Dark Lord delivers. Where are all these Satanists reaping their benefits and raping the rest of us? Can you think of even one Fortune 500 CEO who wears black leather capes and has a pentagram tattooed on his throat? I've checked and there isn't one. It appears that none of the world's richest men needed any demonic help. I would estimate that there is not one billionaire out there intent on world domination and in league with Beelzebub to enslave and frustrate the world. They're more interested in yachts.

Still, that's hardly the point. These imbecilic Satanists want to serve and protect the Evil One. They are aware of his Darkness and embrace it willingly. They all want to be Satan's little helpers. They make a big deal of the will to power, their innate superiority and their contempt for the weak. How odd then that they are mostly embittered social misfits and sexual inadequates. (Orgies are ugly people's way of getting more sex. And while they might provide a certain physical stimulation and hydraulic release - they have no passion, no energy and no value.) So these Satanists boast about their supposed intelligence and awareness of 'reality', yet they want to use magick and borrow the temporal power of the malevolent Lord of the Underworld without realising that there's no such thing as a free metaphysical lunch and you-know-who is going to want unnatural supernatural payback. Hell, they can't even spell magic.

In common with most religions, Satanism has its demonology and hate figures. Indeed if anything their hatreds and 'enemies' are more honest and rational than those of the many splintered protestants, Catholics, Muslims and beyond. The Ian Paisleys, the Ayatollahs, the vicars of Rome are never happier than when denouncing each other for being papists, abortionists, liberals or unbelievers. (It is not the Satanists who keep me awake at night, it's these other guys.) There is no shortage of hatred in the world. At least the Satanists channel it into improving their own Earthly existence and leave me alone. If - God forbid - any of the world's religions happens to be right then, whichever one it turns out to be, there will remain 95% of us who are headed for hell. At least the Satanists want to come with us!

But God dammit, if you believe you have a soul in the first place, the decision to hang on to it, in case you may ever need it, ought not to be difficult one. The whole Christian religion is set up for lost sheep, repentance and the hypocrisy of deathbed conversions. And the more you've got to forgive the better. "Without the shedding of blood there is no forgiveness" (Hebrews 9:22) and there'd be more rejoicing in Heaven over the last minute admission of a Stalin than there would be for a Gandhi. At least Satan has standards.

But you need your own soul to join his party, and telling Lucifer that you have changed your mind about being his perpetual servant and asking if he wouldn't be a poppet and let you have yours back, just isn't going to work, even if you catch him on a good day. Indeed - it is for just such occasions that he practices the deep, mocking laugh for which he is rightly famous.

Believe in evil and you are believing in good too. Once you believe in absolute values and judgement, then it's obvious that you have to behave. Just as you can't have dark without light, you can't have good without evil. But if so, it shouldn't be too difficult to choose the right one. [Hint: Look up their dictionary definitions.] When picking your team, it is worth noticing that all major world theologies have happy endings. That is the point of them after all, reassurance that the world isn't a cold, impersonal rock floating in empty space. If you seek to rebel, seek to think the unthinkable. That might be a challenging place to start. What sort of loser doesn't want to be on the winning team?

Of course, maybe there are no Satanists? Maybe there isn't anyone that idiotic? Maybe it is all fear and propaganda put about by god-mongers intent on subjugation of credulous masses? Maybe Satan himself was created by those so intent on righting wrongs that they wrongly see rites?

I don't want to come over some hand-wringing theist moralist or supercilious nihilist belittling the little people. I have been to Dark Masses and ritualistic orgies, I've seen the Temple of Set from the inside. Sure - I signed something on the way in, but it was perfectly innocent, just a standard disclaimer; You can understand how Black Mages want to protect themselves against frivolous lawsuits from prissy pseudo-Satanists suing because they got the blood of a virgin on their black Armani. I'm not stupid - I read it and there was nothing duplicitous about it - all pretty standard stuff. - *'I disclaim this...', 'I abandon that...', 'I submit to the rulings of Azrael', 'My immortal essence is thine in perpetuity'.* Blah! Blah! Blah! Typical legalistic mumbo-jumbo! Totally anachronistic really. Parts of it were in Latin, for Heaven's sake! I signed it but I doubt it has any legal validity and besides it wasn't even in my own blood.

Daed si laup .. Daed si laup..

CHAPTER FOUR
TELEVISION

I find television to be very educating. Every time somebody turns on the set, I go in the other room and read a book.
– Groucho Marx

Ψ ?

Hazel Cole had never been in a chauffeur driven limousine before. After yesterday's phone call from Shona's personal assistant, she had been expecting a car to collect her but it was something of a surprise when she answered the door to a uniformed driver. Looking past the driver, she saw the absurdly elongated American beast parked in the road, its darkened glass making it look very menacing. She followed the driver down the stairs and reluctantly let him open the rear door for her. She hoped her neighbours could not see her. She climbed in but could not make herself comfortable.

From the moment the door closed behind her it was obvious that she would not be able to travel like this. Unable to find the door handle, she tapped on the darkened window to the driver, not realising straight away that he could not see her. She fumbled with the door some more and succeeded in opening it and climbing out, just as the driver had got round to the other side of the vehicle, climbed in and closed his own door. He took off his peaked cap, placing it on the seat next to him, fastened his belt and turned the key. He checked the offside mirror out of habit and was leaning forward to peer out of his window and check that it was safe to pull into traffic when he found his view was obscured by a person. The same person he had just seated in the rear of the car. Doctor Cole was tapping on his window. The chauffeur pressed the button to lower it.

"I don't suppose you would mind if I sat up front with you would you? I did not like it back there."

He was delighted. Brian had got into driving because he enjoyed talking to people. When he started to get bored of the short hops and repetitiveness of taxi work, he had discovered through a friend that he could make a similar living driving fleet cars for a private hire company. A lot of it was dull too, but for the last year he had regular work for Shona's television company. He enjoyed ferrying minor celebs and other daytime guests to and from their homes and the studios. The studios were north of London, just beyond the M25, and it was a rare journey that did not take at least an hour. Since he also drove the same individuals home, it was wonderful to be able to continue his interview after they had appeared on the show. And because it was television, there was no shortage of interesting passengers, always welcoming another chance to talk about themselves. Tales he could then re-tell to his friends down the Flying Pig. It was Brian's dream job. At least it used to be when he drove a simple executive saloon, but as her ratings had grown Shona had started having delusions of Oprah and had insisted all guests were collected in American black limos. Brian was cut off from conversation by the formal atmosphere and the privacy divider.

"I know what you mean. Hop in," he said cheerfully, removing his cap from the passenger seat.

At the studios, Shona reviewed the running-order for this morning's show. It was all the usual crap. Slightly famous guests with something to sell or promote: A soap star discussing her first serious role, an obscure shrink with a book to plug, and some reality-TV D-lister having to come to terms with the reality that most of the country hated him. It was not exactly Oprah, but she knew that people tuned in to see her, not her guests. Shona preferred it if none of them could outshine her. That did not look like it was going to be a problem today. But it meant that Shona would have to carry the show herself. That was fine. She was as hyped as ever.

The journey from Hazel's house in Peterborough to the studios flew by. Hazel and Brian hit it off instantly. She tried to tell Brian about the psychologist who had put several taxi drivers in a brain scanner. They each had an enlarged hippocampus; the organ of memory, that holds the knowledge of locations and directions. Naturally, being a taxi driver, Brian had heard all about it and this triggered his own reminisces about his early days learning the routes round London. From there, their conversation took many twists and turns.

Brian was having such a good journey that he got carried away. Forgetting that he was talking to a grey-haired old professor, he accidentally told her the story of having to carry a paralytic Spice Girl into her flat and help her change out of her vomit splattered clothes. Hazel did not mind. It took her mind off the butterflies in her own stomach.

•

The man had been a London bus driver once. He had driven a Routemaster. It was a London icon, and he had really enjoyed the job, pleased to be associated with this moveable capital landmark and proud to be doing an important job, carrying London to and from work. Working for London Transport was one of the first times in his life he felt that he had friends, that he was accepted. He got on with his colleagues but he appreciated the distance. He would only see his fellow bus drivers occasionally in the depot or as their paths crossed out on the routes. The conductors he was paired with were generally busy on the runs so he had privacy during the day, sitting up in the cab of this large, useful and friendly machine. He even joined an break-time chess league that ran at the depot. There were some strong players and the man enjoyed a friendly rivalry with several of his fellow drivers. For several years he was very happy.

Unfortunately things turned bad for the man when the buses were deregulated. A private contractor took over the man's routes and depot and, although initially they all kept their jobs, matters went rapidly off the road. The company rearranged the shifts and the timetables so that the drivers had to work harder and had less chance to fraternise with each other. It was only about twenty minutes longer on the road each day but it was that little bit too much. Many of the drivers felt they were pushed too far and were more exhausted than they had been. The changes also meant that shifts often began or ended at the other end of the route. Meaning a driver would have to travel home on his own time. Drivers usually lived near the depots, which was how they had been assigned when they first got the jobs, so starting and finishing work at the depot left them close to home. The new scheme effectively lengthened the working day for the already over-worked drivers.

It did, of course, mean the company needed fewer drivers and initially they were able to reduce the numbers through early retirements and voluntary redundancies. Thereby increasing the profits. But whatever they did one year just raised the bar for their productivity the next. The new bus company was always looking for ways to cut its costs. Naturally enough the Routemasters and their costly surplus headcount were the next to go. Half the Routemaster fleet was replaced with driver-only buses. Conductors were given the choice of retraining as drivers or talking a walk. As a relatively new driver, the man was transferred to the driver-only buses. And it was this change that led to him getting the sack.

Ironically for someone who would shortly later be locked up in a secure mental unit for aggravated assault, the man had lost his job as a bus driver for being too nice. Although the new buses were ugly and utilitarian, they were no harder to driver than the Routemasters. The man quickly adapted to the new vehicles. He could not however adapt to his new dual role as driver and conductor. Firstly, he lost that meditative privacy of a separate booth, where he could concentrate solely on the driving, now he was far more easily distracted by passengers talking to him or merely standing close by in his peripheral vision. He had a couple of accidents and a few near misses. Worse yet, the man was a not man to be dealing with the general public. He tried to be friendly but he never quite got the tone right. All to often he would misread a passenger's cheery hello as an invitation to start a conversation and the bus would often be held up as the slightly bemused passenger tried to cut him off. By far the greatest concern to the bus company, the man was terrible at dealing with fare-dodgers. A victim of bullying all his life, the man had no experience of standing up for himself or telling people what to do. If someone wanted to get aboard his bus without paying, he was happy to let them. The company, however, were not happy and after two warnings and two failed opportunities to adapt the company's 'productivity centred ethos', the man was sacked. It was to be the last time the man ever worked for The Man.

Ψ ?

Shona's assistant, Alice, had talked Hazel through everything carefully. Hazel would be asked a little about the book and a little about herself. There was always the chance that Shona would latch onto something she said and launch into an anecdote of her own, reinterpreting whatever the guest was saying in terms that related better to her. Apparently the audience related to this too, or at least didn't seem to tire of Shona's unhappy childhood. So if a digression came, it was best if Hazel were to go along with it and just agree with everything Shona said. A look of panic that flickered across Alice's face as she said this. Hazel took careful note.

"Thank you, Maggie Daniels. Later on I will be talking to 'Orrible 'Enry recently evicted from 'The Oil Rig'. But right now I am pleased to welcome onto the show, Dr. Hazel Cole." Shona said, standing to greet her guest and giving her perfect TV smile. She wasn't in the least bit pleased. These shrinks always made her uneasy. You never knew how much they knew about you.

"Dr Cole is a psychiatrist, who.."

"Psychologist actually, it's slightly different." Hazel interrupted, smiling sweetly.

"Oh God," thought Shona, "Not one of these pedantic medical types. They are always uncooperative, monosyllabic and make crap television."

Shona smiled sweetly back. "I've just finished reading your new book, 'Help Yourself' " She hadn't. In fact, she hadn't read any of it; she hadn't even seen it before picking it up just now for the benefit of camera three. At lunchtime yesterday, the show's producer had flung a copy at some flunky with instructions to read it and prepare some intelligent questions for Shona to ask.

"Did you like it?" Hazel asked. This was not right. It was Shona who asked the questions and the guests who replied. Those were the rules of the game and any guest desperate enough to appear on this kind of show should surely know that?

"I loved it!" How could she? But it was another rule of the show to be uncritically gushing about everything. Anyway the junior researcher's questions would let Shona bluff her way through. She consulted the bullet points.

"So you are saying we can all be thinner, fitter, better people?"

"No, nothing like that," said Hazel.

The office junior hadn't read it either. He had been out extremely late the night before to some newly opened club and got lucky with a stunning girl who worked in public relations. He had not slept at all last night and he was hoping to see her again that night. To be prepared he was planning to hide in a guest dressing room and spend the afternoon catching up on his sleep. He had flicked through Help Yourself, but the words were floating off the page, so in the end he had just copied and pasted the questions from the notes for another self-help guru they had had on the show half a year ago.

"Treating yourself to a new outfit improves your self-confidence," Shona asked uncertainly, having scanned down her crib for something in the summary that seemed most likely to her.

"You haven't read it have you?" Hazel suggested, still smiling sweetly.

From there, it degenerated badly. And unfortunately for Shona, having just come back from the commercial break, there were many awkward and uncomfortable minutes before the producer could come to her rescue. (What she never found out was that he let the section run on longer than he needed to because car-crashes were always such compelling television.)

The final section with 'Orrible 'Enry had gone moderately well and coming off the set Shona was slightly calmer than she had been during the debacle with the head doctor. But now as she played back the show in her mind she relived the bad bits. Her stomach dropped as she recalled how Hazel had made a fool of her. Shona did not like being mocked. She channelled her anger at her perceived humiliation into righteous indignation and very quickly had turned the situation round in her head. She picked up the copy of the accursed book and looked at the gentle smiling face of Hazel on the back and read the blurb beneath that listed Hazels many qualifications and her time working in psychiatric hospitals.

Slowly it began to make sense to Shona. That shrink had deliberately set out to make Shona look stupid. On her own show! Just so people would think how clever the doctor was and buy her stupid book. The scheming and devious old biddy. You would never suspect it to look at her. But this was so clearly what happened. She would not get away with it. You did not get your own show on daytime television without knowing how to stand up for yourself. Shona was not about to let this insult pass. She grabbed the offending book, had a short scream and stomped out of her rooms and down the corridor.

Shona exploded into Hazel Cole's dressing room.

"I suppose you think it's clever to trick me on my own television show, do you?" She screamed, brandishing 'Help Yourself' as if it were damning evidence.

Hazel Cole had lived through stand-up shouting matches with psychopathic multiple murderers, so she was not intimidated by a furious chat show host.

"I wasn't trying to trick you. I think there must have been some misunderstanding. I am sorry. I expect you get a lot of guests and it must be hard to keep track of everything?" Hazel asked in a clear and steady tone that calmed Shona somewhat.

"Yes, I have to do everything round here or, as you see, it all goes wrong. So it doesn't help if you try to catch me out!" Shona added, remembering that she was still mad.

"I am sorry." Hazel knew better than to argue the point. Instead, she changed the subject "But I bet you've always had to do everything haven't you? Were you the oldest of your brothers and sisters?"

"Second. But my older brother was no use. Just like my dad."

"And it was a big family?"

"Two little brothers, four little sisters and just me and my mum to look after them."

"Yes?" Hazel had calmed the woman in front of her and now sought to draw her out.

For Shona, talking about herself was one of her favourite ways to pass the time but it was rare to find anyone who actually listened. Properly listened and knew when to ask questions or when to let her carry on. Hazel had forty years of professional experience of doing precisely that. Shona talked for a long time. Hazel listened.

•

The man did not own a television that worked. The eight he did own had fallen victim to his inquiring mind. This was probably a good thing because television was not good for someone in his condition. There was too much happening at once. He had always had trouble concentrating and television seemed to be edited to make it impossible for him to follow. The constantly changing sequence of shots and scenes left him reeling. Especially all the hidden messages.

He had once videoed the news and very carefully gone through it using the pause button. He had filled a whole notebook from just the secret codes hidden in that one 15 minute morning news program. He often wondered who the messages were for. It was too much for one person. It had taken him a whole day to go through that one program and there were more news broadcasts almost hourly.

Maybe each code was just to communicate with just one group or person and they were all unaware of each other? How many people was that, out there receiving these instructions? How many more were there these days of satellite and cable? Back when he had done his investigation there were just four television channels and the computer graphics were very simple. Now there was far more crammed into each frame of each program and there were hundreds of channels readily accessible. As he understood it there were over six channels that showed nothing but news twenty-four hours a day. It made his head spin just to think of it.

$$\Psi\ ?$$

After leaving Hazel's dressing room Shona had gone back to her own room, hurrying so no-one would notice her tear-stained face. She locked the door, blew her nose and opened her copy of Help Yourself on the first page. She finished it that same night and the next morning she arrived at the studio carrying two dozen copies. A dozen were given out at the production meeting and everyone on the show was ordered to read it. The other dozen were couriered to (in this order) her agent, her two best friends, her mother, several other friends and two of her sisters. Her other sister, her brother and her father did not receive a copy. (She had learnt a lot from Dr. Cole's book, but it would not work miracles.)

CHAPTER FIVE
CLUBS, A DUCK, TWO WHORES
AND SOME DRUGS

> I wouldn't recommend sex, drugs, alcohol or insanity for everyone, but they've always worked for me.
> – Hunter S. Thompson

*

Eric had asked John to meet him at his club, Black's. John had a great deal of trouble finding it, hidden away at the centre of the maze of Soho. He had even more trouble persuading the openly incredulous bouncers that he was actually supposed to be there. Black's was a club of the very darkest night. Although it was not a nightclub as such. So black that it was off the radar of most of the party crowd.

The footballers and soap stars did not like its poshness, preferring places that were more classy*. Truly huge A-list celebrities eschewed it too. At least it was avoided by those global superstars who burned brightly in the oxygen of publicity. They found its strict privacy policy suffocating. It was the sort of place that River Phoenix wouldn't have been caught dead in. It had its fair share of famous patrons but few of them ever appeared on the front pages of tabloids. And if they came here to party it was because they preferred to keep it that way. Black's celebrities were known for their cerebrity.

On any given evening it was a lot more tedious than the

---
* An oxymoron if ever there was one.

gullible readers for star stalking magazines would care to believe. And if ever they went there they would hate it. The dance floor was only open from Thursday to Saturday evenings but the well-stocked, oak-panelled library was open twenty-four hours a day, seven days a week. Black's did have a first class cocktail bar and an excellent private restaurant that served the best confit of duck in the whole of London. Whatever that was.

Once John had negotiated the distrustful door staff things went more smoothly. Like those who had successfully convinced Saint Peter of their credentials, John found that on the inside, everyone was falling over themselves to help him. A liveried concierge, familiar with his kind, took this confused soul under his wing. Delicately interrogating John he ascertained who he was and what mistake had let him into Elysium. He informed John that Eric had been here earlier but had been called away. He guided John gently into the bar and entrusted him to higher powers.

The barman wore a different uniform. He was clearly in charge of the next cloud up. A plush, well-appointed cloud with thick black carpets and deep red décor. In contrast to the sparking lights of the bar with its smoked glass counter and mirrors, the rest of the room appeared very dark. There were lots of little lights cleverly hidden in the moulded fittings but the subtle light they seemed not to travel very far before being absorbed by the soft dark furnishings. The big dark suede sofas, gathered in four or five well spaced groups, looked too comfy to get up from. Although it must have been possible because currently they were all empty. There were about a dozen stools lined up along the bar; two were in use. Other than John and the barman (the concierge having evaporated) the only occupants of the bar were two young women. Two beautiful blonde angels, who were drinking cocktails at the far right end of the bar.

Out of instinct John headed to the furthest stool on the far left end of the bar. Nevertheless the woman facing his direction caught his eye and smiled. Her smile dazzled and discombobulated him. She leaned into her friend and whispered something. Now her friend also turned round and having to work a little harder also caught John's eye and offered him an equally dazzling smile. John was still too disorientated to react so cast around for assistance. He found it in the form of the cocktail list. He studied it intently without taking in a single word.

"Good evening, sir. ... Sir?"

John became aware that the barman was talking to him.

"Hello."

"Your first time at Black's?"

"It's that obvious?"

"Not at all, but you do seem a bit confused by our drinks menu."

"Yes, what would you recommend?"

"Will you be dining with us, sir?"

"Yes, does that matter?"

"The food at Black's is very rich so you would be advised to start with a short, sharp astringent drink like a whiskey sour or our pomegranate margarita?"

"Erm," John stalled as he hunted these on the menu.

"Or perhaps a simple gin and tonic?"

"No, a whiskey sour sounds great." John had never had either of these but thought that a whiskey sour sounded safest.

The barman moved away and proceeded to make an elaborate fuss over the preparation of his drink. John remembered how to read and found his drink in the menu. Whiskey and lemon juice didn't sound too bad. Though perhaps there were secret unmentioned ingredients because the barman was making a surprising amount of fuss. But maybe that was what made it cost fifteen pounds a glass.

John was ready with his wallet when his cloudy brown drink was placed in front of him.

"Don't worry sir, it's on Mr Hayle's account."

"Right, thank you."

John's first tentative sip was of a drink that didn't really taste of whiskey or of lemon juice. In fact, it tasted fantastic and his second mouthful was more ambitious. He was fortunate to have swallowed it before he noticed that the two blondes had walked over to where he was sitting.

"Hello," said the blonde on the left.

"Hh," said John.

"Hello," said the blonde on the right.

"Hh," said John.

Jayne and Sam taken individually were far beyond any

ordinary man's hopes even to fantasise about. For it would be too unrealistic, too far removed from his experience for him to extrapolate into this stratospheric league. That they were enthusiastically introducing themselves to John, who until a few weeks ago had been an ordinary man, was not getting through to his higher brain at all. Some dusty circuits in a primal part of his brain, starved of sexual contact of any kind for the last six months, had blown. From the moment his cognitive functions had registered that they were talking to him, he'd become paralysed from the neck upwards.

Jayne was a natural blond, as she would gigglingly offer to prove to John any number of times more that night. Sam told him later that she had gone blonde for professional reasons but for other reasons connected with her profession she had no means of proving this. They were both much more intelligent than either men or women normally gave them credit for. Whether for this reason, or some other, they often found that men's intelligence dropped considerably in their company.

"I'm Sam," said Sam.

John managed to nod.

"I'm Jayne," said Jayne.

John managed another nod.

"You're that philosophy friend of Eric's aren't you?" continued Sam.

"He told us all about you," finished Jayne.

"You know Eric?" The shock made him forget that he'd forgotten how to speak.

"Oh yes! Of course," said Sam and for some reason Jayne found this very amusing.

"We were just talking to him now. He was very insistent that we should meet you." Now it was Sam's turn to laugh. "He said he wouldn't be gone long, why don't you join us until then? We can introduce ourselves."

"We don't need Uncle Eric to look after us do we?" said Sam.

"Yes, good idea. I'm John, by the way."

"Yes, we know." They said it in unison and broke into simultaneous laughter.

•

It had started out as a good idea. The man was sure of that.

His flat was a mess and that was making him uneasy. He knew he was prone to getting confused especially once he was already confused. He knew his own mental state just as well as any of his many, many doctors. He disagreed that it was a medical condition. Tidying the flat would be a good way to clear his mind. And once his mind was clear, he would be able to think straight again. Simple really.

The trouble was that his flat, in reality no more than a bedsit, was as cluttered and confused as he was. And it wasn't very easy to know where to begin. It had been getting harder the longer he left the problem. He'd wanted to be methodical. That was important, he'd learnt that from the doctors. But the lack of space made it difficult to keep things orderly and the problem fed on itself. An empty room is, to a first approximation, tidy. A nearly empty room isn't that far off either, whichever way you arrange the few things it contains.

But each new thing you add to a room adds exponentially to the ways they can be arranged. Collect any items over any length of time and you will have untidiness. And all the while the second law of thermodynamics is adding dust, decay and disorder to the pile. Housework is a never-ending war with entropy. And entropy will always win in the end.

Nature abhors the vacuuming.

The man did not even own a vacuum cleaner. But he intended to bring order to the chaos. He could see that his sanity partly depended upon it.

His flat was in even greater disarray than normal. The five broken televisions were lost under shifting strata of newspapers. The floors and all the other surfaces were carpeted in an autumn forest of free leaflets and flyers, collected on the man's daily perambulations but mostly unread. From the waist upwards, his kitchenette was not too bad. The tiny dining table regularly got swept clear for the man to unfold his treasure maps. The cooker and kettle were accessible and the tiny amount of available work surface was too small to support major chaos. Sure, the sink was full of dirty crockery but it wasn't overflowing and it wasn't full of dirty dishwater. (The man had lost the plug for the sink ages ago.) His cupboards were a terrible mess but that was why cupboards had doors.

The kitchen floor on the other hand was not for the faint hearted or the barefooted. Toast, crushed up Crispies, teabags that had missed the bin and other interesting detritus all jostled together with a growing community of stains. The black and white floor tiles were occasionally visible but it was an even bet which was which.

We shall not speak of the bathroom.

The man did not consider himself an untidy or unhygienic person. But the medication made it hard for him to keep on top of things. It meant that he had lacked the energy. But he was getting better. Now, energy was pulsing through him; if anything he had too much of it. This made him a busy person. His time was limited and he had a lot of important things to do. Cleaning could normally wait. But he was starting to feel it get away from him. There were too many wonderful things happening all at once and he was starting to lose track. He was starting to lose focus. He needed to be organised, to stay on top of things. Coming back to this chaotic flat after each day's amazing adventures, he was finding it difficult to get organised. How could he draw up his plans if he couldn't find any paper? How could he write in his journal if he couldn't find a working pen or an empty journal? How could he unfold the maps if there were no flat surfaces available?

He couldn't, of course.

But neither could he carry all this around in his head. There was too much. It got jumbled. He fumbled and his head jangled. Before he made any more plans, he needed a plan about making plans.

And this was it. He had to admit that his flat was a tip. So he would have to tidy it. And this time he meant it. He had started several times earlier in the week but little problems always seemed to get in his way. The sink was full, so was the draining board, and all the crockery cupboards. There was no clear space on which to start re-stacking his newspapers. The bin was too full to be moved but there were no bin bags to transfer the rubbish to.

He had forgotten to get them again today and the shops would be shut by now but he wasn't going to let that defeat him. His mission was too important to be foiled by petty problems. He would just have to set his newly tuned creativity to work.

* ¢

Absorbed into the soft clutches of the dark suede sofa, Sam and Jayne had John surrounded. He had floundered through the conversation for an awkward twenty minutes. He'd been letting Sam and Jayne quiz him on his life so far. And although he was passing the quiz, he was failing the conversation. They both seemed very interested in getting to know him but he had trouble making an interesting story out of his own history. There was little in his life so far that impressed him so he was having a hard time trying to sound impressive. Disconcertingly this wasn't putting them off which in other circumstances could have boosted his ego but right now merely served to make him feel even more awkward. He knew nothing about either of them but he was too overwhelmed by their double-barrelled assault to attempt to turn the tables. Besides, he didn't know which one he fancied more.

His whiskey sour was almost gone but it had yet to turn into Dutch courage. He had some catching up to do; Sam and Jayne were clearly not on their first cocktail. He necked the last mouthful. The empty glass provided an escape. He was attempting to stand up when Eric steamed into the room.

"Don't get up. Ah, ladies, you've met Mr Smith, excellent. William, a bottle of champagne and four glasses if you please. The good stuff." Eric threw himself and his briefcase on the sofa opposite. "So has he told you that I'm going to make him world famous or is he being his usual modest self?"

The champagne was bought and Jayne moved over to sit with Eric, draping herself comfortably across his long body. For the brief time it took them to finish the bottle, Eric held forth on the nature of celebrity and how John could provide an antidote, an interesting alternative. He also set out some of the things he would be doing to make this happen. This was the first John had heard of many of Eric's plans, so he listened as enthralled as the girls. Apparently, tomorrow he was being interviewed on the Radio One drive-time show.

"I didn't know that," John said.

"Well, you do now. Come on keep up at the back. I can't stop and explain everything to you. We'd be here all night."

•

The man had been here all night. He wasn't yet making progress. He had had some interruptions: a couple of crucial notes for his journal, a siren outside the window. He had thought he wanted music while he worked and had turned on the radio. It was still tuned to the news channel so he was going to switch it over but they had a very interesting programme about an East African micro-finance project and he sort of got swept up in it. When it ended half an hour later he remembered what he had been doing and tuned into some bland commercial station that would serve nothing but pabulum. Much better for working. But this was going to be a long job so he thought he should eat something first.

So that was that, whether he wanted to or not, he'd have to start with the sink.

* ¢

Back in Black's, another liveried member of staff had shepherded them through to the restaurant. Passing through the over-brassed swing doors it was clear they were moving up to the next realm of heaven. Everything sparkled: the mirrors, the chandeliers, the glassware and the knives and the forks. Several trolleys supporting silver domes. Even the cakes on the many-tiered cake-stand seemed to sparkle, glazed strawberries glistening like rubies.

"Sam Spade tells me you're no longer a vegetarian, is that right?" Eric directed his question at John, who nodded a confused consent. "Good, in which case, young Mr Smith and I are having confit of duck, you ladies choose whatever you like. The sole and the hake are great. But perhaps you've had enough of wet fish?" Eric said, merrily jabbing a fork in Smith's direction.

"A private detective?"

"Yes, I had you investigated. I want to know about all the skeletons in your closet. The more I build you up the more my competitors will want to tear you down and we'd like to stay a few steps ahead of the pursuing hounds."

"Couldn't you have just asked me?"

"I could do that, I suppose. If I wanted to be bored out of my fucking mind. And that's not going to tell me what dirt other newspapers could dig up on you. They'll be going through your bins and interviewing every girl or boy whose heart you've broken. If it's out there someone will find it and I had rather that someone was me."

"So you hired private detectives to investigate me?"

"Of course, you don't think I could've trusted this to any of my *journalists* do you?"

"And so what have your detectives found?" asked John, slightly angry but confident that ultimately he had nothing to worry about.

"We've got a big, big problem. They haven't found anything. You don't appear to have done anything wrong or interesting your entire life." Eric pulled a red folder from his briefcase and held up a flimsy report just a few pages long. "If we're not careful, I am going to have to start making things up."

John looked terrified.

"I'm joking, I'm joking. But perhaps you can help me check to see if they are doing a good job. Eric turned with relish to the executive summary. For the second time that night, John had to suffer through a catalogue of his under-achievements.

~

If good foie gras depends upon on an unavoidable amount of cruelty to geese, the secret of duck confit is killing them with kindness. Not for nothing is the best restaurant in the world called the Fat Duck. The fatter the duck, the better the confit. And whereas the geese must be force fed to selectively screw with their livers, for a good duck confit one needs a happy, well rounded duck. A duck that leads a full but not that active life, fed all that his heart desires (and yes it is ideally a he-duck because drakes taste better)

But if it is the happiest ducks that are destined for the highest tables, it is not a long life that they lead. For these ducks are rarely out of adolescence before their time must come. Mercifully, it is a swift death. Stress hormones break down the fat so the ducks are killed with the minimal of shock or warning. Chopping their heads off after a hearty meal usually works here. Life as he knew it is no more for the duck but his lifeless body will hang around for a little while longer before his true purpose is fulfilled. The fat, lifeless bodies are hung up to let the blood drain out. No sooner than two weeks but no later than a month and a half he can be confited. The need to be kind has now passed but no less care must be taken if one is aiming for the best.

The legs and thighs are jointed from the body and seasoned with sea salt and black pepper. A large number of garlic cloves and some thyme and bay leaves are placed on top of the duck legs and the whole thing refrigerated for half a day or so. Then the legs are removed and placed in a heavy covered pot with a further amount of fat taken from the carcass. These are then braised in a low temperature oven for up to eight hours. This preserves the legs in a milky bath of their own fat and they can now be kept refrigerated for several months. Eventually the duck will have his day. And upon that day, he shall be taken from the fridge, roasted until crispy and deep, deep brown and usually served with a selection of vegetables roasted in his bounteous fat. And he will, if treated to a happy life and a dignified death, taste absolutely delicious.

* ¢

By the time the food arrived, Eric had got bored of teasing John and had started regaling the girls without outlandish tales of the many celebrities he had met and disliked. It seemed to be most of them but his greatest hatred seemed to be preserved for Hugh Hefner, the Queen and the Pope. Though the latter two were conceded, at least, to have some good taste.

"The problem with Hugh Hefner is that he has absolutely no soul and minimal charisma. He wouldn't know kitsch from cubism. He's okay with curves but he can't cope with crinkles. He airbrushes all the character out of his starlets. He wants to hide us from life's ugliness – perhaps it's because he looks like a failed experiment to cross a coconut with a pumpkin?"

Sam and Jayne were clearly enthralled. John, relieved to be out of the spotlight, started to relax. He'd even managed to chip in with an occasional joke. To John's surprise Eric had laughed and so had the girls. Maybe he was still in with a chance. He still couldn't decide which girl he liked more. Though his choices could be dwindling. Jayne barely noticed he was there and Sam just seemed slightly uneasy.

•

Decisions, decisions, decisions.

The man had decided to start with the newspapers and pamphlets and he knew that it wasn't going to be a straightforward task so, very wisely, he had broken it down into stages. First he would sift all the paper into piles, then he would sift the piles into smaller piles and from those he could start to get things organised, sorting by their important properties like resonance and portent. The first order of business was to have three piles, newspapers, magazines and pamphlets. The pamphlets pile could also include leaflets and flyers. (This wasn't ideal but he could deal with that later.)

First, he needed some space for the piles. The drifts of paper were not so built up beneath the window. The man would often stand there to look out at the world. He would start his sweep from here. He scooped up a clutch of clutter with both his arms and carried it carefully to the bed.

He managed to move a couple of armfuls and now almost had clear spot by the window to start from. As he went he couldn't help reading the topmost sheets. This one announced a meditation class at his local community college, he remembered picking it up; he was going to go. How strange that he had forgotten all about it. This was important. It had better not get lost again in the big sweep. Maybe he needed another pile just for the *really* important things? It would save time in the long run. He let the other papers drop to the bed and looked around for another spot to clear.

* ¢

When the main courses had been cleared, Eric ordered champagne and coffees all round. A few minutes before, a valet had come and whispered something in his ear and now he pushed back from the table and stood up.

Eric gestured to you John. "You, come with me. Ladies, I am not much of a sweet person but perhaps you can find us a few nice things to share? We'll be right back."

John followed Eric out of the dining room. They went back down the magnificent balustraded staircase and across the black marble hallway, into a thickly carpeted corridor leading to the rear of the building. They came to some heavy wooden doors with a plaque that proclaimed 'Private Dining'. They entered a room that was more muted than the main restaurant. Dark oil paintings hung on the walls and a large mahogany table with twelve matching chairs dominated the room. Seated in one of them had been a tall, dark-complexioned man, who now unfolded himself to make their acquaintance.

"Mr Smith, allow me to introduce Mr White, my pharmacist."

John took the proffered hand. Mr White looked Russian, but was in fact seven-eighths Inuit. John assumed that Mr White was not his real name but it was a fairly accurate translation of his Eskimo name. Disconcertingly he had a strong Welsh accent.

"All right there, Mr Smith. Eric here tells me you're planning on having yourself a wild night, are you?"

"Yes" John replied for the lack of anything better to say.

"So what do you need?"

John stalled, not wanting to reveal his pitiful ignorance of all things illegal, "I'm not really sure," he offered weakly.

Eager to collect his own order Eric rescued him. "I'd say he needs Mister White's All-Night Bag of Shite, wouldn't you, Arlvik?"

"Right you are, Mister H, though I prefer to refer to it as Mister White's Original Miscellany." Arlvik started to bring all sorts of bags, packets and bundles out of his many pockets and dropped them on the mahogany table. From deep in one of his inside pockets he got another slightly bigger packet and slid it across to Eric. "And while I'm about it, there's yours Eric."

Eric wasted no time in tearing open the packet, which seemed from where John was standing to contain half a dozen smaller plastic pockets of white powder. Eric stuffed all but one of these into his jacket. He tipped the contents of the final one onto the smooth French polished surface of the table and began making geometrical patterns in the dust. This unnerved Mr White slightly and he went over to bolt the door.

"So where were we?" he said coming back to the table. "You will need a lot of that, obviously," nodding at Eric and passing John two bags of white powder. John guessed these were cocaine.

"Some of these." Lots of little white pills that reminded John of his ex-girlfriend's pointless homoeopathic chalk tablets. He imagined that these would be marginally more effective.

"Although these have more of a kick" A slightly smaller bag of green ones.

"And these," (pink ones), "are more mellow, you know?"

"Yeah" John lied, hoping to sound knowledgeable.

"Be fucking careful with this," (some dirty brown powder), "It is stronger than you'll be used to." John did not contest this.

Next Arlvik handed him a bit of paper folded into a small rectangular parcel. "This will help you out if your horse gets sick, if you know what I mean." John did not know what this meant. But coming from a drug dealing Welsh Inuit, he doubted very much that it was the number of a good veterinarian.

Finally, Arlvik placed two other small plastic bags on the table, one with a colourful selection of pills and capsules in it, the other with a few more little white parcels. "Then these are your medicine cabinets, Traditional and Western." He gestured first at the white parcels. "A range of Mother Nature's finest psychedelics. They are all labelled and they are all divine. So enjoy the ride." He handed the bag to John with some ceremony. John tried to look suitably cosmic. "And if you crash we've got western medicine to pick you back up. Vallies, Viagra, Codeine and a few jellies."

"Thanks," John took the pills and added them to his pile.

"And I nearly forgot, some of this." He reached into yet another pocket and handed John a small sack of dusty green buds. The first thing he had been able to positively identify since arriving.

"Did you need anything else?"

John could quite honestly say that the large collection of

plastic bags now resting in his jacket pocket was more than sufficient. A lot more than sufficient. He very much doubted he would take any of it but not wanting to hurt the drug dealer's feelings, he merely smiled and nodded.

He had tried weed a few times at college and fallen quite peacefully asleep. But woke up deciding that on the whole he preferred alcohol. Of the others, he had only ever taken cocaine. Even that had been only once, at a house party, where he had done it to attempt to impress the bright and perky Australian girl who had offered it to him. And while he had enjoyed the sensation, it didn't have his intended effect. The girl had become even more bright and perky and very quickly wandered off to find other people to talk at.

Eric had not been idle. He had shepherded his white cloud into an intricate geometric pattern that looked like this:

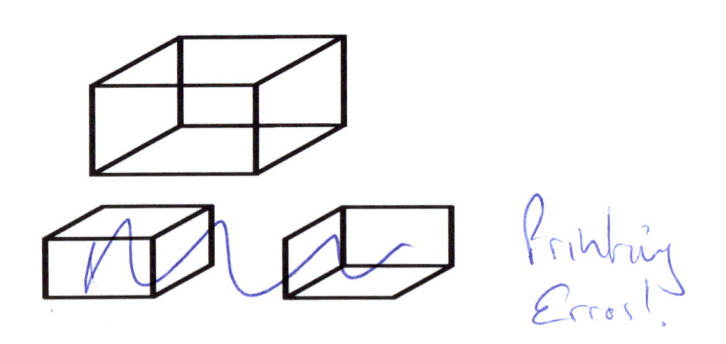

Printing Error!

(but in white on mahogany).

Eric stared at it for some time as if mesmerised. Then he reached into his pocket and retrieved what looked like a small silver candelabra. Just right for two of those birthday cake candles. It must have been hollow because having put the two prongs to his nose; Eric was able to rapidly hoover up most of his construction. He had good lungs and very clear nasal passages.

When he straightened up just two lines of the figure remained.

"They say I should not keep punishing my nose like this but I figure on getting at least another 10 or 20 years out of it yet."

He moved away from what remained, offering it to the two of them. Fortunately for John, Mr White stepped forward. He took a miniature single candlestick holder out of his own pocket. In one smooth practised movement, he bent down, brought it up to his nose and, blocking his other nostril with the same hand, he guided the little silver tube along the left hand line. When it had gone, he straightened up and passed the metal tube to John and once again John found that he was taking drugs purely in order to look cool in front of other people. Peer pressure doesn't stay in the playground.

With one hand John brought the tube to his nose. He tried to imitate the others but this was a little more difficult than the experts made it seem. Seating himself in the nearest chair and using both hands, John managed to seal one nostril while sniffing through the other. It took him only a couple of attempts to clear the table. There was a tingle in the back of his throat but it wasn't all together unpleasant. He handed back Mr White's candlestick holder and tried to compose himself into a cool posture. He just about had it settled when he blew everything by sneezing violently.

Eric snorted at John's poor snorting.

Mr White was more diplomatic. "When you need any more just give me a call." The Inuit handed him a business card. At first it looked blank but as he took it, he felt raised lettering on the front. Holding it up to the light he saw that there were words embossed in white ink on the card.

"Very cool," John had to admit.

"Hey man, I'm an Inuit, we know all about cool." This was clearly a favourite line of John's new friend and despite himself, he found he was laughing quite hard at the cheesy joke.

•

By the third or fourth sub-clearing and on about his thirteenth fish the man spotted that he was going wrong again. He had been making fine progress. He had a clearing by the window to get started in and in addition had cleared several new area in case he encountered any more interesting titbits. He had the space by the window for everything he was going to keep, a space on the sofa for paper that was too important to lose, a space next to that for things that were not only too important to lose but were also extremely urgent. Finally, there was a space in the corner of the room for funny pictures of fish. One needed to keep one's sense of humour or you might go mad.

The fish had been an inspired idea that started with the scissors. They had been discovered when he was lifting yet another armful off the sofa. They had been missing for weeks. He had dropped everything else and done a little dance. Scissors would really help right now. He could chop things up. If he just kept the essential articles and pictures, it would cut his collection right down to a manageable size.

Obviously he mustn't lose them. They needed a very special place. He put them in his pocket while he looked around for somewhere suitable, which was when he spied the goldfish.

It was on the cover of a computer magazine. A big shiny goldfish. It was the only reason he had bought the magazine in the first place. He had no interest in computers and didn't entirely trust them. But he did like fish, they were soothing and funny.

This was such an obvious first use for the newly found scissors that he set straight to work, tearing the cover from the magazine, then carefully cutting round the fish to free it from the page. It looked almost alive.

He cleared a space in the corner and put the fish there. But it looked lonely. So, scissors in hand, he went fishing. Trawling through seas of paper for further fish. There was less fish related news than you might expect. But after an hour of determined effort he had a goodly catch. Though by some miracle the front room now seemed more untidy than ever. He was back to square one.

Absently putting the scissors down, the man sat in the middle of the sea with his fishes and had a little think.

• ¢

From there the evening picked up pace. The beautiful desserts were demolished for a few tiny tastes and the coffee was left to go cold. They let the champagne take the strain. With some prompting from Eric, John had passed a bag of cocaine to the girls, who needed none.

All too soon they were leaving the club and climbing into Eric's limo that had pulled up right in front of the door. And then inside there was some hilarity as Jayne and Eric scrabbled and scrambled on the floor, trying to find a magazine with her in it. This was the first time that it connected in John's head how these girls knew Eric and mostly he was surprised at his own innocence.

From an evening with Jayne it should have been obvious. It was Sam who didn't quite fit. She had been a bit anxious throughout the meal and now rather than joining in with Eric and Jayne's games she sat quietly on the seat beside him, leaning in and giving the occasional shiver, although it wasn't cold. John put his arm around her and his kindness seemed to do the trick. She huddled in closer and seemed to relax as they enjoyed the floorshow.

In short order the limousine reached its destination. Another club, judging by the large gentleman who helped Sam, Jayne and John out of the car and onto the waiting red carpet. Eric remained inside. He waved them off with instructions to abuse his bar tab, while he excused himself to get back to work. Rarely was there a night where he let his editor put the paper to bed without interference. He made vague promises to return in time.

White's was anything but pristine – on a bad night it could actually be quite grey. Infamous as the exclusive haunt of film stars and minor royals, of rockers and high rollers, it was more usually filled with bored and boorish young aristos, uncouth city millionaires and whichever subset of the jet set happened to think they were the only ones who knew about it.

Footballers and soap stars felt comfortable here. No-one would fail to recognise them and no-one would ask them their opinion on anything more challenging than what they thought of each other. Occasional American A-listers would splashdown at the end or more often the beginning of a publicity tour. The door policy was exclusive but nobody stopped the paparazzi from camping patiently on the pavement. A well-timed telephone call from your publicist and a carefully choreographed stumble into a taxi at four AM was all it took to appear in the party pages of the tabloids and the free-sheets. Everyone knew it and they were all happy with the arrangement.

With Eric gone, and with a little assistance from the marching powder and support from a beautiful woman on either arm, John was able to step into the shoes of an alpha male. They were an unfamiliar fit but with each step they felt more comfortable. They were the nicest new shoes he'd ever had.

He tried to guide his girls to the bar but a woman with a cream cocktail dress and a big black ear-mike intercepted them and guided them to a private table; A black marble disc with three ice buckets in the middle. They were expected and they were important.

John slid round to the middle of the white leather seat and Sam and Jayne slid in on either side. There was easily enough space for ten very important people *and* all their egos. Nonetheless the girls both squeezed in close to him.

There was champagne waiting for them but the waiter who opened it wondered if they wouldn't also like some shots. Which of course they would.

Moments later a bottle of frozen vodka appeared with three squat shot glasses nestling in a brick of solid ice. The vodka was a brand he'd never heard of and had a flavour like satanic snowflakes. They had toasted themselves and slammed their glasses back down while the freezing liquid warmed them from inside.

"So," Sam asked, "what exactly is this big idea of yours? I didn't really follow when Eric was explaining and you didn't get a chance to say for yourself."

John paused as he thought of the best way to answer. He felt as clear-headed as that night on the stage. That was a long time ago and in the blur of that time he had been asked many times. But this was the first time since then that he actually had an audience. He was very glad she'd asked.

•

The problem was that rearranging the chaos never actually decreased it. In the closed system of his bedsit, he could only bring order to any one part at the cost of disorder elsewhere. And since the room was so small that, even when he had done that, it was all but impossible to keep the two from mixing together again.

He needed to be able to remove the unwanted noise and extraneous information to leave him with a clearer signal and a view of his own carpet.

But how?

His bin was already full and he could not burn things because he didn't have a fireplace. Then he saw the solution. It was crystal clear and had been right in front of him the whole time.

Getting up from the floor, he went over and threw open the window.

*

It was only when Jayne's mask slipped for a second time, letting her boredom creep through that John slowed down enough for the irony to catch up with him. For the last half hour he had been sitting here holding forth, talking non-stop about how life passed people by, that there was so much to experience and enjoy in every singe moment. He had been witty. He had been entertaining. He had made the girls laugh, at first.

Sam was still with him but somewhere along the way Jayne had fallen behind. She did a good job of hiding her boredom, at least from John. But this time last time he had finally noticed. It stopped him short. His personal revelation held no interest for Jayne.

Realising the mistake she had made Jayne needed to fix it. The usual small talk wouldn't help but she had plenty of tools to her trade. This was her job and she was very good at it.

"Come on, let's all have a dance." Grabbing John's hand she pulled him from his seat and she and Sam escorted him to the dance floor.

On any other night John might have put up more of a fight but in the hands of two professional escorts he didn't stand a chance. Not that he knew this or perhaps he might have put up a fight. It was the sort of this that would have pricked John's conscience as a polyester liberal*. But, even, then he would have lost, in the end. Besides he was a polyester liberal but he was also a man. Sam and Jayne were very, very expensive call girls and they were being paid for with Eric's money. It wasn't a fair contest.

But part of the job of being a very, very expensive call-girl is to assuage the guilt with subtle assurances. She'd made it obvious that was an independent woman for whom this career was a personal choice. She'd lead you to believe that the money was largely irrelevant, that, right at this very moment, she was choosing to spend her time (and your money) being

---

* Polyester liberals are like woolly liberals but with a greater dependence on petrochemicals. They would like to do the right thing but are a bit too comfortable with their lifestyle, so rather than changing it they just feel guilty about it.

with you. If this still would not work, she had a whole arsenal of less subtle tricks that are known to any woman with curves, a cleavage and the confidence to use them.

There were two things that made very expensive call girls different from merely expensive ones. Firstly, they charged you more. But more importantly they made you believe they were worth it. Like all the best high-end retailers they made you feel good about spending your money.

Jayne was doing it because it suited her personality and validated her opinion of men. Sam was doing it because she found it less demeaning or depressing than any other job that was available to her as a tri-lingual humanities graduate with a Masters in Anthropology.

Although Sam and Jayne's time had been bought and paid for, and although they could fake it expertly, they genuinely seemed to be enjoying John's company. The cocaine currently cascading neurotransmitters through his brain gave him the confidence to feel he deserved their attention. And he was not far from wrong; Sam and Jayne were both intrigued by this somewhat artless young man with rich and famous friends. It was a lot less tedious than their usual daily grind.

The three of them danced just for the sheer joy of it.

A text message had come through from one of Eric's assistants. Eric would not be re-joining them but by way of an apology for springing the radio interview on John unannounced he had booked John a suite in a hotel on Park Lane.

Several songs and a couple of lines later, Sam moved in close to John, he felt her breath on his cheek and her hair brushing against her face.

"Maybe we could go back to your hotel now?"

"You and me?" John asked redundantly.

"You, me and Jayne."

So there he was lounging in a large armchair in an even larger hotel suite that cost more per night than he used to earn in a month. A tumbler of brandy in one hand and his legs spread wide, so two gorgeous girls (who also cost more per night than he earned in month) could stand in front of him, wriggling their hips and removing each other's clothes.

If only Kate could see me now, John thought and quickly imagined exactly what might have happened if Kate was here. She would have walked straight out again. Or maybe not. She might have screamed or thrown something first.

John's most recent girlfriend, a serious minded corporate lawyer, had left him about four months after he had quit work to pursue his comedy nightmare. They had never been terribly close to begin with, coming together because they were among the final few of their mutual friends who had not already formed a couple. They ambled ambivalently into their relationship. They stayed together in mutual desperation. Low-level fear that maybe this was the best they could do for themselves.

Kate ended it when John's best had gone from being a moderately ineffectual junior corporate grocer with some prospects to being a highly effectual comedy straight man who worked alone telling obscure jokes about Moliere to people who did not care. Once she realised that John's new vocation wasn't some elaborate joke she walked out of his feeble performance. Making the break she reassessed the rest of her own life and let herself be seduced by one of the middle-tier partners at her practice. It was a mistake she forgave herself for making.

John had felt inadequate and envious when he had first heard that Kate was dating some creep with a corner office and Chelsea flat that was still unfurnished because in the year he had been there he had not had chance to leave his desk long enough to unpack. But by chance he had bumped into them in Soho one evening as he headed home after another unfunny night and they were coming out of some incredibly expensive restaurant. They spent no more than three awkward minutes on the street as Kate and her boss's boss waited for a cab. It had changed his opinion completely. The guy was a balding beanpole with no chin and all the charisma of a middle-tier corporate lawyer. He called her Katherine.

After that, John went from envious to angry. Mad that Kate could fancy something like that. He'd thought she'd have more taste, more class.

A gentle tugging brought him back into the room. Sam and Jayne had run out of clothes of their own to remove. So they were starting on his.

•

The man watched the flyers fly.

He set his freesheets free.

He shed his leaflets and some many newspapers were now yesterday's news.

Suddenly it was all so easy. He dragged the bed across the room to speed up the sifting. There, where the bed had been, was a nice clear space to restart his filing.

*

This was all a wild adventure. For hours now he was exploring uncharted waters, weighing anchor at one paradise after another. Though their ship was largely navigated by the more experienced members of the crew. Or were they mermaids? Sated but still buzzing, his mind drifted off, wondering what had got him here.

His attention was drawn back to the room,. Sam was shaking him awake and, with the Viagra doing the rope work to raise the main-sail, Jayne was encouraging him to negotiate the Northwest Passage.

So this was sex, drugs and rock and roll.

•

It taken some time but the man had brought order to the chaos. Banished nonsense to the outer darkness.

He could see his carpet. He could see all five of his broken televisions. He had about ten piles of paper of varying importance.

He was done. He went over to shut the window when one last thought came into his mind. Did he really need five broken televisions?

INTERMISSION
NECKER

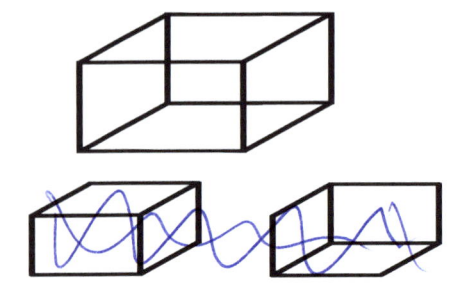

In my professional opinion, this is the best optical illusion in the world. It's certainly the only one that I would have permanently tattooed on my body. It is a Necker cube. A wireframe outline of a cube. But look at for a little while and you should notice something strange. Whichever way it appeared at first, it seems to flip and change, a little longer and it flips back again. One moment you see the front face is coming out of the page upwards and rightwards. Seconds later, it is the opposite way around. The other square is now the front face, coming out downwards and leftwards. Then back, and so on ad infinitum or at least ad nauseam. The flipping never flipping stops.

Trust me, I have had the tattoo for over five years now.

So what is happening? First, let's be clear that they really are different. These are not two different views of the same cube. There's one seen from above and one seen from below.

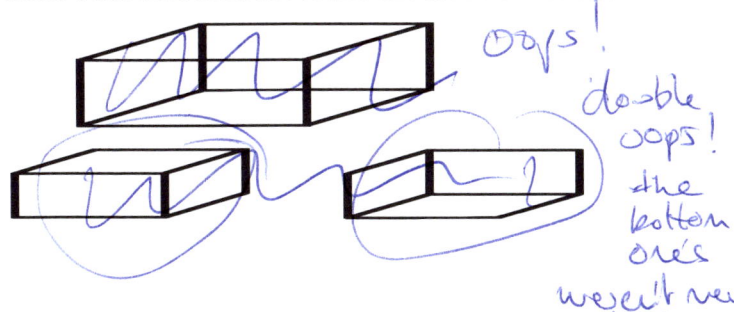

[figure: two cubes with handwritten annotations: "oops!", "double oops!", "the bottom one's weren't meant to be crossed out."]

So which is right? Obviously, they are both right and that's because in fact they are both wrong. What we are actually seeing isn't a cube at all. It is some connected lines on a flat page that give the impression of a cube. Two cubes. The original figure is ambiguous. So on one level, the fact that what we see flips between these two possibilities is a fairly ordinary neurological fact. The visual parts of our brains see the lines on the page. They try to interpret this two-dimensional pattern. Elements of it are strongly suggestive of depth and what we construct is the cube that fits this. There are two possibilities so that's what we see.

I don't think anyone knows quite why it flips at that particular speed. But it might be more than a coincidence that 2-3 seconds is also the length of the personal 'now'. The moving window in which we are constantly experiencing the present. Two seconds ago is the past, in two seconds time the future will arrive but right now this thin sliver of existence is happening. Or so it seems to feel.

There is only one window that you are looking out of. The Necker Cube suggests there can only ever be one. Try and divide your narrative into two conflicting frames and you'll find it can't be done. At first glance this is so obvious that it is often overlooked. But the fact we experience a unified self provides absolutely no explanation as to why we experience a unified self. Or why, as in the excluded simultaneity of these cubes, we can't experience anything else.

At least not with a normal healthy brain or while trying to stay sane. Slice the huge bundle of fibres connecting the two hemispheres together and amazingly you'll survive but there will be two dislocated parts to your personality rattling around inside you. It's very hard to imagine what that feels like but take the right drugs and you can safely experience the disorientation of a kind. Dissociative anaesthetics can give you out of body experiences or twist time and space, while something as simple as too much alcohol can leave gaps in your memory of the night before. You were clearly there experiencing it, so why can't you remember?

If you are unlucky enough to develop schizophrenia or even a simple skunk-induced psychosis, you can experience a disorientation of not knowing that your internal voices are your own. The illusion of a single-self is so strong, so essential that these experiences can drive you mad. Even when you know the cause, it doesn't seem any less real. Self-knowledge doesn't stop the depressed from feeling down. It doesn't help someone with psychosis get a grip on himself or herself. Which self?

The Necker cube gives some clues as to how this self-governing mechanism is supposed to serve us. A well functioning consciousness balances the up with the down, the top with the bottom. Out there in the world is a single ambiguous figure that feeds into the system from the bottom upwards. A flat figure is passed up to higher dimensions, which use their knowledge to impose a fuller form. This happens with everything but rarely do we notice. Most things seem to us to have only one sensible interpretation. But this unruly cube breaks that illusion. Here it is clear that our brains have imposed the sense. Some abstract concepts have been handed down to ambiguous perceptions to tell them what we think of them. Many possible interpretations are always bubbling under the surface but only in rare circumstances does the debate take place before our very eyes.

It's worth thinking about.

CHAPTER SIX
RADIO

In real life, [Diane] Keaton believes in God. But she also believes that the radio works because there are tiny people inside it.
– Woody Allen

• †

The man had woken up early, his brain buzzing with strange and wonderful thoughts. He was definitely getting better.

The man went into the kitchen. He put the kettle on. He was God's instrument. He would do what was required of him, he would be vigilant, wait for the signs and when the time came he would be ready. He sat down at the table, bit into his toast and turned on the radio.

"The time now is ten to eight. In a few minutes, I will be speaking to the Education Secretary Carey Espedair about the government's plans to introduce compulsory IQ testing for all PE teachers. But first here is the morning thought with the Right Reverend Donaldson Cake, Bishop of Enfield and founder of the Families First campaign and pressure group."

"Thank you Peter and God bless you, and good morning everyone and God bless you too. On my way into the studio this morning, I passed through Kings Cross station and I happened to stop at the newsagents to purchase my morning paper, and as I did so, I had cause to reflect on what an impermanent and transitional time we live in. A month ago, no-one had heard of John Smith. Now he is on the cover of every magazine and newspaper. Especially those of Eric Hayle.

"In the last few weeks, in this case, we have seen, like never before, the cynical power of the media to manipulate the public and the unalloyed lure of celebrity. A man with nothing complex to say is elevated to the level of a sage. And then by some strange circularity, because he appears in our newspapers, what they say about him must be true. (For why else would they print it?) To me, it seems that here is a man that is famous for being widely seen as wise. And who is seen as wise because Eric Hayle has seen to it that he is famous. He is offered to us as wise man, a prophet, and yet his message is empty and all we are presented with is packaging and personality."

Having worked himself up to quite some pace, the Reverend Cake took a second's break, after thirty years in the church, he knew how to deliver a sermon.

"I cannot help but think how different this is from the story of Our Lord," he continued. "He did not have a public relations team. He did not grace the cover of lurid tabloids. He didn't hang out in smoky nightclubs mocking everyone. He was not even very widely recognised in his own lifetime. But his message is not instant, it is timeless. A profound and lasting truth that has been preserved and handed down through the authority of the church."

"It could not be otherwise for it is a message that is the Truth, the Light, the Way. But in these darkened times, that Truth is often obscured by the lies of the media, that Light is obscured by the dazzle of celebrity and that hard Way is shunned for the path of pleasure, of instant gratification. But these things will fade and die. Only Jesus Christ can offer eternal and lasting salvation. He is still the prophet for our generation."

Again the Reverend paused,

"God be with you."

"He is", thought the man.

Ψ

Why did Phil Collins cross the road?
To get to the middle.
– Traditional

Jonny Lawson was a leathery old has-been. One might have thought his mid morning show on Radio Two would be a complete anachronism, the sort of middle of the road, middle brow dross that one could only have heard in the dark and hideously tasteless days of the nineteen seventies. That is exactly what it was. After thirty years of presenting his show, he was not about to change the formula now. Especially as it continued to be successful in a way that ought to give pause to those intellectual commentators who claim we have all become far more sophisticated over the years.

Given the choice Jonny would not have changed the music either, but fortunately (or not) Phil Collins, Mick Hucknall and Celine Dion had arrived to widen the middle of the road into a treacle tarmac-ed superhighway of schmaltz.

All the same Hazel was looking forward to appearing on his show. It made her feel nostalgic for the seventies and eighties, for her time as consultant psychologist on several secure special units and in-patient mental health wards. When she had made her morning rounds, Jonny's show would almost always be on in the background of the communal area. Its bland chatter and anodyne music had just the right kind of soporific effect on the mentally unbalanced. Diplomatically, she did not mention this to Jonny. She was learning the ways of the media, though it did not please to see this happening to herself.

He had a great face for radio. His head was oddly angular, with a flat triangular nose and a wide line of a mouth. His eyes were stupidly far apart, almost round the corners of his head onto his temples. When he smiled he looked like a shark. His hair was not his own, nor anyone else's. The last time the glossy black strands crowning his head had been anything resembling organic was sixty million years ago, when as primordial microbes they had begun their long journey towards the shiny magic of plastic.

However, you do not get to host your own show on Radio Two for twenty-seven years without something between the ears of your over-sized headphones. He was an intelligent man. He was warm and genuine. He was slightly witty. There was nothing to dislike about him but he was about as thrilling as Phil Collins' latest album. Hazel did not like Phil Collins. Unfortunately, Jonny Lawson was also lecherous old fool who showed no shame in his pursuit of whatever woman had caught his eye. It was usually the nearest woman. Though some adjustment was made to his proximity criterion to account for age and availability.

Hazel was almost the same age as Jonny. With a well practised eye, he had clocked the absence of a wedding ring the moment he had first met her shortly before the show. Now she was sitting at a microphone four feet away from him and due to be there for the full two hours of the show. Jonny had acquired his latest target. In his mind, she did not stand a chance. The first song of the show was already coming to an end. Jonny Lawson double checked that he had his own handwritten notes on Hazel's book and smiled his shark-like smile at his guest.

Hazel smiled back nervously, matching Jonny Lawson's perfect teeth with her own. Perfectly fake, she thought ruefully. She wore dentures after winning one too many arguments with in-patients on the psychiatric wards. She occasionally forgot one of the many unwritten rules of the mental health world that the winner of a rational argument better watch out for a chair in the face. Hazel felt a lot more on guard at the moment. Her appearance on Shona's TV show had not gone well and the publishers' publicity manager had been lecturing her on the need to be more public friendly.

"That was the ever wonderful Barbara Streisand. Now I would like to welcome my guest for the morning. Dr Hazel Cole. Author of 'Help Yourself', a new book described as a self help book that tells people that they don't need one. Hello Doctor."

"Hello, Jonny. And thank you for having me. I have been listening to your show since my first day working in the NHS 35 years ago."

"Well thank you. Although you don't strike me as old enough to have been with me in the early days. But then it doesn't feel that long to me, time flies when we're having fun. So Doctor Cole, what's this all about? A self help book for people what don't need it. Isn't that like swimming lessons for fish? Or is it more like clarinet lessons for sheep?"

"Well, Jonny, it might be more like flying lessons for birds" Hazel said. "I am not saying that the contents of these types of book are irrelevant for people, something that can't be helpful but more importantly than that I am trying to persuade people not to rely on experts. I believe that everyone can help themselves but not everyone knows that they can."

"So you want to shove us out of the nest?"

"Not perhaps shove, but maybe I can provide some encouragement to find out for yourself just what you are capable of. And helping yourself is like learning flying in that it will not come straight away, it will take practice and hard work. But it is something we can all do."

"Apart from the penguins and emu's amongst us?"

"There will always be exceptions." Despite the uncomfortable feeling of his eyes all over her, Hazel was beginning to enjoy this conversation.

"But the vast majority of us have the ability to get what we want?" Jonny asked. The tone of his voice was innocent enough, but the way he held her gaze told a different story.

"What we want and what is good for us are not often the same thing," Hazel replied, trying to play the same game. "We all know that but have difficulty realising that we would be better off with what is good for us in the long term."

Listening to what she said, Jonny Lawson realised that Hazel was onto him. But completely ignoring what she had just told him, he decided to pursue just like he did with every woman. He loved the chase and besides this had worked for him for the last 35 years. It was not like he needed anyone to help him.

"The phone lines are open, if anyone wants Doctor Cole to help push them out of a tall tree, give us a call and we will see if she can answer your questions? In the meantime, here are the Eagles."

*

> This is BBC Radio 1FM, and if there is any news of the death of Michael Heseltine in the next hour, we'll let you know.
> – Chris Morris

In a studio on the floor above, a hung-over John Smith sat opposite Radio One's Kevv Clarke, waiting to be asked some questions. He had been waiting for some time.

If Kevv Clarke were to shut up even just briefly a person in his company might have some chance to think of some one thing they liked about Kevin. But he never did and perhaps as a consequence, he was widely disliked. He was into his early thirties but acted like a teenager who had just won the lottery. He had more energy than a caravan of Mexican welterweights on crack and talked faster than a cattle market auctioneer. The controller of Radio One, a competent accountant out of place and out of his depth, thought Kevv was the greatest thing on radio since Marconi. He had given Kevv the drive-time show and in the face of all that is decent and good Kevv's show was uncommonly popular.

"Hey that was the latest song from Y-chrome. Innit great? I love it, I'm gonna play it every day until you guys make it number one. Coming up soon I'll be talking to John Smith, literally the 'man of the moment'. But right now I neeeed more music. It's Kylie. Yeah Kylie!"

"You've been saying that for the past hour, when am I going to be on?"

When the songs were playing Kevv would still be talking. He continued chattering away at the same helter-skelter pace. Talking mostly to himself but occasionally to his producer Jo who did not like him and to his mate Si, who probably did but was never observed to utter a word and gave no other indication that he might have an opinion about anything. He was Kevv's best mate from way back and part of Kevv's contract was that Si must have a job on the show. His job appeared to involve eating Mars Bars, drinking Diet Coke and giving Kevv the occasional thumbs up through the glass of the producers booth. He had additional ad hoc duties getting in Jo's way. Making her hard life even harder by getting sticky thumbprints on CDs she was about to play, or simply being large, slow and in the wrong place as she rushed about the booth attempting to keep up with Kevv's continual off-the-cuff revision to the running order. Jo liked Si even less than she liked Kevv.

"Next I'm playing Flow Hectic by Space Noise.. naah, I won't.. I 'eard it on Yozzer's show this morning. It has gotta be the end of that. Jo love, let's have Love Cloud Heart Attack, at least that's still cool... In your own time love, we'll just talk amongst ourselves shall we?"

John thought this might be his cue and leaned forward in his chair but Kevv was already off onto some anecdote about the last time he went drinking with Riboflavin aka B2 the singer from the semi-autonomous electrobeat collective B-Vitamins who were responsible for the cacophony that was Love Cloud Heart Attack.

John worried that he had never heard of any of this music. What did he have in common with this overgrown teen adrenalin gland? This blipvert avatar with the attention span of an electric goldfish in a Japanese arcade game.

Jo suffered the mayhem, kidding herself that she had the best job in radio.

"Any minute now, any minute mate. I've got another hour and ten minutes. Plenty of time. We've got a lot to fit in. It ain't my fault that you come in on the same day as our first play of new Michelle single AND the exclusive new remix by the Warminster Posse is it?"

"And haven't you played both of those?"

"Yeah, but they are so wicked that I am gonna play them again... Okay Jo, love?.. so as I say there's a lot to get in. Don't worry we'll get to your stuff in the time we've got left."

John got up and left.

Kevv did not notice. If he thought about it at all, he might possibly have guessed that his guest had gone to the lav. John had not said anything to Kevv as he left. There did not seem any point.

He did tell Jo as he was talking through the producer's booth to the exit. Ordinarily she would have tried to convince him to stay, if she had not been under her desk, scrabbling round to pick up the next five CDs she was supposed to play that Si had knocked over seconds before. It was another typical bit of unpredictability of the sort that Kevv's show was famous for. His audience loved the on air accidents and mishaps. Having retrieved Banal Love Frogs from the floor and cued them up she went in to tell Kevv his guest had left.

She hated leaving Si alone near the controls but it was the only way to talk to Kevv; if she tried to tell him things over the intercom he had a habit of fading her out. When she had inserted the necessary words edgewise into Kevv's teletype of consciousness he could not care less. In fact, he was quite pleased. It gave him something to talk about in the next hour. He motored into the final hour of drive-time telling his five million listeners how this boring person called somebody Smith had walked out on him. He found it immensely hilarious that anyone could be so stupid as to think they had anything more interesting to do than to talk to him. To be on his show.

He warmed to his theme and started doing impressions of 'the Missing Smith', having both halves of a conversation with Smith about what could be more interesting than Kevv. Since England were not playing football and the Robbie Williams Wembley Concert was not until next week, he concluded that there could not be anything and had 'Smith' admit that he was mad.

He continued down this track all the way through to his six o'clock sign off. He got so carried away he even forgot to replay the Warminster Posse. By the end of the show 'Madman Smith, the Missing Smith' had made more of an impression on the frenetic consciousness of Kevv than he would have ever have managed if he had not vanished. His name would raise curiosity in the minds of Kevv's millions of listeners.

Smith himself should have been curious whether this was a good or a bad thing. But he didn't feel curious about anything. He also didn't feel like going back to his grotty little flat. So he took a taxi back to the hotel, paid for another night out of this own pocket and asked not to be disturbed until breakfast.

CHAPTER SEVEN
NEWSPAPERS

To understand Milton one needs a Bible, an encyclopedia and at least a working knowledge of Latin and Greek. To understand Shakespeare one may occasionally need a dictionary. To understand Nostradamus one is just as well off with a box of frogs.
– ANON

•

The man had had to leave the house early. The walls were starting to sound funny and he did not like the way the fridge kept inching towards him every time he turned his back. It was Thursday and it was sunny so he wore his blue sweater, his green socks and his orange jacket. In case it started raining he put a spare pair of yellow socks in his left hand jacket pocket.

He was going to the library. For the last two nights he had dreamt about a beautiful flying pink horse called Ailsa with no bottom. It had been a most wonderful dream, so good that it had woken him up. The first time he simply lay there hoping to get back to the dream but too excited to go back to sleep.

He never managed to go back to sleep these days, not now he was off the medication. From the moment he awoke, his mind was racing. No matter how exhausted he felt, it was always impossible to get back to sleep. He knew he needed several 'snoozes' but it was never possible because his mind was already heading out on its morning run.

Yesterday's dream had been different. His mind had been racing but sated. As if it was basking in the afterglow of vigorous sex. Although sex itself was a distant memory made indistinct by his many years on medication.

When the dream had returned a second night, it had woken him up just as quickly but this time around he recognised it for what it was and desperately tried to recall the details. But there still wasn't much more than that, a beautiful flying pink horse called Ailsa with no bottom. This was surely a sign. But it did not fit with any of his usual symbology. It did not even connect to any details or events of the last few days. This was not something from his own mind. This was something other, something new, a message sent from a higher power. His heart was racing. He sang to himself as he hurried to get ready, trying to block out the cacophony coming from the wallpaper.

> *Be Thou my Vision, O Lord of my heart;*
> *Naught be all else to me, save that Thou art.*
> *Thou my best Thought, by day or by night,*
> *Waking or sleeping, Thy presence my light.*

It took him a while to find where the sofa had hidden his keys this time but eventually he was ready. He left for the library, as alive as he'd ever felt. He'd been given a message. He just needed to find out what it meant. He would discover this in the usual way, by consulting the clues that had been hidden for him in the headlines of that day's newspapers.

* ¢

For the second morning running Smith started his day seeing the lovely faces of Sam and Jayne staring up at him. Although this time it was more of a shock to see them, barely dressed and in bed together, smiling up at him from the front page of The Scum. The valet had thoughtfully brought him a copy with his breakfast. Reading the headline it took several seconds to realise that the story was about him.

He read the whole thing (continued on pages 21,23-24). He re-read it several times. He looked at the pictures. He sat shell-shocked for a long time. He had a fleeting moment of pride that he was famous, that finally people would know who he was, then he thought about what those people would think of him and he felt a little queasy. He realised that one of those people would be his mother and he had to rush to the bathroom and throw up.

Clearing his stomach cleared his head somewhat and he began to feel aggrieved that he had been misrepresented. They had got his age wrong, he only tried about half the 'cocktail' of drugs they had claimed and he was sure they had all got a little sleep around seven in the morning. "Randy Smith kept us up all night, purred curvy Samantha." Well, maybe he did not mind that but the whole tone of the article made him out to be a ravenous drug-fuelled sex maniac.

Under those circumstances there was only one person to call.

"Eric, have you seen the front page of the Scum?"

"Yes, good isn't it?"

"Good!? What is good about 'GURU GIVES IT GOOD'?" Smith spluttered, "'Our night of sex and drugs with sleazy lifestyle guru John Smith', £2,000 per night vice girls tell all'"

"Yes, fantastic isn't it? I couldn't believe it, the front page, three pages inside, some good photos of you and they even used my headline."

"Your headline!?"

"Yes 'GURU GIVES IT GOOD' – I am quite pleased with that, it paints you in a very positive light. The rest of the article is good too, you must like *that* picture?"

"It is good, but where did they get it?" Smith conceded before remembering he was still angry. "What is so good about being labelled a ravenous drug-fuelled sex maniac? And you still haven't explained what you meant by 'your headline'."

"First of all, calm down. Secondly it is a label that has never done me any harm. Thirdly, you know the old cliché 'all publicity is good publicity' well, it is a cliché because it is true. Fourthly, this story is great for you and fifthly, that is why I planted it," Eric concluded triumphantly.

"You?"

"Yes, we couldn't buy publicity like this."

"Would we want to?"

"Of course! Everyone's a winner! You get onto the front page of a national tabloid. Well, those two lovely girls got the cover but you can't begrudge them that. Incidentally, they also got ten grand each and some really great exposure, they wanted to say thanks."

"Yes, I can see the 'exposure' they are getting 'continued on pages 19, 22, 23 and on an' on an' on," John said testily, feeling somewhat betrayed and that he had been wrong to think they were just nice girls with nasty jobs.

"The girls told me that you saw a good deal more than that on

Tuesday night." Eric said, laughing at his own joke.

"You're enjoying this, aren't you?" John wailed.

"Yes, that's what they said about you." John did not even dignify this with as an reply so Eric continued. "Look, they are just a couple of nice girls in a nasty world. Now, thanks to you and I, they can get out of being fucked flat for cash by rich, fat, stupid Arabs. They have a chance at celebrity status, an honest living and the chance to start sleeping with rich, fit, stupid footballers. And incidentally, they haven't told me anything about what went on in that room, but I do know you made quite an impression. They genuinely like you..." Eric paused ".. Tiger!"

John let the boost to his ego win out over the blows to his dignity. He looked about the hotel room where the night before last he had been man enough to please two beautiful (and extremely self-confident) young women. He felt a little calmer.

"Okay I take your point. But I cannot help feeling you are exploiting us for your own entertainment." John said. "I guess I should have expected that."

"This was the best way to get you noticed and I did not force you to do it, did I? Just like I don't force anyone to appear in my magazines. They do it for money. Sex sells, Johnny boy!" Eric was warming to his favourite theme. "Especially if there's a human interest angle. Look at those celebrity sex video. I make fifty movies a year that are fifty times more filthy than the Paris Hilton video and yet it has probably outsold them all put together. It sold millions and was downloaded millions of times more. That's the good stuff, because it is real, because it gives the public access to someone people think they know. That was great publicity for her and this will be great publicity for you."

"You didn't film.." John interrupted, in panic, unsure exactly how far Eric would go. This amused Eric no end.

"Don't worry, Johnny boy! Your video is for my private collection."

Now John was extremely worried. How far had Eric already gone? He was fairly certain there was no video. But he hadn't exactly been paying attention. How, after all, had they got that photo on page 22? And with Eric Hayle you never quite knew what he had on you. The only way you would ever find out for sure would be an unpleasant experience. In all likelihood a very unpleasant and very public experience. John attempted to replay the night. He didn't think there had been a video camera at any point. Could there have been a hidden one?

"This is why I became a newspaper man to sell stories. True stories. Pornoland deals too much in fantasy. And I don't care much for the pointlessness of Celebrityville either. I prefer reality. I prefer your version of reality. But those idiots out there aren't going to listen to anything we try to tell them, unless they hear it from someone famous. And now thanks to the fucking Scum, you will be feted like a rock star."

Thinking back, John realised that it had been in this room. Holding Eric against one ear, he started hunting around the room to see where a camera might have been concealed. Eric kept on talking.

"Like I said before, trust me, everyone is a winner on this. Heck, I even got five grand for putting the story their way. Not that they know it was me. Not yet anyway, I can't wait to give that bastard Wallace a call and let him know." There was a burst of laughter and John heard Eric shouting across the office at some lackey, presumably to look up the number of the editor of the Scum.

"Look I'm rambling. I told you I wasn't going to tell you everything, didn't I? So you can't say you weren't warned. And right now I am telling you it's okay. The message is this; 'Don't worry John, Uncle Eric knows what he is doing.' Tomorrow, the Clarion will print your side of the story. You better come into the office."

The line went dead.

•

In the library, the man was pleased to find his favourite seat unoccupied. He took just one newspaper like the librarians insisted that he should. He got out his four-colour Biro and his newest spiral bound notebook, already going dog-eared after just a week in use. He was starting with the Financial Times. He started scanning the pages, his red pen poised to mark the significant details.

The librarians had yet to catch him circling words and underlining sentences, but even if they had, it is doubtful if they would have stopped him. They only rationed him to one newspaper at a time to stop fights between the man, the rocking woman and Dr. Donkey Jacket. The librarians weren't that interested in the library rules, mostly they just wanted a quiet life.

The capital's public libraries, being indoors and centrally heated, had always attracted the weird and the feckless. Real research happens in libraries too but for every Karl Marx there are at least four Marx Brothers. And since the government's Care in the Community innovations there had been a large increase in the number of certified card-carrying members of library that the community's librarians had to care for.

Introverted and socially awkward people themselves, librarians were ill equipped for this change to their job description and valiantly tried to ignore the libraries' heaviest users. This unofficial policy worked well.

Mostly the two groups kept themselves to themselves. Rarely would the librarians bother the loonies; who could usually while away the day poring over their favourite periodicals or making complex textual analyses of Barbara Taylor Bradford[*]. Likewise, the loonies did not often trouble the librarians, whom they distrusted for their obsession with silence and their compulsive need to alphabetise everything.

Occasionally members of the two groups would interact, when a librarian might tick off a manic depressive for putting Enid Blyton back in the wrong place or a paranoid schizophrenic might request help posting his latest black helicopter sightings onto the internet.

Today was peaceful and the man was able to work undisturbed. The pinkness of the horse had dictated that he start with the Financial Times, and this in itself was a pleasing omen. He liked the Financial Times with its second section filled with columns and columns of numbers. Normally, he would flick slowly through the paper, his eyes jumping randomly across pages. He'd paused to mark the particular words that resonated with personal occult significance. When he had gone through the whole thing from cover to cover and more carefully from cover to cover of the markets and prices second section, he would transfer his findings into his notebook, colour-coding them as appropriate and attempting to make sense of them as he went.

---

[*] Her popularity with this demographic was a total mystery to the librarians, who observed that the loonies could not stand Catherine Cookson.

Today had been a very good day.

He doubted that he needed to consult any other papers but as he was putting the red and pink paper back, he caught sight of the word GURU on the cover of the Scum. He read the whole story from beginning to end. That never happened.

Normally, the chess column was the only one he read all the way through or took at face value. Not that the Scum had a chess column.

*

John Smith came out of his room and bounced off a wall that had not been there the night before. The wall answered to the name of Parnell Brockgrove.

"Good morning, Mr Smith. I am here to help you pack your things."

"But I'm not leaving."

"The hotel management would prefer it if you did. They do not consider you the sort of guest they would like in their family-friendly hotel." Parnell had walked into the room, leaving Smith no choice but to retreat inside or be flattened underfoot.

"Well, this is not a very friendly way to ask me."

"Please do not shoot the messenger. Your friend Mr Hayle sent me to collect you. To make sure you get safely to Fleet Street."

"Oh, I see. That's it, is it? Very thoughtful of him. Kidnapping me? That is the second 'favour' he has done for me today. What a friend he is, I hate to think how he deals with his enemies. Probably sends you round to help them down a disused lift shaft."

"I am peace-loving man, Mr Smith. I am here as your bodyguard."

"What do I need with a bodyguard?"

"Have you ever appeared on the front page of a national tabloid before?"

"Of course not."

"Mr Hayle is something of an expert when it comes to the gutter press. He thought it best if I look after you. There are quite a large number of reporters and photographers waiting downstairs to buttonhole you. I am Parnell."

Smith shook the extended hand and resigned himself to the slim hope that this apparently reasonable monster was right and Hayle did know what he was doing. Within a few minutes he had packed up his bags and he and Parnell were descending in the lift.

"Your bill has already been settled and we have a car waiting outside. There are about thirty or forty gentlemen of the press between the front door and our vehicle. I suggest you do not say anything to any of them and stick close behind me."

Flashes flashed and shutters fluttered. The reporters started to crowd in all shouting at once. For the first time it sunk in that his 'sin' was not just local gossip filling columns of a county quotidian, a little thrill next to the picture of little Jemima winning the gymkhana. He had assumed that the story might be whispered amongst relatives and passed laughingly around a few old school friends but this was clearly different. Three million people were reading this morning's paper and they would talk to millions more. And Eric was intending to at least double that with his 'counter-punch' tomorrow.

People would point at him in the street, dogs bark at his shadow. John moved in closer behind Parnell and watched with interest as he cleared a path to their vehicle. It was a variety of magic. Since coming outside, Parnell had not broken stride. He had not stopped nor made any sudden movements, he was not touching anyone, he was not even overtly intimidating them but bodies were bouncing away from his presence. Like little magnets flipped into the air by the invisible field of some strong force of the same polarity. The crowd had been close around them but as Parnell passed through it sprung apart. He always inches away from actually touching anyone and yet they leaned awkwardly back or were uprooted in their effort to keep out of his strongly bounded personal space.

John kept as close as he could, filling the gap in Parnell's wake. They made it to a large red SUV with darkened windows that prevented anyone from seeing inside. It had the Clarion logo printed along its side. Parnell shepherded Smith and his suitcase into the back seat and went round to the driver's side. A few seconds later they were pulling into traffic. It had all happened so fast that John had barely registered the flashes and the shouts.

He had been aware of the press. But only as a collective, crowded around him. No one face had caught his eye. No individual word caught his ear. Here he was, experiencing life in the fast lane and it was all just a blur. A thought jumped into his mind and he scrabbled round to see if they were being chased. No, that would be crazy right? He relaxed into the comfy leather seat.

"Thank you."

"You're welcome. It's my job. You did okay for your first time." Parnell glanced back in the mirror. "We'll be at the Clarion in ten minutes. Your heart is still racing. Sit back and count your breaths."

Parnell was right, John was full of adrenaline. He tried to do as Parnell suggested. It wasn't easy but it seemed to help. A few minutes later they were passing through Trafalgar Square and along onto the Strand. John was relaxing and as they pulled onto Fleet Street he was almost enjoying himself. He half-wished the windows weren't tinted so that people could see him.

They pulled up outside the Clarion and Parnell let him out. John glanced about himself but no one was paying them any attention whatsoever. Parnell handed the keys to a Clarion security guard, and taking Smith's case in one enormous hand. He led him into the building. This time, they were waved straight though reception. Waiting for the lift Parnell spoke again.

"Did you know that in the seventeen hundreds the Fleet was still an open river? It was London's gutter, the combined filth of human and animal population oozed down it into the Thames. Tanners and slaughter-men dumped the carcasses of dead animals into it. A goodly number of human bodies found their way there too. The stench was like nothing we can imagine. In the end, everyone got so sick of the foul and disgusting river of filth they buried it underground and paved it over."

"Or at least they thought they did," John said as the lift opened for him. Parnell gestured John inside but stayed in the corridor. He held onto John case and with the other hand held up four fingers. John pressed the corresponding button. "Do you ever get used to the stench?"

Parnell Brockgrove shrugged and turned on his heel, a complex set of movements involving the rearranging of a large number of very solid muscles. The grace and economy with which he did it hinted at the secret of his success as a bodyguard and bouncer. Such was his poise and skill that he could effortlessly deflect any blows that came towards him. The slow moving gentleness and deceptive economy of movement with which he did it left anyone watching with the impression that the attacker had bounced off some magical force field that surrounded this gentle giant. People, punches and all shapes of trouble would literally bounce off him.`

~

The secret of how Parnell did this was open to anyone to learn. All they would have to do would be to spend ten solid years paying mindful attention to their every movement and practising for a few hours each day a simple sequence of Chinese callisthenics. Anyone could learn it. People often made the mistake of assuming that the reason he could perform this magic was because Parnell was a six foot six, twenty stone natural athlete with a build that would give the World Heavyweight Champion cause for pause before coming to blows with Parnell.

The real essence of his methods came from what he had been taught by a sprightly Chinese dentist and a weedy ex-librarian from Slough. For the last ten years Parnell had been learning T'ai Chi Chuan at the school of Master Chou and Master Phillips. T'ai Chi seen by the uninitiated as the ancient Chinese art of directing invisible traffic slowly, to its initiates it was the Chinese art of directing invisible traffic. Having only been invented in the mid seventeen hundreds it could hardly be called ancient by Chinese standards and the 'traffic' was more commonly referred to as 'chi', a metaphorical measure of internal energy to be directed into fluid and effective movement. It need not necessarily be done slowly, but when practising a student has so many subtle adjustments to be aware of that the slower they go the more they can learn and improve. Parnell was one of the school's slowest pupils.

In the ten years he had been going to Chou and Phillips, Parnell had learnt that this size and strength would count for nothing unless they were properly channelled. He had learnt this the slow and gradual way of all valuable knowledge. And if he were to forget to use his mind alongside this body his teachers would always catch it, demonstrating the power of a well-placed twitch of the muscle that sent him flying across the room. Considering that both Master Chou and Master Phillips were into their sixties and about five foot five apiece it was a clear lesson.

Master Chou was a direct line pupil of the Yang family. Master Yang Lu-chan (1799-1872) known as Yang the Unsurpassed, had learnt T'ai Chi Chuan, literally translated as 'Supreme Ultimate Fist', by peering through a fence at the the secret practice of a famous martial arts teacher Chen Chang-hsing. At night he would practice what he had seen, rediscovering for himself the secrets Chen taught. One day Chen saw this young man and recognised his own style being so expertly performed. Ignoring the culture of secrecy surrounding martial arts at the time, he took Yang on as a pupil but was very quickly surpassed by his student. Yang left and founded his own school which flourished and such was his reputation that he even taught at the imperial court. His sons learnt from their father but did not always maintain his tradition with the diligence he would have liked.

His grandson, Yang Cheng-fu (1883-1936) known as Yang the Invincible, was responsible for popularising the family style and gathering a group of very talented and dedicated students. Following the Chinese revolution, several of these including Lee Shu-pak and Cheng Man-ching found themselves in Hong Kong where Chou, then a young dentistry student, started learning their art.

Simon Phillips was born and lived the first 20 years of his life in Slough. He had been a quiet, introspective child. He had first read about the history and mystery of China as a boy in a dusty old encyclopedia from the era of the British Empire. As he grew so did his fascination and obsession, and he devoured anything in print about China. He studied oriental languages at university and had got a job in the university library to have access to otherwise hard-to-come-by Chinese literature. He was too scared to visit the country he loved.

Eventually, in the early nineteen seventies as the Kung fu craze was sweeping the west following the death of Bruce Lee, a friend had persuaded Simon that the two of them should go to Hong Kong. His friend had quickly become bored and after a month had returned to Britain. Simon stayed for 15 years. He had only been planning to stay a little while. He only had money for two months but about six weeks into his visit he met Chou and fell in love. Simon stayed and Chou introduced him to T'ai Chi. He fell in love again.

Such was the intensity of their relationship and their pleasure at expressing their love through the gentle ballet of T'ai Chi that they almost spent every moment of their time together sparring and improving the art. Chou wanted to open his own school but while everyone acknowledged the excellence of both Masters Chou and Phillips; there was local resistance to having a white instructor so they continued as they were. Chou continued to practice dentistry. Simon was unable to find any purposeful or meaningful work, in they end they decided that they would open their school back in England.

And so with the unofficial blessing of the official Yang school they came to London and opened their academy.

Though he weighed more than the two of them put together, Parnell had never once succeeded in pushing over either of his two masters. T'ai Chi sparring consisting of two practitioners squaring up to each other a pace apart and attempting push or pull your opponent off his feet. The force of few ounces can deflect a thousand pounds and a thousandth of an inch is the difference between upright and off-balance. With a slight flick of his wrist at exactly the right time a skilled artist could uproot the opposition and send him flying backwards across the room. At first it seems like some magic or trickery but it had happened to Parnell enough times that he realised it was actually the culmination and consequence of the years of intense learning and practice that Master Chou and Master Phillips had applied.

Always of a philosophical disposition, the challenge of discovering these secrets appealed to him and over the next ten years he became their star pupil. He spent at least several hours every day going through the slow ballet of the Form; the long interconnecting choreographed sequence of the moves and postures of the art. He learnt about breathing, about how all the necessary muscles must be in alignment to function at utmost efficiency, that a light floating touch and posture adapts and reacts to any intrusion into ones personal space. He learned to think in thousands of an inch. (But still was unable to catch up with the continual improvements of Phillips and Chou who spent their mornings and afternoons practising and their evenings teaching.)

* ¢

John found Eric in a conference room off the main newsfloor. The table was spread with papers and newsprint. There were two other people in the room, a scruffy unshaven man not much older than himself and a severe and smartly dressed young woman. The man was seated, flicking through the folder that Eric had been waving around at Blacks. The woman stood, waiting to be given a purpose.

"Mr Smith! The man of the moment." Eric was still just as cheerful. "Welcome to the Clarion. Let me show you how newspapers work. We will set the record straight. Let's hit back at those bastards at the Scum. Let's hit them hard.

"This is Jack Harris, one of my finest." Jack and John exchanged nods. "This is Eva, she reads my mind and organises some of my many lives. She's something of a prude so she won't like *you*." John and Eva swapped smaller nods. "But she *will* bring you a tea or a coffee if you ask her nicely."

"Yes, tea please." Eva evaporated.

"Right, let's not dilly dally. We've got to strike while the story is hot. You tell us your version and we will print the truth."

"What!?"

"Just the plain and simple truth. You had no idea those lovely girls were escorts. Those unscrupulous newspaperman must have set you up. I wonder if you could sue? I'll get one of our lawyers to join us. I wonder what other lies they printed? I see you've got the offending filth right there, may I?" Eric was gesturing at something in John's left hand.

John looked down. He was clutching a tight furled copy of the Scum. He'd been holding it since he'd left his room in the hotel. Slowly uncramping his hand, he dropped it to the table. All you could read was the single word 'GURU'. The world went dark.

The next thing he knew he was sitting down, and Eva was trying to get him to take a sip of tea. It was sweet. He didn't normally take sugar but then he didn't normally faint.

"Too many late nights?" Eric was still there and more amused than ever. "You should slow down."

Perhaps John looked like he was about to cry. Eric suddenly changed tack.

"Look, this is all completely under control. Under my control. You don't have to do anything. Jack and I will take care of this. The mouthpieces of the moral majority, self-appointed spokespeople for what is True and Right would say with the absolute conviction of the self-righteous that I am the worst of the pack. But my papers only print what is true. Or else what would be funny if it were true."

"We'll threatened them with lawyers. It costs them money and scares them away from anything genuinely controversial. But it won't come anywhere near court. Not in my lifetime and I'm batting for my century."

Eric was looking forward to his hundredth birthday because he wanted to see if he would receive a telegram from the Queen after his extremely anti-monarchist papers had spent most of her reign being extremely rude about members of the Royal Family. It would piss him off if he got it from her. He was dearly hoping to outlive the sceptre'd Hag. He took great satisfaction each time one of his enemies died before him. In his long life he had buried a lot of them. But, for some reason, he was always making new ones at a faster rate.

"Watch this. Some kid made a YouTube video combining your performance at the club and sound-bites from the drive-time show, to make it seem like Kevv did interview you. It's quite clever."

CHAPTER EIGHT
TELEVISION AGAIN

But if oxen and horses and lions had hands
and so could draw and make works of art like men,
horses would draw pictures of god like horses,
and oxen like oxen, and they would make their bodies
in accordance with the form that they themselves
severally possess.
– Xenophanes

†

Today, Reverend Cake was having his busiest day since that whole gay boy band furore of the year before. He had already given four interviews (two for local radio and two for local newspapers). Now he was on his way to do several TV news segments. Although John Smith was not his usual kind of bogeyman, there was something about this story that was just getting bigger and bigger. The Reverend Cake congratulated himself on being one of the first to spot its potential and the first and loudest voice condemning the intrinsic nihilism of the Smith message.

For once the Reverend Cake had found a broad range of support for his denouncement. The story was drawing a wide range of commentators both religious and secular, from both left and right, many uneasy with what Smith's message represented. Of course, few of them endorsed Cake's conservative Christian position but they all acknowledged the arguments that he had first articulated against Smith. More surprising was to find himself quoted with approval by an equally large group of more cynical commentators in the liberal media, who normally would have never have sided with Cake against someone like Smith, so clearly one of their own. Behind the intentions of these talking heads, Cake guessed that most of the motivation came not from a sense of moral outrage but from a desire to settle scores with Eric Hayle.

Reverend Cake was out in front in the denouncement of the Smith phenomenon and from the very beginning he had seen through to and condemned the malevolent hand of Eric Hayle. As a result he became increasingly associated with the story. Each day his phone would ring more often as he bubbled to the top of the call lists of more and more of the journalists covering the story. The Reverend was never short of a new quote to condemn the craze. The journalists were obviously pleased with his copy because they usually used it verbatim and never asked him if he thought his own role was not contributing to the continuation of Smith's time in the spotlight. But of course if the hacks started asking questions like that they would soon think themselves out of existence. The newspapers left out the Reverend's evangelism but they were quite good at crediting him as the President of Families First.

The Families First group was first and foremost about attempting to prevent certain people from having families and indirectly forcing them on others who did not want them. They opposed single mothers, surrogacy and fertility treatments. They would not countenance gay couples wanting to conceive or adopt. They were against abortion - full stop. They considered both sex education and contraception inappropriate for teenagers. In fact they could not conceive the goodness in any baby not born to two monogamous, married heterosexual parents doing things naturally. That little baby Jesus was a precedent for artificial insemination and the non-standard family unit was just the exception that proved the rule.

The group spent all of its money and most of its time campaigning against these sins and sinners. At no extra cost to his organisation Reverend Cake would keep his name in the papers by regularly denouncing the latest teenage fashion or promoting with his seal of disapproval the work of 'controversial' rap stars and 'provocative' pop starlets. It was a win, win, win situation. Cake got coverage, corporate controversialists in the music industry got their free advertising and the media got an easy story.

Unfortunately, this did not bring any money into the church. The press would gladly have paid Cake for his sound bites, as would the record companies but Cake was not that stupid nor that desperate. As long as he kept his church in the news, he had plenty of funding. The funding had come in secretly from a similar organisation in the States. That group had been founded by Christian oil barons who literally had more money than sense. Following a tour he had done of the Bible Belt, they had provided Cake with a piddling few million they had lying around and the transfer was arranged in such a way as to make it appear that the Families First group had substantial support in the United Kingdom. It did not. It had Cake, a couple of his cronies and the embarrassment to humanity that was his congregation.

If he had not been a fully-fledged Church of England Bishop, he would have been ignored as just another evangelical crank. As it was, he was an ecclesiastical disaster to a Church hierarchy that always preferred to be ecumenical. Only the last week, the Archbishop of Cardiff had let slip a remark that was widely interpreted as an admission that he did not believe in any of those Biblical fairy stories (though he thought Christianity was still, on the whole, a good idea).

Cake was a canny enough preacher to know when to preach to the converted. His appointment to the Bishopric had been several years ago back when he was still ambitious about succeeding in the Anglican hierarchy. But once it had become clear that he would never process any further in the official family of the church, he had founded the Families First group. Shortly after he had taken his collection plate on a transatlantic flight. He came back with much Good News to declare and several million in secret donations.

Reverend Cake used some of his Southern oil money to arrange for a clipping service to keep track of his many media credits and he sent copies of the better ones to his state-side supporters.

$$\Psi\ ?$$

"Hazel, we're live in 30 seconds."

Hazel had agreed reluctantly to take part in this show. She had felt guilty for inadvertently embarrassing Shona on her own show the week before. When Alice, Shona's personal assistant had called, Hazel had turned them down saying that she did not think it was a very good idea. Ten minutes later she got a call from Evelyn, her publisher's public relations person explaining loudly and at length exactly why it was a very good idea. So when Shona herself called a few minutes after that, Hazel meekly acquiesced to another appearance on Shona's sofa.

The format would be very similar to Shona's usual Friday show; an open discussion in which unhappy couples and dysfunctional individuals worked through their issues on live TV in front of a braying and insensitive studio audience of equally dysfunctional members of the public. Shona would moderate and one of the show's regular experts would offer empty platitudes. Normally each show had a particular theme, eating disorders, compulsive shopping, estranged fathers. Several misfits would recount their tales of woe then spend the rest of the show being accused of being liars, malingerers, perverts, bigamists or worse by the audience. The resident expert would occasionally try to earn their keep by stating the obvious. And whatever the topic (with the notable exceptions of estranged relatives and extra-marital affairs) Shona was usually unable to resist a game of one-upmanship with her own tales of personal hardship and suffering.

For today's show Hazel was acting as the expert and as usual the problems came from the audience. But this week, fired up by her enthusiasm for Hazel's book, Shona wanted to do things differently. So the chronic procrastinators, who had been due to appear, were postponed until the following week (much to their great relief). Instead the problems would come straight from the studio audience. There would be no single topic and no pre-selected panel of basket cases.

There were five carefully screened members of the audience waiting with pre-scripted questions ready to read them out when called on by Shona, with another two standbys in case anything went wrong. However, their problems could be anything and, unlike normally, only Shona would know in advance what they wanted to say. Fad or no fad, Shona had learnt something since the week before. She made sure she had prepared very thoroughly indeed. She wasn't going to let this little old lady ambush her twice in two weeks.

"Hello and welcome to Shona on Friday. I am here once again with Dr. Hazel Cole and today she and I going to be helping you to help yourselves."

Suddenly they were on air. Just Shona and Hazel sitting alone on the sound stage. Hazel was oddly less nervous than last time but with less clue as to what might happen. Before it had gone so awfully wrong, her last appearance had seemed straightforward and predictable. And the production team had been highly reassuring. Used to dealing with TV virgins they had talked her through everything that was supposed to happen and reassured her all the way along. This week she was just one of the team. She didn't feel it but she was determined to do her best.

"Isn't that right Hazel?"

"That's right Shona. I have spent over forty years studying the mind and the brain but I could not tell anyone here, anything about their own minds that they could not figure out for yourselves. Everything that happens to you happens in your head. It happens to your brain and you are your brain. Events may take place 'out there' in the world but it is how you interpret them that makes the difference."

"Can you give my viewers an example?"

"Yes Shona," said Hazel and proceeded to tell the story of the man she had met on the train.

Shona cut this slightly short to tell her own anecdote about how believing in herself had got her onto television. From that they had gone straight to the first case, an unhappy looking woman in her late thirties.

"How can I get my husband to love me again?"

"Do you love him?"

"Yes."

"For how long have things been going wrong?"

"We have been married ten years and known each other for nearly twice that. It has been tough and rocky at times but I still love him. In spite of everything I still get a magical, special feeling from being with him. But I get the feeling that I no longer excite him."

"Have you asked him?"

"No."

"You are able to come on national television and publicly ask me to solve your problem for you but you cannot talk to your husband?" Hazel left no room for an answer. "I am sorry to say there is nothing I can do in your relationship. But I do think that if you are brave enough to come here then I think you can definitely tell him how you are feeling."

"I can't."

"You can tell two million strangers but you cannot tell him?"

Shona winced, wanting to interject that she had nearer four million viewers but she stopped herself.

"I am being unkind. It IS easier to talk to strangers than to people who have known us a long time. The longer someone knows you the less they actually listen to what you say. They assume they know it all already."

The woman opened her mouth to say something but nothing came out. Her brain was too busy thinking. This hardly ever happened. People came on Shona's show to argue why they were right, not wonder if they might be wrong. But Hazel had just removed all lines of attack. She'd moved past the confrontations and appeared to have actually helped this first guest. The woman sank slowly back into her chair. The audience at home could see the advice sink slowly into her.

The studio audience saw it too and the atmosphere in the room became more charged. People shifted, people sat up. Here was someone who really could help. It wasn't clear exactly *how* she was helping. She hadn't said anything particularly unusual or profound but just watch how the woman had sunk calmly into herself told them that it had worked for her. And if it worked for her then maybe it would work for them. Eighty people started mentally rephrasing the questions they thought they wanted to ask.

In the awkward silence Shona sank too. It wasn't supposed to go like this. The first problem was supposed to take them up to the adverts. Yet here they were, still less than five minutes into the show and already they were moving to the next guest. Looking at her notes she hoped this one would be better. Some middle-aged no hoper worried that he had wasted his life. Let's see her fix that in under three minutes.

Shona called the man out and the boom mike moved to hover over his head. Before Shona could ask him anything about himself, he had flung himself desperately into the care of the good doctor.

"Dr Cole, how can I be happy?"

"What is making you unhappy?"

"Life"

"There's no cure for that but we are all in the same prison. Life is complicated, messy and unfair. There is no justice. The best one can do is to understand your own mind. "

"That doesn't help me much. Give me a specific example"

"What would make you happy?" Hazel asked

"You tell me." the unhappy man shot back.

"But it is very different for different people."

"Money."

"It can be an answer but you could make yourself more unhappy as you chase after it. Maybe the best way to be happy is to think of something you can have and think of a reason why you deserve it. And it has to be a better reason than because you are unhappy. You should not be rewarding yourself for being unhappy, that will just teach you to feel sorry for yourself and make excuses to indulge. Find a positive reason, there will be one. Maybe you did something good at work or for your children. You've been on television. That's a brave thing to do."

"Yes," He had wanted to be angry but it was too difficult while trying to concentrate on what Hazel was telling him. It wasn't what he had expected and yet at the same time it seemed quite obvious. Besides, something about Hazel reminded him of his favourite teacher back in school, Miss Norman. She used to tell him off too. Back in the room, Hazel was still speaking.

"Then, before opening that bottle of wine, pause to think about that positive thing. You've bought the round. Your son or daughter made you laugh. If you can't think of anything, phone a friend. You have friends and it's good to speak to them. That can be the reason in itself."

"That's not much," he protested weakly.

"No, but it's better than nothing isn't it?"

"Yes." He said it in a very quiet voice and sat down. Only lip-readers would have noticed the silent 'Miss' he added at the end.

This was bad TV. The studio expert was supposed to provoke the audience into a stand-up fight not cow them gently into their seats with a series of verbal hugs.

There was a buzzing in Shona's ear. Her producer wanted to know if Shona had lost her voice. The realisation that she had not interrupted anyone for ages on her own show was like a shot of adrenaline straight to her heart. She yelped. She twitched. But no words came.

Dr Hazel Cole, MD, PhD didn't seem to notice this seizure.

The show must go on so the producer steered her shell-shocked star through a few more introductions and Dr. Cole did the rest. She soothed. She calmed. She talked people through their problems and guided them gently to their own solutions. All the scheduled guests were dealt with and the back ups. Plenty more hands went up and plenty more people were helped. Their problems weren't solved but their helplessness was being addressed.

All except Shona's. She had recovered somewhat from her earlier fright but this was going from bad to worse. You couldn't make good TV without drama and tension, but Dr. Cole seemed to defuse all the bombs before they even had chance to start ticking. Shona was having trouble finding anything to add. Any place to interject with her own insights and unhappiness. She was not happy about it. But there wasn't a lot she could do.

"We've got time for just one more," the producer's voice came into her ear and she echoed it to the audience. Finally some good news.

It seemed like everyone had had his or her say. But there was a small, shaking hand half-raised on the back row. The floor manager spotted this girl, early twenties and quite frankly not right for television. But by now they were out of other choices. He whispered to the producer, who guided Shona and camera two towards the sad and nervous figure.

"Yes, the girl at the back there. Your hand is up?"

"Yes."

"What is your name?"

"Susan."

"Hello Susan, You have a question for me and Dr. Cole?"

"For Doctor Cole, yes."

"And…"

"My baby just died. She was three months old. What can I do?"

The audience hushed and Shona's heart leapt. She felt much better. At last, here was one that Dr. Cole wouldn't have an answer for. Couldn't.

Camera two tightened on the girls face. Camera four zoomed in on Hazel, who was studying the girl carefully. The producer cut back and forth between the two. Eventually Hazel spoke.

"Susan, what was your baby called?"

A strange look passed across the girl's face.

"Emily," There was a hesitation in her speech. "She was called Emily"

"Susan?"

"Yes?"

"You're lying."

"No!" said Susan.

"Yes!" thought Shona.

"There wasn't a baby was there? ... Susan? Tell me."

"No"

"But something *is* the matter. Please, tell us."

By now the girl's face was wrinkling. Her eyes were watering and fixed firmly on her lap. She wouldn't look up, trying to block the room full of people, lights and cameras. After an age, she looked back to Hazel.

"I'm lonely," she said and burst into tears.

Hazel was already out of her chair. She was climbing the stairs beside the bank of chairs. She reached the girl and wrapped her up in her arms. More tears came. And more. Hazel was crying too. Members of the audience joined in. It built and spread. Little embarrassed wipes of the eyes became full blowing into handkerchiefs. Sobs became howls.

Shona's mouth opened and closed. Again and again.

The producer eventually remembered he was human being and ended the transmission.

The switchboard took lots of calls. Within minutes The Guardian and the Telegraph had both phoned Hazel's agent to arrange interviews. Shona's station knew a hit when they saw one. The executive producer was waiting for them even before they came off air.

~

The procrastinators were put back another week and then another.

Bookshops found themselves being asked for copies of a book they had never heard of. They phoned Hazel's publishers to moan about how unfair it was that their competitors were being given early access to this hot new book but that they had only got one or two copies. Their competitors phoned up and said the same thing. The initial print run had been just 5,000, normal for an unknown author of this type. These had all gone.

The confused but happy senior publishing staff found that there was not even a copy in the office, they had to laser print it from proofs to see what their best-selling book was about.

They spent the morning trying to blame each other for not having been ready for this success and the afternoon fighting to claim the credit for getting this author aboard. At about four o'clock a secretary passing through to clear away coffee cups, asked her boss how many more copies of Help Yourself they were printing and could she get five put aside?

Nobody, of course, had thought of ordering the reprint to commence, but after a further brief flurry of blame-storming they called the printers to put in an order for another 50,000. This was not nearly enough.

†

"And finally tonight we have a report on Exocet celebrity John Smith, who is inspiring idiocy all over the country." The Newsnight presenter managed just the right amount of sneering condescension. "With me in the studio is the Right Reverend Cake, Bishop of Enfield and President of the Families First group. But we go first to this report from our youth culture reporter, Natula Varaskia."

Natula Varaskia, only 24 herself, and a former child pop star, was an ideally qualified youth reporter. Although her previous career was a distant memory and her teenage years had been almost normal. In her first year at university she had started producing short news items for student TV. A contract with small satellite entertainment news channel paid for the rest of her education and set her on her current path. She wanted to be a serious journalist but was seasoned enough to play to her strengths. She went to the BBC the first chance she had to work in 'youth programming'. She worked hard not to be typecast and took any chance she could to do real reporting. Not that she was called upon much by this very middle-aged programme, but when she did she made extra effort.

Her report on John Smith was both highly professional and highly entertaining. The evening before she and her cameraman had gone her old university bar and found a likely group of photogenic students. She followed them through the course of an evening, interviewing them and plying them with drink, as they went along. The cameraman captured their increasingly drunken antics and these were edited down to a three minute package, which Natula spliced together with stills and audio from Smith's performance. The juxtaposition was obvious but effective. Here were people who really did live for the instant, who swept through life with an intense focus on the immediate here and now. They enjoyed themselves and little else and this, the report and selective editing implied, was why Smith's message was spreading so fast through their group. Yet Natula carefully left it open whether Smith and his followers stood for the same thing or whether they were just hearing what they wanted to hear. Back in the studio, the presenter turned to his guest.

"Reverend Cake, what is your reaction to this latest youth craze?"

"I just worry about the example this man sets to our young people. What he is saying is childish and we all want our children to grow up. To paraphrase the apostle John, to become a man you must put away childish things. It is irresponsible to encourage people to just enjoy themselves."

"So people shouldn't enjoy themselves?"

"He-hem, I am not suggesting that, Michael." Cake replied with a little fake laugh. This was how the game was played on Newsnight. "I like music and art. If you came to my church in Enfield you would find that it is full of both. The music and art in my church in Enfield."

"So you see John Smith as just another pop star?"

"Yes and no. His message is as empty of content as any pop lyrics and he is clearly as much a manufactured commercial product as any boy band. But I worry that people won't see him for what he is. By standing up there speaking, telling people what to think, he's disguising the fact that his message is essentially empty."

"Teenagers should listen to you instead, Reverend?"

"It wouldn't be a bad idea if they did, Michael. Not at all" Reverend Cake felt comfortable, Michael Wallis was still playing straight out of the Newsnight playbook. The Reverend had been here before.

"But seriously Reverend Cake, couldn't we argue that this man Smith is articulate and attempting to engage people in genuine existential debate? You personally might not like his message but young people are listening. Aren't you just annoyed that you and the church youth club are failing to compete?"

"I think I know which one will still be around this time next year." A tried and tested defensive move from Cake.

"So why are so concerned about John Smith?"

"Oh, Smith himself seems to be a nonentity." At last Cake spotted his opening. "Nothing more than a puppet for darker, more malevolent forces. Smith's message is nihilistic because he is an empty vessel echoing the words of a dark master. It is not hard to see that it is the Clarion that has manufactured this false prophet. It is their agenda which is really behind this."

"Eric Hayle is the real villain here?" The Reverend Cake had pretty much won. Fire and brimstone always made these BBC types uncomfortable.

"I'm glad we agree Michael." This was too easy. "We at Families First have long argued that Eric Hayle is not fit to run national media and we urge the government to silence the public voice of this self-proclaimed pornographer. This John Smith episode is just another example of Hayle trying to rip apart the fabric of society and destroy good Christian family values." Checkmate.

"Reverend Cake, Thank you." The Reverend Cake accepted the resignation graciously.

CHAPTER NINE
TELEPHONES

Watson, come here, I want you!
– Alexander Graham Bell, making the world's first telephone call to his assistant Thomas Watson, on Friday, 10th March 1876

?

Alice, Shona's personal assistant, was so excited she was spoiling her make-up. She burst into Shona's office, heedless of the standing instruction never to interrupt Shona's post-lunch 'aroma-therapeutic delta-wave energy realignment.'

"We have just had a call from Marina Allan!" she squealed excitedly, waking Shona from her siesta. She had to repeat herself more slowly and in a lower register before it got though to the bleary eyed eighth most important woman in Britain.

When the message got through, Shona was as awake and as excited as Alice. Readers of Chat magazine had voted for who they thought was the best female role model in Britain. Marina Allan had come second. Shona had come eighth but there had been a bunch of pointless celebrities and Olympic medallists in places three to seven. Which in Shona's view made her essentially, the second most important real woman in the country and Marina Allan, the first. Because second was the best any ordinary woman like her or Marina could hope to achieve. No normal woman could compete with Madonna.

Not that Marina Allan was any normal woman. She was famous. She had at least two careers and about six children. She was a very senior figure in the Civil Service and she was on the boards of directors of several large transport consortia and countless charities. She was famously clever and had a style that was all her own. She was also the wife of the Prime Minister.

It would be to under-estimate the size of Shona's ego to think that she herself saw Marina Allan as a role model but more than anything else in life, she wanted Marina on the show. It was an article of faith among the staff of the show that this was the Holy Grail. Shona had interviewed Madonna on three separate PR tours. But Marina did not speak to the media. Marina was not to be criticised or joked about. Shona was to be brought all news items and press photos with Marina in them.

Shona went to the same clairvoyant and the same crystal therapist as Marina but she had not yet bumped into her. Or persuaded either of them to introduce her. She wanted to suggest that Marina came on the show for one of Shona's famous makeovers. Obviously, either Madame Clara or Madame Amethyst had finally mentioned this idea of Marina Allan. And now she was calling Shona.

"She wants to come on the show?" Shona asked Alice, just to confirm she was not dreaming.

"Er.. She wants to meet Doctor Cole," Alice answered falteringly.

"On the show?"

"No" said Alice starting to stop and take stock of her own original enthusiasm for bringing the news to Shona. She had overlooked the overriding importance of Shona in Shona's view of the world. The show came in second place, nothing else came close. Alice saw the fury rushing to Shona face, replacing the all but evaporated elation. And she was the cause of this reversal. It was another accepted fact of life on the show that messengers bearing bad news were occasionally fired.

"They did not say." Alice said quickly, pleading for her lifestyle. "It wasn't her. It was her office. They just said that Marina would like to meet Doctor Cole. They called us to see if we could arrange it. Maybe she does want to come on the show?"

"Maybe" Shona agreed, her internal optimist clinging to this sliver of hope. It was better than nothing. As well as channelling her requests through their shared healer and psychic, Shona had attempted to contact Marina Allan via other mediums. But in the past, all her proposals had been rebuffed by Marina Allan's highly expensive taxpayer provided personal office. In recent months they had stopped being polite about it, not bothering to return Shona's call or even pretending that her messages would be passed to Marina. And now Marina Allan's office was calling her.

Marina Allan was obviously too busy to call in person. As well as her work in the Civil Service overseeing the drafting for the government policy documents in the Department of Transport, she sat on the boards of several of the largest private companies that through a tangled network of subsidiary contracts were now running public transport. This was typical of way her husband's inner circle operated. This did not break the letter of her Civil Service employment contract but it was so breathtakingly in violation of the spirit of them that people were at a loss as to know how to begin to denounce it.

More especially, considering who she had breakfast with each morning. Nor could they understand how he could possibly let her get away with it. Whenever any backbencher or journalist overcame their apoplexy and incomprehension long enough to challenge the Prime Minister on the subject, he would always monotonously recite that in his view was no conflict between the rules governing Civil Service contract and her outside interests, and that every committee that had investigated had declared the same. But since every single one of those committees was ultimately answerable to her husband, the Prime Minister, their conclusions could perhaps be guessed in advance. Everyone else reached the conclusion that the Prime Minister was ultimately answerable to his wife and was only allowed to get dressed in the morning after she had finished with the trousers.

Shona was not interested in political affairs. Successful women were always the victims of envy. She saw Marina as a kindred spirit. Madame Amethyst had said they had the same chakra colouring pattern. She understood that Marina might not want to come on the show right now. But once they had met and seen how much they had in common, felt the connection, become best friends it would be a different story. And this meeting would happen when Shona arranged for Marina to meet Doctor Cole. And after all, it was Shona that had made Hazel famous.

What was more, as implausible as it seemed, this highly successful mother of six, whose husband runs the country, must have seen the show. Shona perked up considerably at the thought that this busy woman with several careers must put aside a couple of hours each morning to watch her show. It must also mean that her husband had forgiven Shona for her affair with his (former) political secretary.

Shona was very happy. Alice was very happy that Shona was very happy and that she would live to work another day. All that remained was for someone to tell Hazel the happy news.

*

John was psyching himself up for a long time before he phoned Eric. He had a question he wanted to ask and for the fifth time that day, he started dialling Eric's private personal line. Eric had given it to him the day before in the Clarion offices. He'd been in an ebullient mood and told John that if ever he had a question, he could call any time. This time he pressed the final number and waited.

"What?"

"Eric?"

"Who is this?"

"It's John."

The FUCK OFF that he received was so primal that John dropped his phone.

¢

"Editor's office"

"Get me, Nichols," Eric said.

The editor's secretary rushed out onto the newsroom floor looking for her boss. Eric was not very happy about something. You did not need to be Hazel Cole to tell that. You did not need even have had to meet him before to tell he was furious. And if you had met him before, you would never be so foolish as to ask him what was troubling him. Even with relative protection of a telephone line between you. Unless perhaps if you were Hazel Cole.

He would probably tell you anyway. Or at least you could pick up the gist by watching to see who was being shouted at the loudest. And picking your way between the profanities, you could piece together his reasons.

"Eric?"

"Nichols, you arse. What do we know about this Cole cunt?"

"The head doctor? Appears on Shona?"

"And in almost every paper today except ours. What the fuck do we know and what the fuck do we think?"

"I don't know. Daytime TV is not something we follow on the news desk."

"Really? Then what the fuck *do* you do all day long? Cos it certainly isn't journalism. There's something big out there and your news desk isn't on it. Wake the cunts up and get them to work."

"Yes Eric."

"Clarke did the Shona and what's-his-face story. I want you and him on a conference call just as soon as you've found a fucking clue."

The line went dead.

*

"John Smith" John answered his phone. He did not recognise the number and was terrified that it was going to be Eric, calling back to shout at him some more. But the silence on the other end of the line sounded nothing like Eric. "Hello?"

"John... It's Sam. Look, I am sorry."

"Oh Sam, Hello... You were just doing your job."

"Yes, but no.. I really am sorry. Look, I got paid. I was doing my job. I didn't really realise.." she paused, "I had a good time."

"So you like your job. Good for you."

"No, I mean I had a good time with you, I enjoyed your company. And you got what you wanted too, didn't you?"

"No, I got what Eric wanted."

"Well, I am sorry. I didn't know.. I did know but I didn't think.. I wanted to say sorry properly. Can I take you for dinner?"

"Okay, and which way will I have to look for the camera this time?"

"Please, I am sorry. I like you. I don't want you to dislike me." She waited but John stayed silent. "I feel terrible..."

"Yes."

"Yes?"

"Yes, I'll come. Somewhere quiet?"

"Somewhere quiet. I'll send you a text. John, thank you."

She rang off.

John's anger with Sam lasted about as long as it took to drop to the sofa. Nevertheless, his reason to catch up with the executive decision of his emotions. Was Sam a good person, he wondered? Your average man can forgive a beautiful woman a lot of things that must make it difficult to be a beautiful woman and still be a good person. Sam is *very* beautiful, so it must be *very* difficult for her to be good. She did seem sorry, so there was some goodness in her. And she seemed to like him, which showed good taste. Maybe there was hope for her?

Maybe he could make her his special cause? Being a source of guidance and inspiration to millions was all very well but it was very impersonal. He needed to connect with his people. He needed to help those around him share in his epiphany. Sam was troubled but with the right nurturing, with his help, she could blossom. He hoped so. He owed it to her to try.

Besides, he needed to show that his message was more than story, didn't he? That it played out in his life, that it made him happy, as well as successful. Maybe, Sam could help him do that? She was right; they had had fun last week. Perhaps he needed her as much as she needed him.

His ridiculous daydreaming continued late into the evening. Filled with this unexpected new purpose he did nothing all day. Just revelled in his optimism. But he did not blame himself. It did not matter; His new life finally had new meaning.

INTERMISSION
THE MEANING OF LIFE, THE UNIVERSE AND EVERYTHING

Life, the Universe and Everything. What's the point?

I have always been interested in this question. I never really knew what the answer might be. But in 2003, I had what I thought was a good idea. I decided to write to every professional philosopher Great Britain and Northern Ireland and ask them.

It happened slightly by accident. I used to be a trustee for the New Humanist, which is a sort of parish magazine for atheists. Despite its name, New Humanist had been around in one form or another for over one hundred years. It was getting rather venerable and we were trying to find ways to boost our circulation. Sending free copies to philosophers seemed like it might win us some new readers. We had previously sent a promotional mailing to several hundred Church of England vicars and despite the fact that New Humanist is a very atheist publication, the magazine got about 60-70 new subscribers! Which is a pleasing fact about the C of E and an unusual endorsement for our magazine. Maybe philosophers would be interested too?

Though I suspect a well written, witty and informative general interest magazine with a rationalist/humanist tilt is the last thing they'll want after a hard day in the office reading dust dry tracts like *The Transcendental Grounds of Meaning and the Place of Silence*, published in the no-doubt excellent **Meaning**

Scepticism. But perhaps we wouldn't be able to tear them away from the slightly more gripping journal, **Metaphilosophy**, which has recently had include *'Some astonishing things'* and *'Some Worries about Normative and Metaethical Sentimentalism'*. Though myself and other readers of **Analysis** are more worried about *'Gruesome Perceptual Spaces'*. But most likely after long hours struggling with *'Realism Detranscendentalized"*, in the **European Journal of Philosophy**, at work, when they get home, they probably just flick on the telly or flip through something mindless like Heat Magazine or the latest Dan Brown. Who knows?

Despite the fine quality of the New Humanist, I couldn't help thinking this was a mundane use for a list of all the philosophers in Britain. I had access to the finest minds in the country, people who (I imagined) were paid to spend all day wondering about the meaning of life, the universe and everything. Judging by the titles of the papers they write, they don't actually do so but in principle if anybody knows the answers to life's great questions it ought to be these fellows & fellowesses[*].

So I decided to spam them again with a letter of my own. I did not expect them to be able to provide me with an answer. Not *the* answer. But if they could not, I thought that, at the very least, they ought be able to provide me with a convincing justification why an answer was not possible. And maybe provide some mildly satisfying alternatives.

Thanks to the invention of the internet, it was easy for me to find the names of every member of staff in all the University Philosophy departments up and down the country. For the price of a few hundred pounds of stamps, I could write to

---

[*] Surely the whole point of realism is that it *isn't* transcendental? (Don't ask me, I am not a philosopher. As will become increasingly apparent.)
[*] Or is that fellatrices?

them all. Never before in human history has a single crank had this amount of access to professionals searching for the meaning of meaning. With great power comes great opportunity for mischief and time-wasting. I did not want to be dismissed so lightly, I took time to compose my letter carefully and politely. This is the letter I sent them. It was not written in green ink.

Professor X / Doctor Y
Department of Philosophy
University of Why
Why-on-Why
United Kingdom

1st October 2003

Dear Professor X / Doctor Y,

As a professional philosopher, I expect that you are often plagued by cranks and lunatics. I am no exception. I have it in my head that you might know the meaning of life, the universe and everything. Therefore, I am writing to ask if you could explain it all to me? Do not be too flattered, I am asking every philosopher in the country!

If God were required to explain Himself, I am sure She could do so in a few eloquent paragraphs on one crisply typeset foolscap sheet, though as an atheist, I have not tried asking Her. You are welcome to go further but I would prefer something more like Meditations than either Either/Or or Being & Nothingness. For the sake of brevity and convenience, please feel free to merely refer* me to a paper you have written elsewhere or perhaps something classic by a dead Greek or German.

One final very mundane point; I am not some highbrow Henry

Root and, in any case, the laws of copyright are on your side. But, who knows, if philosophers turn out to be a particularly witty bunch or if you and your peers disagree strongly then I may collect the responses I receive and attempt to publish them.

I look forward to hearing from you,

Caspar Addyman
caspar@onemonkey.org

*As you know, any letter from a lunatic ought to at least include one split infinitive!

I sent it to 644 professors, readers, lecturers, researchers and post-graduates at 37 different universities. Surely some would take pity on a humble seeker after knowledge, you'd think? Surely? A love of knowledge is part of the job description.

In fact, I received only twenty-two replies. It is now over a seven years since I sent the letter and I've moved house three times so I am not expecting any more. Twenty-two would appear to be it. Less than 4% of the professional philosophers in Britain felt interested in answering a polite inquiry about the ultimate question. Lovers of knowledge they may be, lovers of sharing they are not, 622 of them aren't. The 22 who did reply were great. They took time and pains to explain how stupid I was and how the question I was asking didn't make any sense. But they were kind, funny and thought-provoking as they did it.

Mercifully, I only received one death threat.

Twenty-two Nice Philosophers
Presented in chronological order

Here are all the replies I received, unedited and in the order I got them, with a little information about each of the philosophers who wrote to me. On occasion my correspondents did as I asked and sent me a whole paper of their own to contemplate. I read everything but you don't have to. I haven't included the full papers and I wouldn't dare to try and sum any of them up in my own words. Instead I have where appropriate included some rather lengthy quotations. I am sorry but I am too stupid to do otherwise and besides, that's just the way life works.

Prof. Mark T. Nelson, Westmont College

Mark Nelson was a lecturer at the university of Leeds and has since moved on to become a professor at Westmont College in Santa Barbara. He specialises in Meta-ethics, Normative Ethics, Epistemology and the philosophy of religion. His reply came swiftly by email. It was helpful and informative and suggested that God might have the answer I was looking for. That wasn't the answer I was looking for but it started me off with high hopes.

> From: Mark T. Nelson
> Date: Mon Oct 6, 2003 12:25:11 pm
> Subject: your letter
>
> Dear Caspar:
> Thanks for your letter of 1 October. I'm sorry to say that I can't think of any paper of mine that would answer to your query. I guess I think that a good account of the meaning of life, the universe and everything could not be contained in one crisply typeset foolscap sheet; moreover, I think

it would end up looking a bit religious.

There are loads of book-length treatments of this sort, from Plato to Plantinga, but I think you might find the following an interesting place to start, as they contain short, biographical essays:

T.V. Morris, ed., God and the Philosophers (OUP, 1994)
Kelly Clark, ed., Philosophers Who Believe (IVP, 1993)

Not all of the essays are of equally high quality, but there are some nice essays in both books. In any case, good luck with the search!
Sincerely,
Mark Nelson

Andrew McGonigal, University of Leeds.

Twenty minutes later I received another email from the University of Leeds. This one came from Andrew McGonigal, who had recently joined the department and is still there as a lecturer. He is interested in aesthetics, metaphysics, metaethics, epistemology and the philosophies of mind and of language. He was also honest, helpful and informative and merely referred me to a couple of articles by a living American philosopher. Things were looking up.

> From: "A. McGonigal"
> Date: Mon Oct 6, 2003 12:46:54 pm
> Subject: meaning of life
>
> I don't have much to say that is useful or insightful to say about this topic, I'm afraid. There are lots of reasons why life is valuable, and worth living, but

there may not be any very informative way of collecting them under a single category or heading. There are two good articles by Thomas Nagel which you might find interesting.

> Nagel, T. (2000). The meaning of life. In E. D. Klemke (Ed.), The meaning of life. New York: Oxford University Press.
>
> Nagel, T. (2000). The absurd. In E. D. Klemke (Ed.), The meaning of life. New York: Oxford University Press.

Regards,
Andrew McGonigal, University of Leeds.

Dr. Jens Timmermann, University of Saint Andrews

A quarter of an hour later, a third email arrived from Jens Timmermann. Dr. Timmermann is a senior lecturer at the university of Saint Andrews. He too is interested in Aesthetics, together with ethical theory and ancient philosophy. He is an expert in the work of Immanuel Kant. He was the first of my respondents to attempt an answer of his own. His answer is as satisfying as it is succinct.

> From: Jens Timmermann
> Date: Mon Oct 6, 2003 1:00:22 pm
>
> Dear Mr Addyman,
>
> The meaning of life? That's every philosopher's nightmare of a question, especially over dinner. As you kindly give me the opportunity to answer it in writing, here's a quick reply: Drawing on Kant and Aristotle, my quick answer is that the meaning of life

consists in activity in accordance with reason. So first of all, we must do things with our lives, be active, not fritter it away. Secondly, this activity should be in line with what makes us human: our capacity to think, reason, act and communicate with others like us. This kind of meaning is autonomous and does not depend on God or any supernatural power. Human beings are in charge of their own lives, but they must obey the standards of their own rational and moral faculties.

With best wishes,
Dr. Jens Timmermann, University of Saint Andrews

Andrew Belsey, Cardiff University

A few days then passed before I received my very first postal reply. This was exciting. It came from Dr. Andrew Belsey, a senior lecturer at the university of Cardiff, since retired. His research interests include ethics and he was co-editor of the book, Ethical Issues in Journalism and the Media. I didn't know it at the time but he is also a published poet. This may explain his short but troubling letter.

> Dear Mr Addyman
>
> The meaning of life is preparation for death. I hope that you are well prepared.
>
> Yours sincerely, Andrew Belsey, Cardiff University

So there it was. My very first death threat! I was clearly on the right lines with this project if it was inspiring such animosity from professional philosophers.

I am not one to dismiss lightly the words of a tenured academic so for most of the past nine years I have been on my guard. As you can see I am still here, Andrew and his minions haven't succeeded in their dastardly schemes. In fact I am beginning to wonder if he might have meant it metaphorically. He is a poet, after all. But then again, that might be just what he wants me to think. I better stay prepared.

Arnold Zuboff, University College London

Dr Zuboff is an American philosopher, who works at University College London. He is interested in philosophy of mind, ethics and metaphysics. His research is refreshingly modern and no-nonsense. He thinks there can be answers to the difficult questions and that a philosopher's job is not to luxuriate in pointing out the difficulties but to attempt to find the answers. If I didn't know better from my short correspondence with him, I would imagine him as Dirty Harry, sent back in time to clean up the mean streets of Athens.

> From: Arnold Zuboff
> Date: 07.10.2003, 12:39:16
> Subject: Explanation
>
> Dear Caspar,
>
> I'm attaching two parts of my explanation of things. If you're interested in seeing more, please let me know.
>
> Best wishes,
> Arnold Zuboff

Arnold attached two papers that you can easily find online. The first was entitled "An introduction to universalism." Here I will provide you with just the introduction to that introduction.

Brain bisection, the surgical cutting of the connection between the hemispheres of the brain at the bridge of nerves that normally joins them (the corpus callosum), was an operation that gave relief to epileptics. But experimenters working with split-brain patients in the 1960s discovered an additional result of this surgery that was startling and disturbing. When they fed markedly different information into each hemisphere, the subject would, it seemed, possess two mutually excluding experiences at one time.

Let me dramatize the puzzle in this by asking you to engage in a variation on one of the thought experiments in Derek Parfit's paper 'Personal Identity'. Imagine that by pressing a certain button you could cause your corpus callosum to be anaesthetized, so that the communication between the hemispheres of your brain would be stopped temporarily.

Tonight a concert of your favourite music is going to be broadcast on the radio, but you have to do some tedious studying from audio tapes. Well, why not arrange that the music will go into only the right hemisphere of your brain while the study material will go into only the left after the button has been pushed and the integration of the activities of the hemispheres has been stopped? But then the big question arises: what would your evening be like?

The ordinary understanding of what a person is does not allow that you could be both enjoying the concert and suffering through the studying, since each of these experiences seems to exclude the other. Yet it cannot be that you only enjoy the concert or alternatively only suffer through the studying or that you somehow experience neither. For following a more extensive anaesthetizing, or a stroke, that completely incapacitated one hemisphere you would certainly have had whichever experience was in the remaining functioning hemisphere. The concert would be yours if there was only the right hemisphere and the studying would be yours if there was only the left. In our case there are both.

The answer must be that you will experience both the concert and the studying, *though each will seem falsely to be the whole of your experience.* I shall contend that it is this same false seeming, the same illusion, that hides the fact that *all* experience actually is yours. This is a view I call "universalism". All the experience in all the separate nervous systems of the world is yours, *though what is discovered in each necessarily seems falsely to be the whole of what is yours.* Next I shall argue for this larger claim, but the case of brain bisection has shown this much already: that seeming limits of experience can mislead you into thinking you are less than you are. Then what is it that really sets your limits? What, really, are you?

Well, what are you, PUNK?

Arnold's second paper assumes you have overcome your problems with self-identity and moves on to tackle your bad attitude. He wants you ask yourself one simple question. "Why should I care about morality?".

> Let's inquire into the nature of morality--and, more particularly, into the authority that it seems to have in the judgments of most of us. I think a certain story can help us in raising the question of where it gets that authority.

Imagine that someone we shall call Gyges, after the character similarly used by Plato in a basically similar story, is seated at a table. Just before him on the table is a small console with a single button on it. Let's say he knows that if he pushed that button a distant stranger, who would otherwise be fine, would be killed. Gyges also knows that if he pushed that lethal button, he, Gyges, would be given £10 that he otherwise would not have. We are going to look into whether Gyges has any reason based purely on morality not to push the button.

It is vital that we rule out of our story, if it is to be useful to our questioning of the authority of morality, any possibility that Gyges be punished if he pushes the button or that he in some way be rewarded if he doesn't push it. For if we give him the fear of punishment or the hope of reward as reasons not to push the button, we have not then clearly isolated whether he has a reason not to push the button in its being morally wrong to do so. We are wanting to know whether morality in itself has an authority here for him, but his own punishment or reward carries only the authority of the sort of obvious self-interest that is often distinguished from moral motivation. Therefore we shall say something like Gyges can be sure that the death he might choose to cause would have the perfect appearance of an accident having nothing to do with Gyges. So Gyges would be perfectly safe. Let us add that the remoteness of the stranger ensures that there would be no other possibilities of personal loss or gain for Gyges in either the stranger's death or his continued life.

The question, then, is this: Gyges has a slight but undeniable reason to push the button, the self-interested reason that he will by doing so acquire £10

that he otherwise would not have. But does he have a
reason not to push the button?

In case you don't know the answer, I won't spoil it for you by giving it away now but we shall come back to this later.

Tim Chappell, The Open University

Professor Chappell is director of the Open University Ethics Centre. At the time I wrote to him he was at the University of Dundee and he has worked at quite a range of universities in England and Scotland. As might be guessed, he is interested in ethics and also in a little bit of epistemology. He's written or edited ten books and he also writes poetry. Least you imagine him trapped in a library, bear in mind that he also likes climbing some mountains and skiing down others.

From: Timothy Chappell
Date: Tue 07 Oct 2003, 13:33:45
Subject: the meaning of life

> Dear Mr Addyman,
> For the meaning of life, see the attachment.
> Best wishes,
> Tim Chappell

His article was entitled "How should we live?" At last, an answer! And he'd not been completely whimsical. He is quite courageously trying to provide the Answer. It is only six pages long so if we printed very small and printed on both sides we could certainly squeeze it on a single sheet of foolscap. I'd like to quote it at length but it's somewhat technical and so perhaps it's best to skip over the justifications and get right to his conclusion:

> How should we live? Well, here's a framework answer: respect every good you meet, and pursue any

good you like. That answer's a bit sketchy, of course, and we need to add to it some considerations about the agent's need to make their own agency coherent over time, by incorporating each choice she makes into a continuing narrative of self-creation. Still, the framework answer will do to be going on with. Whatever its faults, its sketchiness in general, and my omission to give any examples of failures to respect any good in particular, the framework answer does, I think, at least have one important virtue: namely, truth.

He sent me that in 2003. But I can't help wondering what he would tell me, if I asked him again today. In 2008 while climbing Ben Nevis, he took a nasty bouncing fall in an avalanche, bouncing for seventy uncomfortable metres down into a gully. He was seriously injured but happily survived and has since recovered. Like any good philosopher would, he wrote a paper about it*. It is an interesting reflection upon what it is like to face death. Both what it is like in that precise moment when it appears to happening and what it can mean when that fear creeps up on us at other times. Professor Chappell's experience of the moment was, in common with many others, one of calm detachment. He describes his main emotion as he fell as an admirably British feeling of embarrassment at making such a fuss.

More troubling for him, as a Christian, was the challenge of Richard Dawkins and others as to why a Christian should ever fear death. He agrees with Dawkins logic that there really isn't anything for a Christian to fear on the other side of death. But, reflecting very honestly on his own experience of fear while waiting to go under anaesthetic, he wonders if what is

---

* Entitled, "The fear of death" it will appear in a forthcoming edition of New Blackfriars. You can also find a copy on his Open university homepage.

actually frightening them is that loss of control that would accompany the moment of passing. He concludes, perhaps surprisingly, that his fellow Christians should take a little more time to consider both death and Dawkins.

Harry Lesser, University of Manchester

Professor Lesser is based at the University of Manchester. He too is interested in ethics.

> I don't think anyone has the answer to this or claims to--as no doubt you know. Nor have philosophers normally tried--philosophy is normally about the more modest questions of what we can know and what we ought to do, and has not solved either of these, though I think it has made useful contributions. Incidentally, there is no reason to think that the contributions of dead men are any less useful than those of live men. The sensible thing to do, as you probably know, is not to worry about this, but to give one's life meaning by spending it, as far as possible, in doing things which one finds worthwhile--satisfying to oneself and helpful to others. Some of us think philosophy is among these, but because it helps with some problems rather than giving an overall answer!

Best Harry Lesser, University of Manchester

John Haldane, University of Saint Andrews

Professor John Haldane is director of the Centre for Ethics, Philosophy and Public Affairs at the university of Saint Andrews. He is interested in the philosophy of mind and the philosophy of religion. His home page has some interesting pictures of him meeting famous people, including the present Pope and Madness frontman, Suggs[*].

Dear Mr Addyman,

Thank you for your interesting letter. I hope the promptness of this reply may compensate for its brevity.

Your question is 'what is the meaning of life, the universe and everything?' Noting that you describe yourself as an 'atheist' I am that the following answer is one you will reject; yet it is the one I believe to be true. The universe of things, events, properties and processes, material and immaterial, concrete and abstract, is the product of an all-knowing almighty, all-loving Deity that created human beings in order that they should know and love it now and for eternity.

If you are tempted to consider this answer further, particularly as it relates to contemporary philosophy you may care to look at the following which contain my own elaborations of the reasons for believing it to be true:

ATHEISM AND THEISM, 2nd Edition by J.J.C. Smart and J.J. Haldane (Oxford: Blackwell, 2003)

and

AN INTELLIGENT PERSON'S GUIDE TO RELIGION J.J Haldane (London: Duckworth, 2003)

I am sure whether my saying so will bring comfort or disappointment but I do not regard your letter as

---

* Not, alas, at the same time.

cranky or lunatic and I hope that you receive an interesting set of replies.

(Incidentally, letters from lunatics are usually written in green biro or typed in small font running close to the margins. Also, the contents often continue on the outside of the envelope.)

Yours sincerely,
John Haldane

Michael Rush, University of Manchester

Michael Rush lectures at Manchester and Bolton and for the Open University. His research interests are primarily metaphysical but his Masters thesis was on the topic of gratitude.

Dear Caspar,

I find myself all too infrequently pestered by self-confessed cranks and lunatics; your honesty is refreshing. Or it was, and then I looked at your website and discovered that the claim of lunacy was just a subterfuge. Still, never mind. I couldn't work out whether your real aim was an answer to your question or the collective humiliation of all the philosophers in the country.

If the first, I fear you'll be disappointed; it's a pseudo-philosophical question asked by non-philosophers, and any philosopher claiming to have an answer for you is cheeky, misguided or, possibly, both. If the second, I'm bound to say I hope you'll be disappointed, if only by those respondents that admit to having no answer for you. This isn't humiliating but, in its turn, refreshing. We never claimed (well, I for one never claimed) to be trying to answer that question, so you can't catch us out there. It'd be like saying, 'Ha! Bloody useless! No explanation of the meaning of life, and they call themselves milkmen?' (to milkmen).

Most people asking for the meaning of life really want to be told the purpose of life, which is a subtly different thing. It seems clear to me that there really isn't one, but equally clear that we shouldn't be in the least bit troubled by this. Anyone tempted to think that God has a design for it all should be urged to remember that there is a species of frog that spends something like eleven and a half months of every year asleep, buried in the sand in Arizona, or some such place, because otherwise it would burn to death. This can't possibly be in accordance with any sensible plan. And I'm sorry, boys, but telling me it's ineffable just won't cut it as an explanation. The really important question is, 'how should we behave?' In this respect ethics is the most important branch of philosophy, though I think we'll need to get the metaphysics sorted out before we can finally do the ethics properly. Aristotle might just have been right in saying that politics is the highest of the sciences, but he failed to add that it is in many ways the most boring.

I think it was Philippa Foot who said that if you ask a philosopher a question they talk for a bit and you go away no longer understanding your question. So there you go. So, if we can't ask about the meaning of life, and if we buy the claim that there's no purpose, what's left? Only to quote those well-known, kooky funsters, Bill and Ted: 'Be excellent to each other, dudes.' Aristotle might well have agreed (once we'd settled on a suitable Greek translation of 'dudes'). And I think we can all learn a lot from that.

Yours, Michael Rush, University of Manchester

I have been trying to decide who is my favourite philosopher. But like all things in philosophy, once you examine the question, it rapidly becomes more difficult than you suspected. I have always admired the lyrical style of Nietzsche. I like the outlook of boggle-eyed frenchman, Jean-Paul Sartre. I think Socrates was a wonderful man. As a result of my philosophical investigations, I have discovered the wonderful penetrating clarity of Derek Parfit, and been reminded of the whimsical wisdom of Thomas Nagel. But they were all good for different reasons that are hard to compare.

Then I hit on rigorous criteria by which to judge it. Which of them would be best company on a night on the town? By this measure, and judging only by his letter, Michael Rush must rank quite highly

Derek Parfit, All Souls College, Oxford.
Derek Parfit retired in 2010 having spent almost all his working life as a fellow at All Souls College, Oxford. His 1984 book Reasons and Persons was a hugely influential discussion of morality and identity that ran to over 550 pages. Despite the weightiness of his tome, much of his popularity is due to the clarity of his writing and his vivid thought-experiments using examples from Star-Trek and other science fiction. He has just finished another work weighing in at over 650 pages, provisionally entitled, "On what matters."

Dear Caspar Addyman,

As it happens, I have written a paper which could be broadly said to be about the meaning of life and the universe. You may have seen this already, but I enclose it as an attachment in two formats.

There's nothing wrong with the occasional split infinite, as Fowler himself said.

With best wishes,

Derek Parfit, All Souls College, Oxford.

Dr. Parfit attached a *short* paper of his on the existence of the universe. It's called "Why Anything? Why this?" The full version was published in two parts by the London Review of Books in 1998. It's worth reading. And it's worth quoting the opening and closing at length.

> Why does the Universe exist? There are two questions here. First, why is there a Universe at all? It might have been true that nothing ever existed: no living beings, no stars, no atoms, not even space or time. When we think about this possibility, it can seem astonishing that anything exists. Second, why does this Universe exist? Things might have been, in countless ways, different. So why is the Universe as it is?
>
> These questions, some believe, may have causal answers. Suppose first that the Universe has always existed. Some believe that, if all events were caused by earlier events, everything would be explained. That, however, is not so. Even an infinite series of events cannot explain itself. ...
>
> Suppose next that the Universe is not eternal, since

nothing preceded the Big Bang. That first event, some physicists suggest, may have obeyed the laws of quantum mechanics, by being a random fluctuation in a vacuum. This would causally explain, they say, how the Universe came into existence out of nothing. But what physicists call a vacuum isn't really nothing. We can ask why it exists, and has the potentialities it does. In Hawking's phrase, 'What breathes fire into the equations?'

Similar remarks apply to all suggestions of these kinds. There could not be a causal explanation of why the Universe exists, why there are any laws of nature, or why these laws are as they are. Nor would it make a difference if there is a God, who caused the rest of the Universe to exist. There could not be a causal explanation of why God exists.

Many people have assumed that, since these questions cannot have causal answers, they cannot have any answers. Some therefore dismiss these questions, thinking them not worth considering. Others conclude that they do not make sense. They assume that, as Wittgenstein wrote, 'doubt can exist only where there is a question; and a question only where there is an answer'.

These assumptions are all, I believe, mistaken. Even if these questions could not have answers, they would still make sense, and they would still be worth considering. I am reminded here of the aesthetic category of the sublime, as applied to the highest mountains, raging oceans, the night sky, the interiors of some cathedrals, and other things that are superhuman, awesome, limitless. No question is more sublime than why there is a Universe: why there is anything rather than nothing. Nor should we assume that answers to this question must be causal. And, even if reality cannot be fully explained, we may still make progress, since what is inexplicable may become less baffling than it now seems.

It ends like this:

> The existence of the Universe can seem, in another way, astonishing. Even if it is not baffling that reality was made to be some way, since there is no conceivable alternative, it can seem baffling that the selection went as it did. Why is there a Universe at all? Why doesn't reality take its simplest and least arbitrary form: that in which nothing ever exists?
> If we find this astonishing, we are assuming that these features should be the Selectors: that reality should be as simple and unarbitrary as it could be. That assumption has, I believe, great plausibility. But, just as the simplest cosmic possibility is that nothing ever exists, the simplest explanatory possibility is that there is no Selector. So we should not expect simplicity at both the factual and explanatory levels. If there is no Selector, we should not expect that there would also be no Universe. That would be an extreme coincidence.

These philosophers had given me plenty to worry about and made me fear for my life. But it was probably Derek Parfit who gave me most to worry about and came closest to killing me. He almost made my head explode when he handed over more than the universe in that article. Carl Sagan, the astronomer and science broadcaster used to make the world seem small when he went on about this pale blue dot lost among the billions and billions of stars in our galaxy. Itself just one of billions and billions of galaxies in the universe.

Which is big but Derek Parfit thinks bigger, much bigger. He doesn't just consider this universe or even a mere multiverse of similar universes with similar laws and similar physics that might have existed in its place. He considers every possible universe, every universe that isn't impossible, not according to our local laws of physics but according to the laws of logic and mathematics. He thinks about them all simultaneously and wonders innocently if this super-set of universes might somehow be a "simplest" that one can conceive of and that can actually have transpired*. Would leaving nothing out paradoxically be the most parsimonious explanation for what is left in?

As it happens, no. But I personally haven't got a parsimonious reason why.

Stephen Butterfill, University of Warwick

Stephen Butterfill is an Associate Professor at the University of Warwick. He is interested in the philosophy of mind.

> From: Stephen Butterfill
> Date: Thu Oct 9, 2003 7:33:25 pm
> Subject: your letter about the meaning of life ...
>
> Hi Caspar (if I may),
>
> Thanks for your letter of 1st October. I'm studying questions about belief and action such as "How do changes in our environment or situation lead to changes in our views about how things are?" I think this sort of question ultimately bears on your question about the meaning of life &c, but not very directly. That said, I'd welcome the chance to discuss it if

---

* There is a simpler universe of universes, an empty set that never even existed. But since this place does exist, that is not where we live.

you're interested.

> The recent philosophers who I think of as addressing your question more head-on are people like Bernard Williams, Tim Scanlon and Chris Korsgaard. My favourite is David Velleman who has a short piece from "The Possibility of Practical Reason" (published by OUP, 2000) on the web at: http://www.oup.co.uk/academic/humanities/philosophy/viewpoint/velleman/
> I suppose the meaning of life &c is a problem we all face in one way or another; what's your take on it?
>
> Best,
> Steve

These days Steve is interested in development psychology, the beginnings of tiny minds and how they start to form beliefs about others.

Christopher Norris, University of Cardiff

Christopher Norris is the Distinguished Research Professor in Philosophy at Cardiff University, He has many interests in the philosophy of language, the philosophy of science and literary theory. He has written numerous books on topics as diverse as quantum theory, literary theory and Spinoza. He sent me a copy of interview that he had done several years before with Tetsuji Yamamoto on *'this, that and the other.'* His summary of Spinoza gives a good summary of his own perspectives

Pretexts: literary and cultural studies, Vol. 8, No. 2, 1999
CRITICAL RESOURCES
Tetsuji Yamamoto
Points of Intervention: Interview with Christopher Norris

Extract:
TY: Which philosopher do you like the best?
CN: Well, I have great admiration and affection for Spinoza. [...] Spinoza, seems to me a model philosopher in many respects. He was a highly intelligent, single-minded and utterly committed thinker but at the same time live a life of exemplary virtue. You know, he was never angry. Well, on just one occasion he did become angry, and I think justifiably so, when the mob attacked and murdered his enlightened patron and defender, Johann de Witt. But he himself was attacked, vilified, persecuted, excommunicated, subject to constant slander and abuse at the hands of his religious opponents. He had to put up with some terrible treatment, and yet he remained calm, composed, good-willed and forgiving; and this had a lot to do with his basic philosophical convictions. Spinoza was a thoroughgoing determinist and he thought that, insofar as you came to understand other people and the causes of their action, you could see our way beyond hating or despising them for what they did. At the same time you could reach a better understanding of your own beliefs, desires, thoughts, and actions, and thereby achieve the kind of freedom that results from enhanced self-knowledge.

Jonathan Gorman, Queens University, Belfast

Jonathan Gorman is Professor Emeritus of Moral Philosophy at Queens University, Belfast, retiring in 2010. He has written many books on the theory and philosophy of history. He is also an expert on the philosophy of law and moral philosophy. He sent me a copy of his entertaining paper, "Some astonishing things".

I believe that, when each of us reflect on the nature of

the particular individual person we happen to be, we do so in the light of certain beliefs, puzzles, speculations and feelings. These beliefs, puzzles, speculations and feelings lie deep within us. Reflection on our individual nature involves reflection on two sets of characteristics: first, those which we may suppose to be common to all individuals; second, those which are distinctively our own. When we reflect on our individual nature, it is not, for most people, for the sake of abstract philosophical interest or psychological curiosity. Rather, it is as part of the means of answering the question what we ought to do with our lives. ...

II The search for explanatory and justificatory completeness of self-understanding is a paradigm of philosophical activity. It makes use of analytical skills. I propose in this paper to examine one particular problem: the place, in our conception of ourselves and our relation to the world, of a sense of astonishment at our existence... [Gorman1991]

Jonathan Gorman, Queens University, Belfast

Michael Proudfoot

Michael Proudfoot retired as Head of Philosophy Department at the University of Reading. He is interested in aesthetics and Wittgenstein. And as a former international competitor in the Modern Pentathlon, he also has an interest in the philosophy of sport. It is unknown to me how much he applied this when he coached Team GB in both Modern Pentathlon and separately in water polo. But one of his Pentathlon teams won gold in the Montreal Olympics. It is always good to find philosophers who lead interesting lives.

Dear Mr Addyman,

As you suggest, I receive a considerable number of unsolicited letters from members of the public, of varying degrees of sanity.

I would recommend to you a book by one of my colleagues, here at Reading, John Cottingham. The book is appropriately titled 'The Meaning of Life': it is available in paperback at around £8 and was published last year by Routledge.

Yours sincerely,
Michael Proudfoot

Norman Geras

Norman Geras is a emeritus professor of Government at Manchester University, though his interest in Karl Marx and politics does not preclude him from being considered philosophical. Similarly, retirement in 2003 did not slow him down. He started blogging and has been widely read on the internet ever since. He has written ten books, some of them about The Ashes test cricket matches.

> From: Norman Geras
> Sent: Sat Oct 11 18:23:18 2003
> Subject: your letter
> Dear Caspar Addyman
> Thank you for your letter of 1 October. On my weblog, which you can find here: http://www.normangeras.blogspot.com/ I offer daily reflections on this and that. You might even call them meditations. Please feel free to visit it and sample them whenever the mood takes you. Whether I've managed to crack the meaning of life, the universe and everything is not really for me to say. But you could try the item 'I can't blog a rainbow' which I posted on October 5 and is here: www.normangeras.blogspot.com/2003_10_05

Best wishes,
Norman Geras

I read it. It's a sweet story of a football fan disturbing a passing motorist. I guess the message is that some profound feelings aren't always easy to communicate. Although I could have got that completely wrong.

Max Steuer

I was also slightly wrong to write to Max Steuer, who turned out not to be a philosopher but an economist and world record breaking hot-air balloonist. He was born in New York City but has been based at London School of Economics since 1959. Nonetheless, as he himself says, why should the philosophers have all the fun and get all the glory?

> From: Steuer, M
> Date: 15 Oct 2003, 17:40:28
> Subject: Life's Meaning
> Dear Caspar
> I'm an economist, not a philosopher. But it is not for that reason only that I wonder if philosophers are either particularly privileged or interested in the question of the meaning of life.
>
> In my view, words and other symbols mean something, but being alive is not a word or a symbol.
>
> Last weekend there was a conference here on the Place of Values in a World of Facts. That might have been right up your street. Perhaps you attended.
>
> I think the universe came about through natural causes, not divine or conscious creation of any kind. These causes are understood by some people better than others, and even the most informed probably

know little compared to what might be known. But still, I'm pretty sure that it is natural, not magical.

I think 'values' is more to the point than 'meaning', and for many purposes nearly the same thing.

We all know the difference between pleasure and pain. I know what I prefer. At the same time, most, not all, of us have views about right and wrong. We can debate about these matters by making reference to some agreed objectives and observations.

You say you want humour as well. So solving the riddle of the universe is not enough!
Bye, bye
Max

David Harvey
David Harvey is a professor of Agricultural Economics. I can't quite remember how I managed to include him in my original cast of philosophers but he and I are both glad that I did.

> From: David Harvey
> Date: 16 Oct 2003, 13:13:11
> Subject: The Meaning of Life?
>
> Caspar,
>
> In common with at least one other respondent, I now understand why a free copy of the New Humanist arrived on my doormat, so thanks for that.
>
> In exception to at least one other of your respondent's, I do not accept that the question is

beyond the scope of philosophical inquiry – if that were to be so, then there are limits to the scope of enquiry – what are these? Are the answers to this question then some form of answer to your question – a matter of faith and belief, but not of sensible enquiry? This answer, then, is: whatever you want to believe.

Finally, I'm impressed and not a little flattered that whatever search engine or method you used should identify me as a practising philosopher. I am trying (very, according to many of my colleagues) – though without the benefit of any formal specific training in the art.
I am also trying to creep up on an answer which satisfies me (if no one else). You can find the products of this creeping search at: www.staff.ncl.ac.uk/david.harvey/DRHRootFolder/DRH_research.html#Concept

I suggest that a starting point in this rubbish might be found under the ESRC/Prospect sub-heading, especially "Knowledge: How do we come by it and what does it mean? – an essay on the origins of everything submitted as the second of a quintet of essays to the Prospect challenge (but rejected, of course).

On this basis, my provisional answer is: To self-realise within the patterns and fabrics of universal self-realisation, – meaningless unless you follow the story and find it at least partly credible.

Good luck with your search, and let me know if you find anything useful.

What a nice chap.

David Papineau
David Papineau is Professor of philosophy at Kings College London. He is interested in the philosophy of science and the philosophy of mind. He is the author of seven books and over seventy papers.

> From: David Papineau
> Date: 16.10.2003, 15:13:50
> Subject: the universe etc*
>
> Dear Caspar Addyman
> Thanks for your odd letter. If you are really interested in how I think the universe might be, you might look at 'David Lewis and Schrodinger's Cat', which is on my website in the KCL Philosophy website.
> Best wishes
> David Papineau

Again the paper was quite technical but the summary is simple enough to read, if not necessarily understand.

> In 'How Many Lives has Schrodinger's Cat?' David Lewis argues that the Everettian no-collapse interpretation of quantum mechanics is in a tangle when it comes to probabilities. This paper aims to show the difficulties that Lewis raises are insubstantial. The Everettian metaphysics contains a coherent account of probability. Indeed it accounts for probability rather better than orthodox metaphysics does.

For more accessible versions of the same ideas visit his

---

* I wish I received more emails with titles like 'the universe etc' homepage at Kings College London. David maintains a large audio and video archive of his public talks and radio broadcasts.

Mark Sainsbury, University of Texas
Mark Sainsbury is a professor of philosophy at the University of Texas. His main interest is the philosophy of language.

> Caspar,
>
> Life has no meaning, but individuals can make their lives meaningful by thinking what they would most like to achieve and then trying to achieve that. Self-awareness among *cranks and lunatics* is a rare and valuable quality indeed!
>
> With good wishes,
> Mark Sainsbury, University of Texas

Fiona MacPherson
Dr. MacPherson is senior lecturer in philosophy at the University of Glasgow, where she is also Director of the Centre for the Study of Perceptual Experiences. She is interested experience and its discontents; illusions and hallucinations and things like ambiguous figures.

> Dear Mr Addyman,
>
> Thank you very much for your letter asking about the meaning of life, the universe and everything. I cannot provide you will an answer but I hope to show in what way philosophy tries to contribute towards an answer.
>
> Philosophers investigate questions about the nature

of many different things, such as, what exists, what is possible and impossible, the nature of mathematics, logics, ethics, value and knowledge, to name but a few. I am a philosopher of mind and I study the nature of perceptual consciousness. Thus, I do not directly address the question of the meaning of life, the universe and everything. Nonetheless, I believe that my work has bearing on this issue, as I shall explain.

How would one arrive at an answer to your question (if indeed there is one)? I suggest that we would need to know what everything was (that is find out what exists) and find out what the nature of the universe is (that is find out the nature of everything that exists). We have a good idea of what life is from science, but life seems to get much of its meaning from an aspect of life we know very little about, namely, consciousness. Find out answers to these sub-questions is often what philosophers attempt to do. The frustrating thing is that investigating answers to these questions often raises many other and equally difficult questions.

As you will no doubt be aware, in The Hitchhikers Guide to the Galaxy, where the question of life, the universe and everything was famously posed, the answer was said to be '42'. In the book, those who had asked the question could not see why this was the answer, so they set out to investigate in more detail what the question was. I think there is a moral in this story, as I hope is brought out in this letter.

In my work I investigate the nature of perceptual consciousness. I don't know what it is but I am trying to find out by asking questions about the relationship between intentionality and consciousness and about the differences and similarities between the senses. I hope that some to the answers I get will be a small part of the larger puzzle about what the meaning of life, the universe and everything is. I am not optimistic that an answer to the big question will be reached at all soon but answers to parts of the question are valuable in their own right, which is why I study them,

Yours sincerely,

Fiona Macpherson, Girton College, Cambridge

Nancy Cartwright

Nancy Cartwright holds a professorship at the Institute of Advanced Studies, London School of Economics and another at the University of California, San Diego. She a recipient of a MacArthur Fellowship and is world renowned for her work on the philosophical foundations and implications of quantum mechanics. Her first book was entitled "How the Laws of Physics Lie". If anyone could answer my question.... Surely..

Dear Mr Addyman,

I'm sorry. I haven't a clue how to help with your question!

Yours Nancy Cartwright,
London School of Economics.

Ay Carumba!

Tim Mawson

Tim Mawson is fellow in philosophy at St Peter's College, Oxford. He is author of one book and over twenty papers, the most recent of which is entitled "Sources of dissatisfaction with the Answers to the Question of the Meaning of Life." Interestingly that came about some years after I was harassing him. I hope I didn't provoke him, he seems so nice.

> Dear Caspar (if I may),
>
> Thank you very much for your letter of the first of October last year. I am sorry to have taken so long in replying to it. Initially, I had put it to one side pending a time when I could give it the attention it deserved; I'm afraid to say that it has only moved back to the centre of my attention now because I have realized that such a time will not arrive until the summer. What delays me is the need to focus on finishing my book for a deadline at the end of June. I'd like to feel that I might refer you to this forthcoming book as itself being likely to contain the answer to your question, but - to give the plot away - its argument is to the effect that readers interested in your question should address it to God, the very procedure which you - being an atheist, quite understandably - report yourself not to have tried; and from your report of not having tried it, one may perhaps infer you will remain unwilling to try it. In the event of you considering yourself more flexible on the issue of whether or not you'd ever attempt this, I mention the book's title and publisher - 'Evidence of Things Unseen', OUP - which should be enough to enable you to track it down in due course.
>
> When my pupils ask me, 'What is the meaning of life?' I tend to say to them, 'State of functional

activity characterized by organic metabolic reactions.' And then I follow up quickly by asking whether what I've just said has answered their question. If rather more is required for an answer to be a satisfactory one than that it removes from one's questioner any desire to ask anything similar, then one might reasonably think I rather fail my pupils here - just as I am in this letter failing you. But asking oneself why this isn't a satisfactory answer to the question might in itself go some way towards one's putting oneself on the right track to find an answer to it that will be genuinely satisfactory. That - pending my book and divine intervention - is the best I can do I'm afraid. Sorry not to have been more help and best of luck with your continuing investigations.

I am yours sincerely,

Tim Mawson, St Peter's College, Oxford

His publishers Oxford University Press changed the book title to "Belief in God: an introduction to the philosophy of religion."

~~~

As you can see, a lot of them challenged me to find my own meaning and I concede they are correct to do so. One should not take the word of some professional philosopher, whose job, career and calling had been to dedicate his whole life to answering fundamental questions about the nature of knowledge and existence. Highly trained professionals, Doctors of Philosophy with genuine, guaranteed, certified degrees. Each one paid by you and me, the taxpayers, to sit in a centrally heated office with a big library down the corridor and free access to the internet. He or she is paid to sit there and think, to decide what thoughts are possible to think and which are impossible. I guess they do this by trying to think thoughts and when they hear the satisfying thunk, they know they have thought it. They tick that box and strain and grimace trying to push another one out. But despite all that, do not take their word for anything. And especially not about something as important as the answer to the biggest question of them all.

Listen to me instead.

I am untrained and highly unprofessional. I am sitting in my bedroom in my underwear and I am making this up as I go along. Someone whose only qualification is that he once took some magic mushrooms and thought he saw it all clearly.

One more thing: If at the end of it, you disagree, please tell me and tell me why. I am not handing down tablets of stone, not imparting knowledge granted by God Alone. I am advancing broken inarticulate hypotheses. If you feel that these will not work, please do not cast me out into the darkness, but provide me with some enlightenment. Tell me where I fucked up. Better yet, suggest an improvement.

In order to keep this short, I have made many assumptions. The biggest and most dubious one is in assuming you agree with me about the basics; maths and physics and that kind of mumbo jumbo. You don't have to agree on or even understand any details and there won't be a test but if we could agree that in some way or another that these things are basic, in the sense of being foundational, then we safely ignore them and move to more interesting things.

The world is everything that is the case but do not take my word for it. It cannot be proved by anyone less than God and (even if She were to exist) Her certainty does not translate well into human terms. Our world is unreliable. The laws of nature certainly seem to be law-like. But they are also fiendishly complex and so our world is unreliable. Our perceptions of it are fuzzy and vague. Even our minds are not to be trusted. Operating on our messy biological wetware with its pragmatic toolbox of some bounded rationality and a lot of innate heuristics, we fall a long way short of the perfection conceivable of celestially manufactured automata.

When discussing any of the 'big' questions, it is helpful and important to keep in mind that we are all merely monkeys, little more than monkeys. Bright monkeys with opposable thumbs and linguistic talents, but not so far out of the trees as we would like to believe.

If you want an experimental confirmation of how stupid you are, take a bottle of vodka & a mixer of your choosing and work steadily though it. Very soon, long before the bottom of the bottle, you will be very confused and irrational.

There are three mysteries the origin of the universe, the origin of life and the emergence of consciousness. What we might call the why, the wherefore and the why me? The first two are somewhat mundane questions that are of only academic interest, the narrow specialisms of two branches of science. So widespread is the agreement about the basic Darwinian mechanism that not even the Pope bets against it.

Physicists look after the cosmos. Why is there something rather than nothing? Why is there a universe? And why this particular one, one that welcomes life and has this style of interior décor. These days they see the universe a giant quantum computer. They are interested in the computations that it runs.

The origin of the universe is of even narrower academic

attraction. Only a crowd of mathematicians care about the nitty-gritty of which inflationary theory kick started the construction of coalescing clouds of gas that became the stars we see sparkling in the sky.

To be fair, some philosophers get quite excited about the various choices available previous to there being a universe too. They care about how it could all have been so very different. They do not care too much because at five o'clock the end of the working day, they lock up their offices and head home to watch EastEnders. But during the day they speculate on how the universe might have been doughnut shaped. Or why we have only one axis for time, when it is perfectly plausible there were several. It would be very hard to conceive of what this universe looked like and lunch breaks would probably quite complex things to take, but is this because it is an intrinsically implausible idea or is it only because we are accustomed to and designed for this kind of existence?

Even the fact of our existence, that here we are and that there is something rather than nothing is an overlooked conundrum that they feel we ought to worry about.

Let them worry; I cannot get too enthusiastic about speculations on concepts with no possible confirmation and alternatives that I have no opportunity to take. I will forego the thought of what a luxury it would be to live with an extra spatial dimension and be able to see into my own intestines, or know some moments earlier and apart what choice I would soon make for dessert at a lunch hour spread over two dimensions of time.

Ignoring all that, as far as I can tell there are three just perspectives on the existence of the universe that you or I could take. I call these the Bomb, the War and the Peace. The

Bomb asks you to think of the universe as a bomb that just gone off in your immediate vicinity. It helpfully suggests that asking why this happened won't help you survive the immediate aftermath. The Universe has already happened, get used to that fact and get on with life instead.

But is the universe more like a war? Where the better you understand the motives of those who started it, the better your chances of getting out of it alive. The chances are only marginally better because a war is bigger than you. You may get swept up in currents that are too strong. However well you understand them you can't control them. But the chances are very high that you will never understand them. And you might be fighting for a long time.

Peace, for some us, is a preferable alternative to war. In Peace, the universe is not something to be fought against. You don't have to fight a war to win peace. You choose peace and with luck you get it. Without luck, life may still be yours to enjoy occasionally.

So what about life? Once the origin of the universe is taken as given then the origin of life in its simplest form is essentially inevitable and it merely remains to explain the mechanism. A handful of biochemists care about the flavour of primordial slime but I recommend you just accept that there once was slime.

With a handful of slime, a big enough petri-dish and plenty of time then the theory of evolution is leads you almost inevitably to where we are now. It effortlessly assembles eyes, brains and even wits. Once the struggle commences, the simplicity of Charles Darwin's competitive equation almost guarantees that in the self-replicating arms race, some devious and ingenious creature will appear afore too long.

It explains the appearance and genesis of each and every species we have found so far, circa two million. Not to mention everything else surviving at the moment and every fossil we have ever found as well. To some extent it can explain behaviour too. Evolution has made it much more obvious why we are so obsessed with sex, status and sugary foods. Maybe it explains everything else too?

A lot of these appetites arise before you are as sophisticated as you and I. Over ninety-nine percent of those millions and millions of species would place sex at the top of their lists of their most favourite of favourite things. And those that do not it like it are those boring bacteria and such other tedious creatures who prefer their own company and can clone themselves. The rest of life is at it like rabbits. (Especially the rabbits.)

If survival is a high priority, it is only at the expense of reproduction. The males of some species put up with getting their heads ripped off in order to get their end away. And childbirth and motherhood is always a precarious business.

If you disagree with me and the Pope on this, then in the words of the Bible, you can go forth and multiply. Or to put it in the vernacular, Fuck Off.

Sugary foods are popular with energetic, hot-blooded type, the birds and beasts. Especially with bi-pedal walking super-computers like us. Feel the heat your desktop computer generates as it crunches the numbers to enable you surf the web for knowledge, pirated music and pornography. The massively parallel soggy calculator that is in your noggin has thousands of time the computing power. It works slightly differently or your hair might burn off and your eyeballs evaporate. Nonetheless it is power-hungry. It enables you to search the world for knowledge, entertainment and, of course, sex.

Your brain is there to solve the problems that matter to you. This wonderfully simple concept is, of course, spectacularly complex in practice but even the Pope agrees with the basic idea. Mind you, it does not quite explain you and I. The stumbling block is not our formidable intellects but being able to look out of our own eyes; our subjective feeling of what happens.

This is the third and biggest mystery. Why am I "me" and what gives me the miracle of this instant, for it is a privileged moment in my existence? Of all the time in history I could have been alive, why now? In all the time of my personal history why I am currently experiencing this little bit? Why have I experienced any of it? As far as the notoriously parsimonious processes of natural selection are concerned there does not seem to be any need for the little man looking out. We might just as well be zombies.

Well, we're not. We're monkeys. (Remember.)

CHAPTER TEN
HOUSE OF GOD

> Suddenly there came a sound ... of a rushing mighty wind, ... And there appeared unto them cloven tongues like as of fire, and it sat upon each of them. And they were all filled with the Holy Ghost.

– Acts of the Apostles, 2: 2-4

†

Traditional Church of England vicars were always very embarrassed when the subject of God came up. The feeling may well have been mutual.

Your typical C of E vicar was very happy talking about church fêtes, harvest festivals, weddings and whatnot. He would gladly go into an infants school to tell them Bible stories. He may even offer some grave opinion on the tragic state of world affairs to anyone who cared to ask, but try to pin him down on matters of theology and he would likely as not get very hot under the dog-collar. He would start reeling off a lot of slack in the lines of thought he professed to follow, he would wheel out all the best empty qualifications "I may be wrong..", "I like to think..", "It is all very complicated.." With typical English politeness, the common or garden Church of England curate was more afraid of causing offence than of incurring the Wrath of God. (Even the ones who believed in God in the first place.)

Maybe thinking that God was just another kindly old parish vicar who diplomatically overlooks his parishioners casual blaspheming and heathen lives in the hope that they may at least come to the Easter service. They probably imagined Heaven to be a little like Victorian England. Because to the Monarchy was almost as important as the Almighty in their pantheon. And the Queen certainly outranked the Virgin Mary. They believed in the Empire because they believed in the past, a wonderful time and place where everything had been wonderful.

Of course, they admitted, not everything was perfect in Victorian England, but it was being perfected. The principles and values of those times had been largely right. And it was a plain fact that the loss of those values to our present society was directly responsible for the many problems and failures of our Britain today. If people had maintained the values of those times, we would not be witnessing the malignant sickness of modernity; single mothers, insolent youth, homosexuality, multiculturalism and post-modernism, divorce and abortion.

It was another Sunday and once again Reverend Cake was condescending from high up in his pulpit. He told simple tales and for him, the ends were more important than the means.

Somewhere under the complex hypocrisy of his public preaching and his private failings was a real faith in God. This brought one highly simplifying short cut to all life's complex conundrums. Given the Gordian knot of some contemporary moral dilemma, the likes of Cake would tangle for a while, trying to tease out a straight forward holy point of view before become frustrated with the fact that life is a little more intricate than that, and finally slashing out with their Sword of Burning Gold. Unaware that the delicately woven fabric of contract, complexity and compromise is actually what life is really all about.

He might not be able to reason through stone-clad justifications for what he believed about gays, unwed mothers or female priests but he knew that by God's Grace he had access to the eternal truth and that excused him from examining the tedious reasons for everything.

It could get so tangled when you attempted to take on the 'oh so clever' nihilists in their language. They were so self-evidently wrong in their moral relativism and over-extended scepticism that it was often impossible to even know where to begin disabusing them. So he did not. They were already doomed; the Devil had their ears so Cake did not discourse with them. Instead, he abused them for the benefit of his less critical congregation.

He did not believe in the Devil of the literal cloven hoofed, fire and brimstone school but these liberals were lost to the darkness. No matter how bright he shone his light they would never see it. Far more fruitful to work on drawing in those in the half-shadows and in keeping hold of the enlightened.

Most people want the world to be simple. Some know that it is not and try not to be too smug about things. Socrates was one of these; the Oracle at Delphi informed him that he was the wisest man alive. A shrewd and modest fellow he didn't really believe this could be true but also didn't think it was his place to question an infallible Oracle. Unfortunately for him, he solved the conundrum. He decided that only thing he knew for certain was that nothing was certain. Since no one else had seemed to have realised, this made him the smartest man alive. For being called stupid, the rest of Athens turned against him and he was sentenced to death.

In many ways the Reverend Cake worked completely the opposite way round. He was certain that he had all the answers and that his entitled him to condemn everyone else to a fiery death and eternal agony in the pits of hell. Cake liked to think that original sin rather than ignorance was the price of knowledge. As he often told his congregation, Hell is God's kitchen. Before birth our souls are all prepared in the cooler of Satan's ovens; Steam cooked in the devil's *bain*-marie. Millions of little souls poaching gently in individual coddling pots, shielded from the true heat of Hell, but there to experience a hint of what awaited them if they failed to lead good lives. The dark, smoky knowledge of right and wrong infused into them as they cooked.

Satan's ovens weren't perfect. The temperature was even and so we were born with different knowledge of Evil and hellfire. A few souls were very underdone, very little right and wrong got into these half-baked atheists, whilst a handful of others were overcooked, spoiled and evil through and through. Most were somewhere in the middle, with enough evil to be original sinners but far short of perfection. Only right there at the golden mean were the saints and saviours, who rose to perfection. Deep down, Cake knew he was one of these. He had certainty baked into him.

•

The man had been on a reconnaissance trip to the British Museum. It had gone well. They had everything he needed and they hadn't suspected a thing. Had they? He had to been very careful from here onwards. Perhaps they were going to follow him home? They were good.

What, he wondered, was his next step. He really should get back to base to write up his findings while they were clear and fresh in his mind. But what if they followed him? Everything would be lost. He had already reached Tottenham Court

Road, busy with shoppers by the time this thought occurred to him. He spun round wildly but he couldn't see anything. No, that wasn't the problem. He could see lots of suspicious looking characters. But he couldn't see his pursuers. They wouldn't look suspicious. This was going to be difficult. Which ones were 'THEY'?

He crossed the road and turned north, glancing back as often as he dared. That one with the pushchair? Possibly. What about that man with blue hair. Too obvious. Or is that just what they wanted him to think? No, not on Tuesday, that wouldn't happen on a Tuesday. It was Tuesday, wasn't it?

This was getting out of his control. He was afraid. He wanted to run but he fought against it. A bus slowed and he ducked aboard. He stayed just inside the drivers door watching. The woman with the pushchair hurried to try and catch up but the driver didn't wait for anyone else to get aboard. He watched her into the distance shaking her head and saying something rude. That had been close. He leant forward to talk to the driver.

"Thank you. Where are going?"

"Angel. And can you get back please, you're not safe there."

"I know," said the man and climbed the stairs. His good luck continued. The best seat in the house was unoccupied. He sat down in the front right seat, just above the driver. It wasn't the best seat on the bus, but it was the best he could do as a passenger.

It was only when the real driver came upstairs to ask him to leave did he notice that the bus had arrived. The journey had been calming after the excitement of the city centre but they had not travelled far. Now the man was standing on an equally busy street not far from Angel tube. This was less heavenly than he had hoped. The buzz of the afternoon crowd all rushing around shopping and shouting into their mobile phones was not what he needed. There were hundreds of pushchairs and, out of the corner of his eye, he started glimpsing suspicious characters, people watching him.

He had to get away, further away. The buses were once again his salvation. He was not sure which one he should get. His head was swirling but he forced himself to focus on the map and worked out which was the longest route. It was the 137 to Enfield and he hoped it would turn up soon because he did not think he could managed to decipher the timetables.

As it was, he only had to wait a few fitful minutes before it arrived. He practically threw himself inside and hurried up to the top deck. He was so flustered that he even forgot to watch out for pursuing pushchairs.

At the end of line, life was more sedate. Having had its Sunday lunch, most of Enfield was sleeping it off. The man had a look around. It didn't take long. There wasn't much to look at so he wandered further. In the distance he heard people singing hymns. He moved towards them and found the church. Evensong was already underway so he quietly joined the small congregation somewhere near the back, and loudly joined the hymn somewhere among the tenors.

• †

The Right Reverend Cake looked up from his notes and down on his congregation. The usual losers were held rapt by his performance. He was perpetually disappointed that these were the faithful. Basket cases, inadequates to a man, woman and child.

How different it had been in America, thought Cake. In

America, normal people went to church. Normal, well dressed, well adjusted people with real jobs and traditional families. Some of them were millionaires, and even a few multi-millionaires. (Although most of the multi-millionaires who went to church had their own churches. Ones they had started themselves before they became multi-millionaires.)

The church was powerful. The church was influential. If he was in America, he would be powerful, he would be influential. There would be some hope.

In the sparse congregation, there was a face he did not recognise. Not a great prospect, a scruffy unshaven man who could not seem to keep still. But who was paying very close attention. He was even taking notes. He would listen for a short while, leaning earnestly forward in his pew. Then at junctures that put Cake off his stride, the man would suddenly start writing very fast, his knuckles straining white as he gripped his pen and almost tearing through his paper. He would write about half a side in a battered flip-over reporters notepad then he would stop and go back to staring at Cake. The man had burning eyes and Cake could not decide if he approved or disapproved of what he was hearing.

Cake wondered if he was some sort of atheist news reporter, here trying to find some dirt on Cake. There was some, but he felt safe that this man would not find it here. Although judging by his appearance he was used to digging in the dirt and raking the mud. He must be anarchist, thought Cake. The two being close to synonymous in his lexicon. (Along with nihilist, modernist, socialist and liberal) Certainly there was something anarchic about his thought processes. The points in the sermon that set him off on one of his furious scribbles had no pattern that Cake could make out.

Still at least somebody was listening. The church was dying; it was four funerals to every one wedding. And though many of those marriages begat offspring, there were fewer and fewer Christenings. So few of those church weddings involved actual Christians. They had bluffed their way in for the style, for the venue or simply to please the Bride's mother.

And one could not help but wonder; of such Christenings as there were, how many parents were thinking of their child's future in Christ's Kingdom and how many were thinking of his or her future in Christ's Kingston, the local church school with a good academic record and cynical selection policies. Schools pretended to take children whose parents were of the appropriate sect (there were Jewish, Muslim and Catholic schools too) but actually selected on academic ability to keep high in the league tables. And parents pretended to be religious but actually cared about the same league tables. The opinion of the children was not entered into. The government that is used to saying one thing while doing another declared the policy a great success.

Today's sermon had been 'False Prophets' - always a very easy one to adapt and especially at the moment.

"Today, I want to talk to you about False Prophets, about pretenders to the Throne of God, those who would attempt to usurp the Crown of Thorns. The Jews and the Mohammedeans know something of God." The Reverend Cake liked to be inclusive. "But they wallow in ignorance of the Truth." But the truth was he did not know how.

"They will not hear the Good News that Christ is come. They are damned.

"Our Catholic brethren have seen His Light, the Glory of Our Lord, but you must pray for their souls because they venerate False Gods and raise one man in Rome above all other men.

That is a sin. There is Our Lord and then there are all of us. And we are all equal."

At the end of the service, the congregation was invited to join the Reverend for an informal chat. It was something he'd picked up in America. And he'd brought it back in an effort to be different from his colleagues. They didn't have the facilities of those super-churches so a little table with biscuits and a tea urn were set up at the back of the church. They didn't have the numbers either. The attendees were three elderly widows with no one to go home to and two sets of new parents and their terminally bored children. Put on display to earn a place in the borough's better school. Today, there was also the man.

"I liked your sermon, Reverend. I liked it very much."

"Thank you, my friend. When I am in the pulpit, I always like to speak the Truth as I see it. I have to. It is my duty. Up there is where I am closest to God and where I am closest to these people, and to you, my friend." There was something about the intensity with which the man attended to him that unsettled the Reverend. Far more than the man from Newsnight ever could. Cake moved away from the man, and went over to strike the fear of God into a seven-year-old girl.

Reverend Cake looked out for the anarchist the last of the congregation came out of the service. But he was not among those leaving the church. There was no one left in the church when he and his curate locked up. Cake assumed he must have missed the fellow and was fairly relieved at the thought.

In fact, the man was sitting in the pulpit. It had long been his habit to stay in church as long as he possibly could. A habit from his unhappy school days where Chapel was a haven and leaving it only returned him to a world that disliked him. Besides, Reverend Cake's sermon had given him a lot to think about, and unfortunately he had missed a few parts of it. He had an abundance of questions

He would have asked his questions directly to the Reverend, but it was too risky. THEY might be listening. Or the Reverend himself might not understand just who it was he was talking to. (It had happened before.) Instead the man had gone up into the pulpit to see if the Reverend had left behind his notes.

The man was in luck. The Reverend had not left his crib sheet but that was fairly dull anyway. It was a skeleton script of the sort handed out in classes at theological college. It was vague and non-specific and could be adapted to a wide range of occasions and topics. The Reverend had a collection of about thirty different ones and for ordinary services like this one.

For big occasions and for his radio appearances he made the effort to come up with new stuff. But even this was not really necessary, When you had been doing these things two or three times a week for thirty years, you could often get by on a wing and prayer.

For any given Sunday, it was his habit to pick at random a subject he was fairly sure he had not used in the last month or so. If he thought of some way to adapt it, to relate it to events in the news or topical issues he would scribble down a few reminders of what he wanted to say about it. These were on the post-it notes. In a typical sermon, he would normally aim for about seven of these (a good Biblical number) and include three Bible quotes for the Father, the Son and the other one. During the course of the sermon, he would peel off the little yellow stickers as he went along to avoid repeating things and as a way to pace himself.

It was a great pile of these little yellow post-it notes that the man found on the floor of the pulpit. An autumnal forest of them. He studied them intently. There was a lot to take in.

Too much, it was hard to keep his concentration on one thing, without some other significant and important but unrelated thought bubbling up and beginning to clamour for his attention. He had to write fast to be able to keep up. This was far better than the way it had been before, when he was on the medication. When he had been on those powerful pills he had been tricked into taking. When his own thoughts could not get through to him because of the Infernal Mechanisms inside the pills that travelled into his brain and kept locked from him the secrets of his Destiny

At least Church was a safe place to think. Safer than he realised. He had so much to think about that it wasn't until past midnight that he realised he was locked in. He tried for a few minutes to find a way out but quickly resigned himself to spending the night. He didn't mind.

He ate the flapjack he found in his pocket and had a glass of water in the vestry. He curled up in a nest he made out of vestments and surplices and slept soundly

Eight hours later, the Reverend and the curate unlocked the doors to prepare for the primary school service. Before they could enter, the man had cascaded out and hurried away at a shuffling half-run.

Reverend Cake watched him go, hoping he had stolen the silverware so they could claim on the insurance. (They were covered for everything except Acts of God.) It would also be a great opportunity for publicity. The Reverend could denounce the gays, anarchists and drug-users responsible and launch an appeal to raise funds for the church.

He was to be disappointed. The man would never attempt to steal priceless artefacts from a church. To him they were part of the church. In any case, he was in too much of a hurry. He must get home and consult his other notebooks.

And if the man's plan was true, Reverend Cake need not worry about his publicity, his collection plate or the churches worldly treasures. There would be far, far greater revelations and rewards. (And probably a few Acts of God too.)

Strangely, as he left the man had taken the Reverend's hand and spoken to him.

"It says in the book of John. 'You must be my protector.'"

INTERMISSION THREE
DOUBLE PLUS UNGOD

Religion bad! Humans good!

In which I disagree that the positive social or spiritual contributions of religion make any difference to whether it is a 'good thing'.

[Note: throughout I use the term 'you' but don't take this totally personally, whoever you are!]

After all, belief in Santa Claus is a 'good thing' for children, it makes them happy and maybe even makes them less naughty and more nice (for a few weeks in December at least). As such, it is a lie adults are happy to perpetuate, but none of them choose it for themselves.

I think there is a strong parallel to be found in many of the liberal apologias for religion; 'it isn't necessarily true but it's good for society', 'my own faith is complex but churches shouldn't confuse people with subtle points of theology'.

In my view, if you are religious then you are obliged to grapple with the theology. More than that I'd say you are obliged to be a fundamentalist. You believe in an absolute, you believe in good and evil, right and wrong. You ought to be able to apply this to everything, you ought to try. After all you believe that there is a hell of a lot at stake (not just life and death, but eternal life or death.) Your initial assumption, that God exists (and happens to be of your denomination) is such a massive claim. It goes against all the available evidence. It massively complicates the world around us. Raising extremely difficult questions:

- how does god fit into a world described by modern physics?
- how does the soul interact with the body?
- when did souls evolve?
- why are we spending 3 score years & 10 on a quiz to win eternal life?
- why are you the chosen ones?
- why should you believe your priests?

If the answers come down to a matter of faith, then I have one more question for you: why should anyone else in the entire world agree with you? Because it's true? You haven't established that! Either everyone must agree with you or else no one is obliged to. And if you disagree with the extremism, then you must retreat to a totally personal religious standpoint. You may not be totally permissive of other points of view (I'm not) but you cannot argue from religious premises (you've admitted that people can have their own interpretation of matters spiritual).

By contrast, if you have no religion you are obliged to be liberal. All knowledge is provisional. Every decision must be won by reasoned debate, not appeal to authority. There is a method for establishing not what is true, but what is our best approximation to the truth. It's called the scientific method. And this is where I get absolutist; I challenge anyone to come up with some problem not amenable to the scientific method.

I don't think any moral imperatives need to be predicated on theological grounds. There are (or at least ought to be) rational reasons for the laws of the land. Similarly for the arrangement of society. Most particularly for your personal conduct. Look for the human reason for doing what you are doing, look for your inner motives, question yourself. There is no outside authority, you are the final arbiter of your actions, you are responsible. So is everyone else. Society is built up from personal freedom AND personal responsibility.

"What about the meaning of life?" I hear you cry. (I'm sobbing a little myself.) But if living in a godless world means that life has no meaning then so be it. This doesn't make me want to jump off a tall building, it is just another challenge. After all nothing is certain so maybe I haven't found it yet? And if there is no god then there can be no afterlife. This life is the only place you will ever find meaning. If you get my meaning.

CHAPTER ELEVEN
HOUSE ON FIRE

You shake my nerves and you rattle my brain
Too much love drives a man insane
You broke my will, oh what a thrill
Goodness gracious great balls of fire
– Otis Blackwell and Jack Hammer, loosely based on Acts 2:2-4.

•

What would be ideal for this job would be a milk bottle. But he had not been able to find one. Last time he had a milk bottle, although that was a long time ago now. Twenty years? These days his milk came in cartons or in one of those plastic bottles. One of those would have to do, and on the plus side they were bigger. You could get a four pint one. He decided that this was what he wanted.

He didn't want to waste the milk but after drinking the first three pints, he admitted defeat and poured the rest carefully down the drain at the edge of the forecourt. Filling the flimsy bottle was more tricky than he'd anticipated but by the third or forth attempt, he had the knack.

When he went to pay, he had got a funny look from the guy behind the counter at the twenty-four hour garage. But they sold him the petrol anyway. It was the same man who had sold him the milk.

*

Getting ready to go out, John put his hand in the pocket of his jacket. He felt something plasticky and pulled it out: Mr White's all night bag of shite. It looked up at him. Accusingly or conspiratorially? He couldn't decide which. He kept staring but no answer came. He looked at his watch. He did not want to be late. Guilty he thrust the bag back in his pocket and put his keys in the other.

Sam had invited him to the Burlington Grill. He had got there on time to find Sam already waiting for him at the bar. She was more conservatively dressed than last time, but still looked stunning. The conversation was going to awkward wherever they did it, so they decided to stick to small talk until they both had a drink and were shown to their table. This happened swiftly because the Maître D' had recognised John when he came in and had been hovering by his shoulder since he arrived.

They were seated within minutes and sat opposite each other in silence as the waiter described the specials. Without Arlvik's drugs in his system, John was terribly nervous about the impression he'd make on this date. He also had to stop thinking that this was a date. Concentrating on the menu and ordering quickly seemed to be the only way to fend off the attentions of their over-enthusiastic waiter. Once they had decided and their menus removed, leaving nothing between them and the conversation they had been dreading.

"We deceived you. I deceived you and I am sorry. I want.."

John held his hand up.

"I forgive you. I will forgive you on one condition. Will you tell me your real name? It's not 'Sam', right?"

"No, it's not. And yes, I will, I promise. But not yet. Will you hear me out first? I've been feeling terrible about this and I want to explain as best I can." It's true, she did look pale and ashen. She did not seem to have been crying but her eyes were slightly pink as if she'd not slept.

"Go on."

"I am not going to apologise for my job. My conscience is clear about that but what I did to you went beyond that. I am sorry about that. I didn't think it was going to turn out like it did but even so I didn't have any business doing what I did."

"You could have thought it through…"

"There wasn't any chance. Jayne only called me a couple of hours before we met you. She was very excited saying Eric Hayle had a great job and she needed my help."

John started to speak and it was Sam's turn to hold up her hand.

"Just hear me out please? Jayne said Eric had a friend who needed exposure and needed two girls who would be okay with a kiss and tell. I've never done anything like that but I have heard about it happening."

"He didn't say that I didn't know about it?"

"Jayne didn't mention it. Eric told us both when we met him at Black's a little before you arrived. It didn't really have time to sink in."

"It's not a small point."

"I know, but I was more worried about myself. What I was

getting myself into."

"I don't understand."

"I've been doing the escorting for a while. A year or two. I've never wanted to see my name in the paper."

"You and me both"

"It was Jayne. It's different for Jayne. She has been in quite a few of Eric's magazines. She has even made a few films. She's wanted something like this for a long time... the exposure. Don't get me wrong, she is a lovely girl and she's a good friend." Sam paused and took a sip on her wine. "She asked me to help her out. It was a job, a well paid one too. But it represented a lot more than that to Jayne. I wasn't keen. She knew that. I wasn't the first person she'd called about it but no-one else was free. I was her last resort. I actually said no. This was still when I thought you knew about it, that you wanted to be in the papers. When she first called I turned her down. I told her no. She understood.

"But I thought about it and a few minutes later I called her back. It's funny. The reason I agreed was because I didn't want to be a hypocrite. I've always told myself that I am comfortable with what I do, being an escort. But here I was not willing to help my friend because I was ashamed. I didn't want to be publicly associated with what I do. I realised this and I called her back."

"What a good Samaritan" John said. Sam looked pained "Sorry.. I didn't.. carry on." Sam took another sip of her wine.

"So that was how I was feeling when we got to the club and Eric told us that you didn't know what was going on. I should have thought a bit more about you but I was confused enough myself. I couldn't let Jayne down. She really wanted this. There she was sitting opposite Eric Hayle, can you imagine what that represented to her? Well you saw in the restaurant. Eric was promising her all sorts of things: a front page, a contract at one of his magazines, a film of her own. He knew how to play her."

"I've been noticing that."

"If I am honest, he played me too. He told us that you were determined to be famous; you *would* do whatever it took but that you didn't really know it yourself. But that's why you had put yourself in his hands. He said it would work better if you were kept in the dark. If you didn't find out until afterwards. He said it was just a little trick he was playing on you. He said you were a little afraid, that you'd chicken out if you'd known."

"Yes, I wouldn't have agreed" John paused. "Is that how you saw me, a chicken?"

"You were... sweet. Yes, I suppose it was a bit like that." She laughed. "You were terrified when Jayne and I first approached you." John had to smile.

"Eric also said you really needed to get laid and he was right about that, wasn't he?" She laughed again and held his eye. "You pretty much know the rest."

"Yes, I was there..." John took a sip of his drink. "But were you?"

"Yes, no, it's complicated. There's a part of me.." She stopped herself. "Can we not get into that right now? I enjoyed myself, I enjoyed your company. I'd like to enjoy this."

She gestured around them and then held out her hand for him.

"I'm Natalie."

•

A more alert shopkeeper might not have sold a box of matches to a confused and oddly dressed man smelling strongly of petrol. But then again, he might decide that if he didn't, someone else would.

Besides the man had also bought a pocket A to Z. He was probably just lost.

*

After they had ordered the dessert, Sam/Natalie asked him if he'd like anything else sweet. He didn't understand. She asked if maybe he needed to use the bathroom. He still wasn't really getting it so in the end she just handed him the wrap of cocaine. Embarrassed that his mind had been going down an entirely different path, John took it and hurried away. He wasn't going to take any but, well, maybe just a little. To be sociable.

They had already been getting on like a house on fire but the cocaine poured petrol on that. But then Natalie suddenly stopped talking. John looked round to see what it was that had stopped her. There were two policemen talking to the Maître D'. Just at that moment the Maître D' scanned the room and pointed out their table. In the next moment, the shorter, fatter policeman locked eyes with John. And removing all doubt that it was him they were hunting for, this mean and ugly looking officer and the Maître D' started over in their direction.

Feeling instantly guilty, John's heart leaped to his mouth, he was desperate to make a break for the rear door. They could have made it too if John's legs had not just turned to jelly. Some consideration was given to sliding lifelessly to the floor, hiding under the thick white tablecloths of the Burlington Grill. This was rejected on the grounds that his whimpering might give him away. That and a vestigial need not to humiliate himself in front of Natalie. The small part of John's brain that was not engaged in full-scale panic was trying to persuade the rest of him to keep calm. It was almost succeeding when another small residual rational corner of his cortex piped up in a tiny frightened voice to remind him that he still had over half of White's Original Miscellany in his jacket pocket. Those of his internal organs that had not previously abandoned hope could now be felt jostling and pushing their way to the lifeboats.

The policeman and the Maître D' had paused halfway as the officer asked the restaurateur to leave him to tackle Smith on his own. The Maître D' clearly did not like this trumping of his authority and was upset he would not find out what the law wanted with this customer. He needed to know. It might be necessary to bar the outlaw from returning.

Realising he could not get away and having been brought up to fear and obey authority and especially of the blue uniform wearing kind, John was ready to launch into his confession. Hoping that coming clean with an instant and contrite confession would go better for him. Maybe some crying might help too.

"Mr Smith?"

"..s"

The policeman was clearly senior, he wore a peaked cap rather than a helmet and his uniform was not fluorescent blues an yellows but still of the heavy old fashioned style with lots of silver crested buttons. Tucking his headgear under his arm, he reached in to his upper left chest pocket and removed his regulation, black covered, fold-over notebook.

"Mr John Smith of 43a Havenhand Avenue?"

"..s"

"Hello, Mr Smith. I am Detective Inspector Lipton from Herne Hill Police station."

"..s?"

"Mr Smith I am afraid your flat has burned down."

"What?"

"It appears someone has set fire to your house."

"Oh, is that all? Thank God!"

"Sir?" The inspector asked uncertainly.

"Oh, yes, terrible, terrible" Smith said to reassure the officer, this wonderful policeman who did not want to arrest him. This lovely policeman who was not going to take him down, lock him up and brick up the door. This glum looking policeman who had said something about his house being on fire.

"Hang on, that IS terrible. What happened?"

"It appears that someone set fire to your house, Sir. I understand this must be a shock to you." said the inspector not really understanding why this odd man was so jumpy but reassured that he was now acting the role of the inconsolable victim of crime more accordingly.

"We are not sure Sir. On first impression of the Fire Scene Investigation Officer, it would seem that someone broke your front window and threw a petrol bomb into your front room."

"I can't believe anyone would do that!"

"There is a lot of scum out there Mr Smith," said the policeman, with the weary tone of a man who a had a lot of professional contact with the aforementioned scum.

"When did this happen?" asked Smith.

"Mid-morning, sir. We had been trying to track you down all day. There are quite a few John Smith's in London." said Inspector Lipton.

"Yes, how did you find me?"

As the inspector explained that a journalist from the Clarion had seemed interested in the story and had helpfully established his whereabouts. Smith reflected that this was probably the least bad way to find out your house had burned down. Sitting on a comfy banquet in a Michelin starred restaurant, a pre-dinner cocktail swimming up to your head and an excellent bottle of red recently opened. Much better than getting home from a hard day's rat-racing to find you no longer had a home. Or worse yet waking up in bed, sitting up just long enough to breath a lungful of smoke, exhale 'Oh Bugger' and expire.

"Tell me the worst, I am ready. How bad was it?" He said, toying with his chocolate and white truffle ravioli.

"Very bad, I am afraid Mr Smith."

"Oh well, pull up a chair super-intendant and tell me all about it," said Smith chirpily, the cocktail working its magic and his heart considerably happier now it knew they were not likely to spend a night in the cells. "Can I get Marcel to bring you anything?" Gesturing to the Maître D', who had all the while been edging closer.

"Nothing for me Sir, Thank you." Nonetheless, Detective Inspector Lipton took a chair and consulted his notebook. "The front room was utterly gutted. It was burning fiercely by the time the fire brigade arrive and there was nothing they could do. Besides the petrol bomb, there was a lot of accelerant material scattered about the place." John thought of all the books, newspapers and pizza boxes that normally littered his sitting room and imagined how well the room would burn.

"The bedroom was less badly affected but it is not likely you will be able to save anything." The inspector turned the page but that was all that he had, it seemed that this odd if well-dressed man who was of interest to the papers and ate in extremely expensive restaurants with an attractive and immaculate blonde lived in a one bedroom basement flat in a nasty part of Lambeth. Maybe he was gigolo, thought Lipton.

"The rest of the building suffered from smoke and heat damage but mostly your neighbours escaped unscathed. Do you know who might want to do this to you? An ex-lover? An aggrieved husband?" The inspector asked untactfully pursuing his gigolo theory.

"No, no-one I can think of, no-one like that." John paused. "Eric mentioned there had been a few death threats but he said not to take them seriously. God, what if he's wrong?"

Inspector Lipton watched as John's demeanour took another U-turn. "And who is this 'Eric' person?" he asked reaching hopefully for his policeman's biro.

"Eric.. Eric Hayle." For a moment the inspector's gigolo story was looking better and better, then two added slowly to two in his straightforward policeman's brain. He realised that this man was the overnight publicity machine John Smith. It dawned on the inspector that he was dealing with a 'celebrity'. No wonder the chief had insisted that he went, rather than sending a couple of constables. But someone might have warned him.

In the presence of a personage known or believed to be famous, the attitude of typical wet behind the ears police constable changes from the practical but surly menace they extend to the general public into a helpless slack-jawed star-struck fawning. With time they learn that celebrities are just like everybody else except with bigger egos and less common sense. They also have better lawyers. The attitude of your seasoned detective inspector changes from his normal patronising sarcasm and a barely disguised mild derision to one of debased sycophancy and deeply hidden extreme suspicion and dislike.

This was why the chief superintendent had sent Detective Inspector Lipton, a well-salted veteran of many years' service. There was no other officer under his command whom he felt safe sending to interview a man who had barely been off the front pages of the tabloids all week. Sure enough, D.I. Lipton rapidly adapted to the situation adopting the ingratiating tone he saved for his superiors. Meanwhile he tried to remember why this man in front of him was famous. He could not think of any reason other than that he was famous and a new theory started to form in his crime-fighting mind: Smith had probably started the fire himself for the publicity.

•

The plan was a good one but the man with the plan had forgotten a few details. He realised now that he ought to have waited until the False One had come home and gone to bed before he had done it. But once he had got into the flow of his inspiration he had decided to follow it and it hadn't occurred to him that the other actors in his drama might not be hitting their cues as appropriate.

Besides after three pints of milk, he had needed the toilet quite badly. So he rushed through the attack and rushed off to find a toilet. By the time he got back there was a little crowd and big fire. The man felt quite pleased with himself. It was not until around the time the fire engine arrived that he realised the Enemy had escaped again.

The firemen were very quickly in control of the fire. The flames had been pretty but now there was nothing to see. So he took a walk in the park to think things through. He would not be discouraged. He was a fool to have thought that fighting the forces of darkness would be a walk in the park. It would be tough. It was a challenge and that was why he had been Chosen. After all had not everyone always told him he was special? If he was to do this he needed to do it properly. It was time step up a gear.

¢ ?

Shona had arrived at Saint Helena's School for Girls by taxi and paid the driver too much before trying to duck stealthily inside. The solid and secure school-doors prevented her. Eric Hayle had answered his intercom promptly enough but she was kept waiting for what seemed like an age. She was sure he was doing it deliberately. It was late, past 10pm so there weren't many people on the streets, but that made her presence all the more conspicuous.

Relieved to be finally inside in privacy, Shona did not take in too many of Saint Helena's distinctive features as Eric led her into his study. Eric, himself, was still in his suit. A soft grey, pin-striped three piece, but his waistcoat was unbuttoned and his tie was gone.

She wanted to get this over with but Eric was not going to be rushed. He took his time preparing her a drink, Chinzano with ice. She hadn't wanted to come but was sufficiently ambitious and astute to know that you didn't make Eric Hayle any more of an enemy than he needed to be.

"Shona, out of the harsh glare of those studio lights you look ten years younger."

"Please." Her voice was harsh but she was already resigned to the fact that Eric was going to have his fun.

When she had taken his call earlier that day, he hadn't said what this was about. And while she knew that she should not even consider any proposal he could make she knew even more clearly that she would. That decision had been made a long time ago, well before he called again this evening and ordered her into the back of a taxi to meet him in his home. It was as if she and the Devil had signed an agreement in principle and now were just haggling over terms.

"Do you see much of Nigel these days?" he asked.

"What do you want, Eric?"

"Not much, not much, we'll get to that. But there's really no need to take that tone. Yes, I want *some* things from you but I am quite prepared to pay a generous price."

"I don't want *your* money."

"Oh, I know … It's not money that I am offering. Not *just* money. I know you, don't think I don't. I know your weaknesses."

Shona sighed and rolled her eyes. Why did men always have to be so melodramatic.

Shona's craving was for fame, and when indulging her vice was she was not nice. Indeed, it would be a bold or perceptive therapist who could tell which she enjoyed more the recognition of celebrity or the opportunity to be bitchy. The unrelenting niceness of Hazel Cole and the annoyance of having been upstaged both began to gnaw at her.

Yes, she had resolved, thanks to Hazel, to be nicer but the thing about resolutions is that they are very easy to make and very hard not to break. Especially once the craving hits you and you realise that the self righteousness of doing the right thing is nowhere near as rewarding or as fun as the vice which you have been denying yourself. Shona's heart was already racing.

"This is about Hazel Cole, isn't it?"

"All in good time. Come and join me" Eric had gone to sit on one of the chesterfields. Shona hesitated long enough to make it see like she had a choice and then went to join him, seating herself instinctively in the chair on his left. Stage right. As she walked over, she noticed for the first time that there appeared to be two people asleep in the bed.

"Isn't this nice?" Eric asked. "I feel like a guest on your show. What say we try and solve my problems? You and me together?"

"I am listening." Shona said, though her tone was not one ever heard on daytime television.

"You have your show and you have a shitty column in the Scum, how much do you get for that?"

"Two thousand pounds a time."

"Bollocks, you get six hundred if you write it yourself and three hundred the rest of time. I will give you two thousand a go, whoever ends up writing it, and that's for a weekly not fortnightly column. And that is just the beginning of what I could do for you."

"But?"

"Well there are a couple of things you will have to do for me."

Shona said nothing but let him continue.

"That Hazel bitch is queering the pitch for my golden boy, I want her off the field. Her navel-gazing and 'oh-so-reasonable' attitude to everything undermine the tale we are trying to sell. It just confuses people. The public don't have fancy Pea Aitch Dee's in psychotherapy or whatever la-di-dah lunacy she psychobabbles. They don't need some old biddy opening up their heads and peering inside. They want something simple, something immediate and direct. *Mr* Smith and the newness of nowness not *Doctors* Cole, Freud and fucking Frankenstein. I want her out of my way and I want you to help me."

"Hang on, she is a phenomenon too. My viewing figures are huge. Double what they were even at the height of that shitstorm your papers stirred up about me."

"We only printed the truth and look at you now, it didn't do you any harm, did it?"

"It lost Nigel his job."

"Yeah, well you can do a lot better for yourself than a junior treasury minister. He wasn't ever going to go anywhere anyway. And if he did, he wasn't going to leave his wife. So either way, I'd say I did you a favour" Eric became more conciliatory. "Look, I want her finished but it doesn't have to be straight away. We play them off against each other and we can both benefit."

Shona thought about it. "It won't work . She loves everyone and your moon-faced loon is in a world of his own. They're both ungovernable."

"We won't be working with them, we will be working with the public's perception and that is the easiest thing in the world to manipulate. You could ask Nigel, but I expect you don't talk to him much these days."

"Bastard."

"Come, come! You do these two simple things for me and you will not be sorry."

"How?"

"I don't know yet, but when I do, I will expect you to be there for me. Obviously I can't sign you up to my paper while you are still behind that witch. But I can give you a little taster now," he said handing her a folded piece of paper. Glancing at it, she saw a few meaningless numbers. "You'll find that someone has opened a discreet account for you in the land of the cuckoo-clock. There is not much in it at the moment, but

I find it is always useful to have a few florins tucked away out of sight of our wonderful Inland Revenue."

She gave it another look and tucked safely into her purse, as she looked back up Eric was adjusting himself in his seat.

"And two things? You've only mentioned one?"

"Oh, I think you know" he said, his eyes falling then rising to meet hers with a cruel sadistic glint.

"Bastard," she hissed under her breath. But she could see everything that he was offering her and she wanted it so badly that she could almost taste it. If you wanted to get ahead, sometimes you had to make sacrifices. You had to swallow your pride. This wouldn't be the first time.

One last swig of her drink and she was down on her on her hands and knees crawling steadily across the rich carpet to where Eric was already unbuttoning his flies. All the while there was a fierce gleam in her eyes, like a panther who sees her prize.

It was over faster than she'd anticipated. It was bad but wasn't as bad as she'd feared.

Eric was quickly to his feet and threw her some handkerchiefs as he rearranged himself. He moved to beside the door, eager to get rid of her. She was just as eager to leave.

"Well, that's all decided then. I'd offer to shake hands but I don't think there's any need. You have your down-payment. And I have mine. I haven't decided how this is going to play yet but when I do, you will get a phone call. And when the end game is in sight, you'll get a contract and then I will want to collect my full price."

"But, that … "

"Like I said, that was a down-payment." Eric was laughing as opened the front door and ejected her into the night.

Her departing "Bastard" was mostly for his benefit. As she played everything back, it hadn't gone at all badly. She'd got a very good deal and Eric Hayle was better as a friend than as an enemy. Besides, he wasn't holding all the cards. He clearly knew nothing about her blossoming relationship with Marina Allan.

*

The fire left John quite badly shaken. The policeman had gone but John's nerves were still jangling. Natalie moved her chair a little closer and took John's hand in hers. She couldn't think of much to say so she just stroked the back of his hand. It seemed to help.

Marcel, the Maître D' had not been quite close enough to hear everything but he pieced things together. He did his bit to help. Two coffees and a large brandy appeared silently in front of them. And they were left undisturbed until it was time to close the restaurant.

Natalie took John back to hers. He didn't object. There was nowhere else to go.

CHAPTER TWELVE
PRIME MINISTRESS AND DEATH THREATS

Most powerful is he who has himself in his own power
– Seneca

Ψ

Hazel did not want to meet Marina Allen. Marina's husband was bad enough, his government had come in a massive mandate and the goodwill to change the way things were done. They had made some steps towards change, but mostly they liked it just the way it was. As more time went by it became obvious that they were just as bad as the last lot: Acting for ill-defined reasons of political expediency, bowing to the knee jerk reaction of some fictitious middle England. The wants and needs of the vast majority of the party's core followers were ignored. It looked like Charles Parson thought they would vote for his party no matter what. The equally large majority he got at the most recent general election seemed to confirm that and he moved ever further to the right.

His wife was not her husband, but she was one of them.

But Hazel would not be intimidated. She reminded herself that her professional life had fared worse. She had faced down men who had killed infamously. She had attempted to understand those whom even a mother couldn't love. She had connected with near catatonics and extreme narcissists. She could manage Marina Allen. Therefore, Hazel prepared for the dinner as if this was a clinical encounter. She had read what case notes she could find. The opinions of Wikipedia were not quite as good as a consultant psychiatrist but at least she could read the writing.

* ¢ ?

The day after the fire John had received a call from Eric.

"I thought you'd be calling."

"Great news about the fire, wasn't it? I think we must be getting through to people," said Eric.

"So you're calling to make fun of my situation?"

"Actually, you called me about something a few days ago. You didn't call back so I assume it wasn't important."

"I had a question." John said. It didn't seem so important any more. Not after someone had tried to kill him. Maybe if he could just get out of this. But telling Eric he wanted to quit was no better as an option. He'd have to work his way up to it.

"Yes?"

"I cannot understand how you can pay me so much. How are we going to make any money out of me?" John asked.

"Aha, an excellent question Mr Smith. Maybe we will make a rock-star out of you yet. Do you know who is number one on Mick Jagger's speed dial?"

"Keith Richards?"

"No, it's Rupert Löwenstein, his accountant[*] Come to the

office, I have a surprise."

In the Clarion offices, Eric was ready with another lecture.

"You are selling a lot of newspapers, which is always good. We released the video package and license some broadcast rights we will be doing okay. But as I told you, I am doing this for principle rather then money. But, there is no reason in principle why one can't have both.

"I have a little dirt on just anyone you care to mention. Though the secrets of politicians and celebrities are not nearly as interesting as you might think. And you have probably heard them all down the pub anyway, along with a load of utter rubbish. That is the difference, I know which tall tales are true and often I have even seen the pictures that prove it. But I do not see fit to print this tittle tattle.

"So what if some national television weatherman has a gambling problem, that spokesperson X of her Majesty's Loyal Opposition likes to take late night walks on Clapham Common, or this disc jockey has a nasty disease? Seventy percent of any given political party are incompetent and as many again have abused their authority. Chase after too many soft targets and you discourage the well meaning from ever signing up and you're just left with the real bastards. Only a tiny minority are pro-actively corrupt or criminally hypocritical. They are the ones I go for in print.

"I have met Gandhi, Kennedy and Martin Luther King, and try as I might I didn't like any of them. They all had the same flaw: great though they undoubtedly were they could never stop being politicians. I think every politician who has

---

* This may or may not be true. But what is a fact is that before the band took off Jagger had a scholarship to study business and accounting at the London School of Economics.

succeeded has the same flaw. However strong your principles when you start out, once you enter the political game it is going to change. Sooner or later you are going to have to compromise one or other of them. And when you've done it once, you'll do it again. At first, you can rationalise it, because you can't change the world if you don't have power. So a little idealism must be sacrificed at the altar of expediency. But the further you go the more you do it. You become a bigger and bigger hypocrite. I fucking hate hypocrisy. "

Eric paused. If this rant was going anywhere, John wasn't aware. Maybe Eric was drunk. Or maybe he was just old. It was easy to forget that a man was 91 when you had to run to keep up with him.

"Where was I?"

"I'm not sure. Something about money and principles and bastards?"

"Ah yes, let's forget about the bastards. Money and principles. That was your question wasn't it? You are big. Just like I said you would be. A bunch of students in Leeds have renamed their bar after you and in Dundee University they are nominating you for Vice Chancellor. Some idiot in Swanage has got you tattooed on his back. Though you are wearing England football kit and scoring a goal because he had started getting Wayne Rooney and changed his mind after seeing a video of your performance. Apparently there are even a couple of people have changed their name to John Smith."

"What? Who? Why?"

"And 'where' and 'when'. You're getting the hang of this."

"Why would they do that? Who would even know?"

"But who *won't* know? Meet a new John Smith, there's always a chance he'd changed his name to yours. That's what makes it great story."

"So my job is just to keep on selling papers?"

"No, you happen to sell papers because that *isn't* a job. You have principles not a product. The students like you because they see you as a rebel. They'll never rebel themselves but they don't know that yet. Everyone else wants to know what you'll do next, ready and waiting for you to fail. They'll follow your story and they'll pay money to see you because they simply can't guess what happens next. Right now almost no one is listening to what you actually said. Your popularity is your unpredictability."

"That's mostly *your* unpredictability," John said.

"Parlour tricks. We need to get their attention before we can tell anything. Before you tell, another performance, bigger, better, more shocking. Then people will listen. And everything else will follow."

"Money? I don't see how."

"The fastest way to make money is to start your own religion. This is the next best thing. Just ask Jagger. That reminds me, what music do you like? What bands?" Eric asked.

"All kinds really. Almost everything, except Phil Collins, he's dreadful." John replied unsure what sort of test this was.

"Yes, he's a cunt. Let me put it another way; who would you like to open for you at Wembley?" said Eric, springing his surprise.

Ψ ?

It was only after long thought that Hazel had agreed to have dinner with the prime minister's wife. She convinced herself that Marina Allan could not be all bad and not very scary. But Hazel kept coming back to the fact that she was some high flying corporate warrior queen, who reminded Hazel of Snow White's evil stepmother.

Shona tried to suggest that the meeting took place at the studio. Marina Allan could watch the Friday show where Doctor Cole and Shona solved the audience's problems and she could meet the pair of them after. She was told that Marina Allan was far too busy. Fortunately the alternative arrangements that Marina Allan's office suggested was extremely acceptable to Shona. Marina Allan would like to meet the doctor for dinner at some fashionable and expensive restaurant. And it was suggested that Shona's company could pay. (Although she could easily afford it, Marina Allan was not the sort to pay for her own dinner if she could avoid it.) This was a perfect compromise for Shona. If Shona was paying then no one could stop her attending and the meeting would be highly public. Especially once Shona had tipped off the press. (Though she did not need it, Shona was not the sort to pass up the publicity if she were dining with the Prime Ministress.)

When Marina Allan arrived, she was swept into the building in a swarm of six or seven menacing close protection officers. Unknown to Shona and Hazel, there already another eight in the building. Every entrance and exit was secure, armed officers sat at each of the tables on either side of them pretending to be businessmen having dinner. Crop-haired muscle bound businessmen wearing para-boots and drinking only mineral water. To be fair to them, that was their point.

They were there as an obvious deterrent to anyone who might be looking for them, but not so obvious as to spoil the rich atmosphere of Crivelli's for everyone-else. Entering into the spirit of their roles, they even ordered food. (Which Shona would be billed for.)

One final officer patrolled the kitchen, alert to anyone attempting to sabotage the food destined for 'the baggage'. He made sure that no 'terrorists' or other kitchen radicals tried to poison her with strychnine, cyanide or balsamic vinegar. Especially not balsamic vinegar. Her Bach Flower therapist had expressly forbidden it. In a double Michelin starred modern Italian restaurant it was a clear and present danger. His presence also discouraged the deliberate adulteration of her food with human bodily fluids. A more common occurrence than you, she and especially her Bach Flower therapist might like to think.

"Julio, the twins personal fitness instructor, had a copy with him during their junior Pilates class the previous week and he was so enthusiastic about it that I asked Esme what she thought," Marina explained.

Esme O'Brien was a tabloid editor's dream. She was Marina Allan's best friend and her husband's worst nightmare. She was a former glamour model with even fewer O-levels than Princess Diana, any number of dodgy friends and an outlook so New Age that it was almost as if she had been born yesterday. She may well have been - re-birthing was an almost monthly activity for her. She was Marina's most trusted friend and closest confidante. She advised Marina on everything; her wardrobe, her aromatherapy selections, probably even on Government policy.

Shona hated Esme O'Brien.

"Esme said that you possessed deep knowledge and wisdom but that you repressed your spiritual essence, but then that's normal of Taureans," Marina said.

"Really?" said Hazel biting her tongue, in a way not typical of Taureans. But then she was not a Taurean.

Naturally, Esme had not read 'Help Yourself' but she did like the title. As someone who did not have the mental capacity to think too much about anyone else, it had appealed to her. She worried when she flicked through it and found there were no pictures. Not one diagram mapping chakra meridians. Not even any rainbows or flowers. But when she had looked at the author photograph on the back fly-cover, she had sensed that Hazel was a good person. (And that she was a Taurean.) And Hazel was a good mother earth pleasing name, so the book had passed the Esme test.

Marina Allen reached into her brightly coloured authentic Bedouin Ha'goof and brought out a copy of 'Help Yourself'.

"Look, I've got your book." She said to the frosty atmosphere at the table.

"Have you read it?" Hazel asked politely in a tone that Shona could not help but recognise. She dropped her fork.

"Oh no, I am far too busy," Marina replied and the knife went too. "I was hoping you could tell me about it?"

Shona's dreams hung on this answer. She saw a pained look flick over the doctor's face. Then Hazel glanced fleetingly in her direction. When Hazel had agreed to this meeting, she knew she'd have to be on her best behaviour. She smiled a fake smile and had her first ever go at the cynical art of diplomacy.

For the first course she managed it. She spoke in empty statements. She ignored the absurdities that came back. She deflected difficult questions. She involved Shona as much as possible. Her food was most probably delicious but she had no respite to enjoy it. Her wine went down quickly.

The main course went better. Marina gave up on Dr. Cole and reluctantly conversed with Shona. To Marina's surprise they bonded quite well. Shona was eager to agree with her potential new friend. They knew a lot of the same people. How funny that Madame Amethyst, a terrible gossip and name-dropper, had never mentioned that Shona was a client too. She and Shona spoke the same language. They talked it among themselves and left Dr Cole to enjoy her cod and her Chablis.

It was only at dessert that something snapped. Perhaps it was all the talk of crystals and auras. Perhaps it was listening to the checklist of ingredients that Marina Allan wouldn't eat. Perhaps it was the three glasses of wine. In any event, Dr. Cole decided that she was a therapist, not a diplomat. The prime minister's wife had just said something preposterous about happiness and Hazel could stay silent no longer.

"I am afraid I don't agree."

"I'm sorry?"

"Mrs Allan, Marina, you could not possibly be more successful. It seems to me that you have everything you could wish and have succeeded at everything you have attempted and yet you want something more? If the newspapers are to believed you go to psychics and healers. But surely you are the very last person that should need any help."

"Oh, I disagree, we could all use spiritual help."

"What you want is someone to tell you it's okay? You want approval? Be successful because that is what you are supposed to do but when you close the office door and there is no-one watching, what then? That's what you are scared of. You've reached the top and there is no one left to set you tests."

"There's God." Marina Allen QC was not about to fold under cross-examination.

"Oh please, Can't you see that God is just another father figure for you? You cling to Him because you need someone bigger than you, better than you to turn to when it all gets too much. To tell you it's going to be okay."

"I ... my husband ..." The moment she said it, she and the rest of the table knew it wasn't true.

"Mrs Allen, It's okay ..."

There was a very long pause. Shona couldn't read it at all. Her nails dug into her palms. At length, the prime Ministress spoke.

"My father died when I was thirteen..."

"And you still really miss him?"

"Every day"

"What about your mother?"

"She wasn't really there. She didn't cope very well."

"But what about now?"

"I ... We don't speak. It easier. We don't get on."

"Mrs Allen, you have to stop this, stop worrying. You are doing okay. You are an inspiration to many, many women." Hazel gestured at Shona "Shona is incredibly successful and has an amazing career but she looks up to you. She sees what you do and it inspires her. It is what you have done. What you have achieved, yourself."

Thankful for the attention, Shona nodded earnestly. She crept her hand up onto the table. In reaching distance, should Marina need it.

"You have to believe in yourself too, as a woman. No man will ever replace your father, so there's no man who's approval is going to give you peace. You have to do that for yourself." Hazel waited a second. "Your mother must be very proud of you too."

There was a silence. And then, Marina Allen, the most powerful woman in the country, second only to Madonna in the eyes of Chat magazine, dissolved softly into tears. They were quiet and they were small but there wasn't a person in the restaurant that did not notice.

* ¢

Apparently Eric was deadly serious about Wembley stadium. It was booked in four weeks time and tickets would go on sale as soon as they had selected a support act. It was only at the end of a very long day that John remembered he had another question.

"Eric, have there been any more death threats?"

Eric sent him in the direction of the letter editor.

It was one thing to ask Eric but putting the question to a total stranger, he reflected how ridiculous it would sound.

"Do you have mail for me?"

"Oh yes, so you are John Smith?" the letters editor chuckled to himself, "You have had fifteen proposals of marriage, and inevitably a fair number of far more indecent proposals, which are usually accompanied by helpful explanatory photographs. That is just the emails, I have not touched the mail bag, there's a lot of angry looking ones and some of those parcels are just a bit too squishy for me."

"Angry?" John asked worriedly.

"Yes, well there have been surprisingly few death threats."

"There have *been* death threats?"

"A few but that is e-mail. Even deranged psychopaths know not to sign their names to their threats."

"But there have been some?"

"A handful ten or twenty maximum by email. Judging by the bad spelling and atrocious grammar, none them would be bright enough to launch a decent assassination. They might manage an assault, which could be quite ugly judging by what they can do to the English language." With some distaste, he gave John a sheaf of printed emails and handed him a grey mail sack.

John took his time to go through everything. It was pretty much like the letters editor had said. None them stood out as the sort of person who might set fire to your house. Though he wasn't sure he knew how to spot that. He needed to speak to an expert. The policeman of the previous night entered his mind, and was summarily dismissed. John realised he was putting off the inevitable.

"I wouldn't take any of them seriously." Eric said. "But it shows you are on the right track."

"For martyrdom?"

"Well, I guess that depends on how serious *you* are."

"Death is the proof I'm living, not the prize"

"Okay, okay. Don't worry about the death threats I've been getting them for years and I've not known a single writer who meant it."

"But someone was actually trying to kill me."

"There you are then, the chances of two crazed assassins..."

"And look at this one 'Life is preparation for death, I hope you are well prepared.' What is that? It's not some froth-mouthed, arm-chair assassin, this person has an education".

"Lots of people hate me. I don't worry about it. Neither should you."

"Wait a minute, you drive around in an armoured limo."

"That's business. I don't have enemies, I have competitors. They'll only try and take me out if makes sense on the bottom-line. But the funny thing is, the more ruthless my competitors the better I seem to be able to do business with them."

"I wonder why"

"You are in the religion business. If anyone wants to take you out it will be an Al Sharpton or the Vatican. But you are not even on their radar yet. And I doubt they would write to you in advance."

"So, in summary, I keep going until I offend Opus Dei?"

"That's the spirit. Speaking of which, Wembley Stadium needs a little more showmanship than a Covent Garden basement. We'll need a miracle and a sermon on the mount."

？¢

Maybe Eric was right about Dr. Cole. She was dangerous. Shona dialled Eric's number.

"I'll do it."

"I knew you'd see it my way."

"I do," Shona said. "You know how in the films Hannibal Lecter is supposed to get inside your head? Well Hazel Cole is a bit like that except that as far as I know she doesn't eat any of her victims."

"Who has she 'helped' this time?"

"Well she hasn't helped me. She made Marina Allan cry in front of everybody at the best table in Crivelli's."

"Really? Perhaps I was wrong about Dr. Cole. Not that it matters, she's queering the pitch for my boy and we've got to do something about it." Eric paused as if checking something "The money will be in the account by tomorrow. I hope you are in a taxi."

"No, I'm at home already."

"Well, get in a taxi and get over here. There were two conditions to this deal. Remember?"

INTERMISSION
ABSURDITY

Life is absurd enough already without recourse to astrology, homeopathy and other fantasies. Not only are they ridiculous but the don't even offer anything of reassurance in the face of existential dread. You would be better off climbing into and eventually out of a nice hot bath and then wrapping yourself in big fluffy towel.

On one level the world makes perfect sense. The laws of nature set everything nicely in motion and it all just happens from there. But on another, it is completely absurd because all those laws don't give the place any meaning and when we are dead we're gone and haven't changed the grand scheme of anything. But if only more people realised this then the world would be a hell of a lot better place; people would be forced to stop being so petty-minded. The gods of the Christians and all the rest are ridiculous simplistic, small-minded caricatures of ourselves, showing a complete lack of imagination compared to the grandeur and complexity of the universe revealed by science. There is no better argument for equality and morality than the argument from insignificance.

Philosopher Thomas Nagel and many others have pointed out that life is absurd. Why are you alive right at this point in history? Any other could have been equally likely, you could have been alive in the last ice age or living aboard a space station in the far future. Instead you are here and now and that is worth considering. Even more absurd, why are experiencing this precise moment in time? In your life right now? At this exact second there is someone looking out of your eyes and experiencing the world as you experience it, and that person is you. But you are also the person who experiences your life a minute ago, or last week or when you were thirteen and it is the same you as will see the world in a week's time. Or laugh and cry in years to come. They are all you, but there must be something particularly special about the present you. Because that is the one to whom, right at this moment, I am speaking to and who is reading these words.

Nagel tried to find what it was that made each instant special of each of us. Every moment in time is just like any other and yet there is only ever one present. He concluded that there is nothing that explains it. Ultimately, it is just absurd.

CHAPTER THIRTEEN
BUS STOP

Law I: Every body persists in its state of being at rest or of moving uniformly straight forward, except insofar as it is compelled to change its state by force impressed.

Law II: The alteration of motion is ever proportional to the motive force impress'd; and is made in the direction of the right line in which that force is impress'd.

Law III: To every action there is always an equal and opposite reaction: or the forces of two bodies on each other are always equal and are directed in opposite directions.

– Isaac Newton, Philosophiæ Naturalis Prinicipia Mathematica, 1687

• * ¢

The Mercedes Chancellor is a marvellous vehicle, the best European made limousine you can buy. More elegant than its American counterparts and more reliable than its Russian comrades, it has all the features one would expect from a very important people carrier. Comfortable seating for four or cosy seating for six. Eric's car was the absolute top-end version with an armoured body and bulletproof glass. The passenger compartment was hermetically sealed to protect the occupants from gas attacks and the car's fuel tank was specially constructed to be leak-proof and safe from explosions. The steel lined tyres could still run flat if punctured and with a 6-litre V8 beast of an engine, it could outrun most danger if the need arose. Most European heads of state had one of these, at least, those that could afford it. Russian billionaires and Middle Eastern oil Princes were among the few other customers who could afford such a luxury or could justify such security. If you wanted to attack someone in a Mercedes Chancellor, your best bet was to follow along patiently behind and run them over once they had stepped out of their car.

The London Routemaster was for its time a remarkable piece of British engineering. Beautiful, functional, robust and built to last, it symbolises the hectic yet historic nature of the city. Originally designed in the 1950's, it was a product of some highly innovative engineering and proud craftsmanship. The Routemaster has an integral strengthened body removing the need for a heavy fixed chassis.

With a 97 break horsepower engine and a fully automatic gearbox, it could, when London's roads allowed, attain a good head of speed. Some of those early models are still going strong, and they inspire strong feelings in many grease-covered men who underneath are still small boys. The man was one of those men. And he was pleased to back behind the wheel. He had kept a few keys and it had been a simple enough business to steal this bus.

Thanks to the mayor's mania for bus lanes, the man had a satisfyingly clear run now and was able get quickly away from the depot and into the centre of London, without anyone being any the wiser. Before setting out he'd changed the sign to 'Not in Service', despite the fact this simply wasn't true. This bus was in the service of the Lord. It would smite down his enemy. The man drove on humming hymns and thinking this happy thought. After about half an hour, it occurred to him that he had absolutely no idea where the Evil One would be.

So he did what any sane person would and drove to the library.

He parked up round the corner and went in to ask at the reference desk. The librarian on duty recognised him as one of the regulars and so listened patiently to what he said. None of it made the slightest bit of sense but there was nothing new in that. Carefully cross-examining him and employing the fine mind that she had previously been occupying with a crossword, she ascertained that he was interested in John Smith. Knowing him as she did, she found it rather sweet.

She showed him that day's papers with the lurid story of Smith's narrow escape from death. But he seemed to know it all already. He was clearly quite a fan. The man seemed to want to know more about Smith than the papers could provide. There was no crime in that; in fact it was quite understandable really. She hated to disappoint him, but despite what he seemed to think the library did know everything about everyone, if only you asked in the right way. She tried explaining to him that this wasn't the case in several different ways but it didn't seem to sink in.

Then she had a revelation. Maybe the man wasn't beyond help. There was Google.

Within a few clicks she had found the unofficial fan forum where Smith's most fanatical fans swapped whatever snippets and slivers they could find out about their hero. She showed the man how to navigate the site and where to find the most up to the minute gossip and speculation. This, at last, seemed to satisfy him. She left him happily clicking and scrolling and went back to her crossword.

The rest of the morning was uneventful and she managed to finish the whole puzzle. She had only had to google a couple of clues. Going off for her lunch, she saw that the man had gone too. He'd forgotten to close the windows he'd opened on the computer and left the mouse mat at a ridiculous angle. She quit the browser, straightened up the workspace and shook her head. These loonies weren't too much trouble and one liked to help them out but they sometimes went too far.

ER1C pulled up to the kerb. Not used to waiting for someone to open the door for him, John had joined Eric in the back before Eric's chauffeur Dave could get out to let him in. They were picking him up from his latest hotel to take him to Wembley for a look at the facilities. John ducked inside and as before, the floor was strewn with porn and the resident pornographer was lounging comfortably with a large whiskey in one hand and a cigar in another.

"Morning, shithead. Let's get moving." Eric greeted him cheerfully and the car joined the busy morning traffic. A little distance behind it a big red bus indicated too and pulled away from the kerb.

The 1965 RML that the man was driving had unladen weight of 7 3/4 tons and by the time it came into contact with rear-end of the stationary Mercedes it was travelling at slightly over thirty five miles per hour. Sir Isaac Newton's wonderfully elegant laws of motion saw to it that a large part of this kinetic energy was transferred into the boot of the Mercedes, crumpling it's crumple zones and sending it skidding forwards through the red light and across the box junction. The equal and opposite reaction made a few slight dents in the front of the Routemaster and brought it to halt straddling the pedestrian crossing. Meanwhile, the Mercedes continued forwards joining the counterflow of traffic somewhat earlier than everyone would have liked.

For a few exciting moments, it looked like it would sail unscathed between the traversing taxis, but one driver was changing lanes and travelling a little too fast. He swerved but was unable to avoid clipping the mangled rear left side of the limo. It sent both cars into a complex sliding clockwise dance that still obeyed Newton's laws though the mathematics was now a lot more complicated. Shortly thereafter, it became an interesting and non-trivial N-body problem, as any number of other cars coming in both directions were now unable to avoid joining the dance.

Piccadilly Circus was busy to start with. The normal marauding hordes of shuffling tourists and impatient Londoners all hurrying in every direction. More often, in the case of the tourists, ambling a few steps one way before changing their minds, turning through ninety degrees, taking a few more steps in this new direction before finally deciding this was a good spot for a photograph and taking a few steps back to point their cameras up at the bright advertising screens. All to the annoyance of the gritty and grimy locals who had just danced this way and that trying to get past and then at the last moment, just as they sped for a gap, four hundred pounds of flabbiest sub-prime American bovine would step back to frame his shot and flatten the slight and wiry Cockney.

Right now everyone was a sightseer, hundreds of cameras were capturing the photogenic column of black smoke and hundreds upon hundreds more people where crowding in behind these, all eager to see what was going on.

The traffic was jammed in all directions. Lots of the drivers thought that honking their horns would help the situation and these annoyed other drivers, who sounded their own horns in displeasure, which upset a few more. Others amused by this music added their own lackadaisical syncopations. The whole place was chaos. It was like Piccadilly Circus.

The Routemaster's radiator had broken from its mountings and water was hissing gently from it. This was hardly interesting compared to the multi-car pile up in the middle of London's famous Piccadilly Circus. None of many the tourists watching noticed the bus driver hang his jacket on the back of his seat, climb down from his vehicle and wander off.

* ¢

Things might not have been so bad for the Mercedes and its passengers if it were not for Eric's untidy reading habits, his huge Cuban cigar and a rare lack of ice aboard ER1C. The first impact knocked his heavy tumbler of neat Bourbon out of his hand and the next sent his glowing Havana flying after it. Unadulterated by ice, the firewater caught fire easily and doused the magazines that littered the floor of the vehicle. Too many of these caught fire for Eric's stamping to have any positive effect and so he satisfied himself with kicking the burning papers away from himself. This had the effect of spreading the flames further but it allowed Eric and John to bundle out of the passenger door without getting too badly singed.

Out on the road, they shut the door behind them and surveyed the scene. The back of the Mercedes was slightly crumpled.

"I still get two or three death threats a month but those are mostly from fundamentalist Christians and other fruit-bats. I don't take them seriously. You should read some of them; they threaten me with plague, pustules, pestilence, and pillars of fire. All that Old Testament crap, not much interest in

Loving thy Neighbour those lot. But they are very funny, I am thinking of collecting the best and publishing a book." Eric looked back at this flaming Mercedes Benz and the slightly dented Routemaster. "I cannot remember any of them threatening me with a London bus."

Eric was the most cheerful John had ever seen him.

"Isn't this what you wanted?" Eric asked. "To face death and feel alive?"

"I can't decide."

"Where did the driver go?" Eric was only half listening; he was hunting around and quizzing bystanders on what they might have seen.

"Why do you assume it was for me? I would have thought you would have many more enemies that me? Haven't there been several attempts on your life before?" John asked.

"If you discount the war and certain other episodes I would rather not talk about then yes two or three people may have tried to kill me. But the last one was over thirty years ago. Today, I am seen as just another businessman. I don't have enemies, I have competitors."

"I don't."

"Maybe you do." Eric was lost for just a moment. "Anyway chop, chop, we've still got to get to Wembley. Let's leave Dave to sort out this mess. Which do you think is quicker, bus or tube?"

•

The man was as disappointed as when mummy forgot to flush

the toilet and he found out that Simon the goldfish had not gone to live with the other fishes in the river.

That day he had also found out about death and how even people you thought you could trust will lie to you.

Simon the goldfish was the only pet the boy ever had. The boy had loved Simon. He could watch for hours as Simon swam from one end of his rectangular little tank and back to the fake plastic weeds at the other. Each circuit of his home a little different from the one before never hurried and never worried. It soothed the boy's nerves to watch the light reflecting off Simon's golden scales. With his inscrutable black eyes it was hard to tell what Simon was looking at, much less what he was thinking about. But the boy knew that Simon could recognize him. And that Simon knew that the boy was his friend. He was sad when Simon was dead. He kept Simon's tank with filled with water. Even without Simon there it was a special place. It looked so calm, peaceful and colourful the plastic weeds could not be more green while the pebbles seemed to have every colour under the sun.

First his own mother, and now that priest. No one could be trusted. He really was alone.

Somehow he made it home. He lay down and wept.

Eventually, exhausted, he slept.

INTERMISSION FIVE
CASPAR'S WAGER

Blaise Pascal invented the mathematics of gambling. His own most famous bet was a pretty big one; commonly know as Pascal's wager:

> Let us weigh the gain and the loss in wagering that God is. Let us estimate these two chances. If you gain, you gain all; if you lose, you lose nothing.   Wager,   then,   without hesitation that He is.
> – Blaise Pascal, Penses, 1670

It is basically the same logic that we use to decide if we are going to buy tickets in the National Lottery. The prize is huge, the stake is small. The chances of winning might be slim, but if you don't enter you won't win squat. The clever bit, in Pascal's mind, was that however infinitesimal you believe the chance that there is a God, the jackpot is so HUGE that you would be crazy not to buy a ticket. Unfortunately, this is completely wrong.

I propose instead Caspar's Wager, which runs like this.

> Let's see; a whole bunch of Sundays on my knees, or a fuller life lived as I please? Good god, I wager that anyone who keeps herself so carefully hid does not wish to be bothered by me.
> – Caspar Addyman, Help Yourself, 2013

Actually, I made the bet quite a long time ago. A lot of people do. Even tiny children will ask the Fathers and Rabbi's why it isn't enough just to live a good life.

Oh how simple life seemed when we were young. I remember when I was about eight years old and our class were asked by our sociological jurisprudence counsellor to give three examples of absolute rules we lived by. I can vividly remember the answers I confidently provided

>   Never start a major land war in Asia.
>   Never have sex and livestock in the same sentence.

and

>   Never bet against a co-discoverer of probability theory.

Well, time tells that it would have been a nincompoop who pooh-poohed Pierre de Fermat's Last Theorem, but I do choose to take issue with Blaise Pascal's last hefty bet. I disagree completely with his reasoning; I'll wager he's got it completely backwards.

In fact, I'll stake my terrestrial and my eternal life on it. Every now and again I am reminded, as politely as possible, by my religious 'friends' that unless I repent my godless ways I will be damned to burning hell for all eternity. I tell them it's a price worth paying for my Sunday lie-in. But this irreverence does little to dissuade them.

Smiling ever more broadly, they casually suggest that I join them for their Tuesday evening study group, where their priest/rabbi/Sufi/Baphomet can tell me some really great things about Jesus/Yahweh/Mohammed/Satan. I meet their expectant hopefulness with a slight curl of my lip and explain that I don't let men in dresses tell me what to do. (Well, there was that one time, but I honestly didn't realise he was a man.)

Alas, I tell them, in good faith, I will never be able to join their happy band.

But like all purveyors of opiates, they are wheedling, pushy and persistent and won't I just think again? I just say no. Sensing my steely resolve but still possessed of a glimmer of zeal, they change tack and mention Pascal's prescription for people of precisely my persuasion.

No! And I can prove it.

CLAIM: We ought to act as if God didn't exist.

PROOF: There are two possibilities to consider.
    Case 1: Assume God doesn't exist.
        Trivially we have done the right thing.
    Case 2: Assume God exists.
    Again there are two cases to consider.
        2B: God is good.
        Not to Be: God is evil.

If God is evil then he's played the Ace of Spades and whatever we do we're going to lose. Again there is no point worshipping him/her/them/it/us.

If God is good then we've been put on Earth to live. Let's get on with it. Praising God adds nothing to the worth of our own achievements. Furthermore, despite an exhaustive search, there has of yet been no evidence of God's existence. Therefore, we might conclude that it is irrational to waste what little time we appear to have on worship of one particular imagined incarnation of an extremely elusive deity. We would decide it was better to try and figure things out for ourselves, spend the time as if we didn't have an eternity more of it to use later.

Of course, if Not 2b then we were wrong, but whatever we've

done, God will understand our honest mistake. And, being good, he won't be a dick about it. So that's okay then.

Q.E.D.

Of course Pascal argued from assumptions in classical probability whereas I am arguing from the meaning of 'good' and 'evil'. But we can go beyond good and evil because there's an even shorter version of this argument that uses Bayesian statistics. It starts from the easily demonstrated fact that :

"Absence of Evidence *is* Evidence of Absence." [*]

Alas, we don't have the time nor the inclination for a lesson in Bayesian statistics. Which is a shame because of this proposition, I have wonderful proof. And the margin of novel is too small to contain it.

It's a better argument too since most of everyday thinking happens using some unconscious approximation to Bayesian reasoning. Grossly stated, Bayes theorem says,

"Before you leap to any conclusions, consider how well they fit the facts."

Imagine a fearsome creature with talons and leopards spots looms towards you somewhere dark and gloomy. You haven't got time to wait for conclusive proof so you have to act on incomplete evidence. You have to take an uncertain leap one way or another, but your conclusion still has to fit all the facts. Those other facts may change the odds dramatically. In the forest you might leap one way, in a nightclub quite another. And knowledge of which nightclub you are in helps you estimate the probability that this woman *is* a woman.

Take that Pascal. Take that Original Sin.

---

[*] No, it really is. Look it up on the internet.
http://oyhus.no/AbsenceOfEvidence.html

CHAPTER FOURTEEN
LOAN GUNMAN

Zeroth Law: You must play the game.

First Law: You can't win.

Second Law: You can't break even.

Third Law: You can't quit the game.

– Ginsberg's Theorem a.k.a. The laws of thermodynamics

The man lived at the top of a very tall building. The bedsit assigned to him on his conditional discharge from the hospital was on the 19th floor of a decrepit council tower block. It might have seemed foolhardy to house a former mental health service user so close to an easy means of suicide. But for once social services had done their homework. At times a danger to others, the man was not and never had been considered a suicide risk. The pills reduced his danger to others and no one thought he would ever get access to a high-powered rifle with telescopic sights. The man liked his tiny one and a half room flat. He liked the views. He liked the pigeons that would sleep on his window ledge. He liked the relative peace, up here isolated from the noise of the city. Best of all, he felt was closer to God.

Eric had investigated the hit and run. Despite his blasé attitude to the many death threats he received and his gleeful excitement at the ram raider attempt on his and/or Smith's lives, Eric had been sufficiently interested in who might have done it. And after trawling his memory through a long list of his possible enemies he could not think who might be behind it. So he had hired a little known but well staffed and highly respected firm of private investigators, Vernon Associates.

God knows how they did it but they tracked down the man responsible. (I could at this point invent some reason and could bore you with a long explanation of the native cunning and hi-tech computer wizardry able to reconstruct a composite facsimile image of the man as he left the scene of the crime from camera footage, and then at tedious length connect up the trail that led them to him. But it would interrupt the flow of what I want to get to: the meeting of Eric and the man. Besides by this stage in the book I feel that I have made enough creative input and so would prefer it if you invented your own way for them to find out that the man, former bus driver and more recently former mental patient was behind the wheel of the Routemaster in question. Do not worry if you cannot or will not think of a reason either. There is no right answer and it is not as if it matters anyway. None of this is real. It is all made up. But if you simply have to know email me caspar@onemonkey.org and I will tell you how it worked.)

They had traced the man and let Eric know what they knew. He let them know that he hoped they knew that he would prefer it if they did not let the police know what they knew. But they knew that already. That was the way it usually went in top end private investigations.

The police naturally had not discovered any of this for themselves as yet. Although both cases had made the front pages of several national newspapers, separate teams in the areas involved were still handling them. As far as the police were concerned, one was a traffic accident in the borough of Westminster, the other an arson attack in Herne Hill. Even though, after each incident, the deputy Metropolitan police commissioner had been forced to hold a small press conference at New Scotland Yard. Once the brief flurry of interest had died down, the cases sat unprioritised on separate desks in separate divisions in separate boroughs.

Duffled up against the weather and recognition, Eric had Dave drive him there, in a spare Mercedes. He climbed the stairs to the man's apartment.

Eric Hayle had never backed away from a fight in his life. More than once, he had crossed the globe to get into one. His philosophy had always been the best defence is pre-emptive violence. That there is no problem so complex that it cannot be simplified by violent confrontation. Now he was standing at the door of a man whom his investigators informed him was a schizophrenic with a history of violence. A man who had already tried to kill him once and Smith twice. There had been lightness in Eric's step as he bounded up the nineteen flights of stairs to the man's council-provided one bedroom flat. He had rung the bell merrily.

Eric had read Vernon Associates' report on the man. He had been disappointed because he saw instantly that it was John Smith, not him, who was the man's target. The extensive report had listed his times in secure mental wards, sectioned following violent attacks motivated by delusional religious mania. With Smith being denounced by Reverend Cake and other religious loudmouths, it did not take a genius to work out that this man might jump on the bandwagon. Especially this man.

Much as he hated all things to do with religion, Eric was an enlightened individual. He understood the complexities of mental illness. He knew that the man could not help the way his mind malfunctioned. So Eric had refrained from sharing his valuable information with the authorities and chose to handle this in his own way.

Moreover, his wartime experience in counter-espionage had taught him that every crazed lunatic was a potential recruit. He had decided to pay the man a visit. But Reckless Eric was not being entirely reckless. He had a gun in his overcoat pocket.

When the man opened the door, he was wearing a trilby coated in silver foil. He was highly suspicion of Eric, as Eric knew he would be. But knowing enough of the man's history from the medical files that Vernon and company had 'obtained', Eric knew how to appeal to the man's mania and indulge and extend his delusions. He told the man that he had a dream that he should come here. He said he knew the man had a mission but he did not know what. But he had been told he must help the man complete it. He also hinted that he was not all that he seemed. (This much at least was true, although not in the way that it seemed.)

The man had not had anyone believe and support his worldview before. Occasionally, in his time on the wards, other patients would go along with him a little of the way, but mostly they were wrapped up in their own complex confusions. Besides they were crazy. The man was completely taken in by this tall, extremely elegant white haired figure, who had been sent to help him. Eric was rapidly absorbed into the man's Grand Scheme of Things.

Welcoming Eric into his worldview, the man had explained, in a highly disjointed and incoherent fashion (for his condition was getting worse) that he was God's Avenger. His Holy mission was to stop the False Prophet, the Anti-John. Eric hinted that he knew this, and indeed, it did confirm what he had surmised. The man told him how Reverend Cake's sermon had made it clear that the Non-John must die. The man told that he must end the False One's rise and then he would be recognised for what he was.

Eric reiterated that he was here to help. All this time, they had been standing in the chaotic kitchen but now the man left and went into the other room. He returned carrying an armful of spiral bound notebooks. He brushed the dust of a thousand dead Rice Crispies onto the floor and laid the notebooks out on the kitchen table. He began flicking through them, seemingly at random, to find certain passages and diagrams that explained everything in greater detail. Eric indulged him.

The man's plan to kill Smith was as ingenious as it was unhinged. It could not possibly work but it might have been entertaining to watch him try. It involved breaking into the British Museum to steal a special sword, helmet and breastplate, which been revealed to him as the Righteous Artefacts of his Manifest Destiny. The sword, a twelfth century Crusaders broadsword, was the only thing that could kill John Smith, protected as he was by 'THEM', dark forces that had yet to reveal themselves. The helmet, a bronze centurion's helmet from the time of Emperor Constantine, that would shield his thoughts from 'THEIR' mind-satellites and allow him to get close to Smith without 'THEM' realising. The breastplate was a ceremonial golden breastplate that once belonged to one of Charlemagne's infantry commanders. Somehow its shiny golden brilliance would reflect light and prevent people from noticing him. Thus, would this unbalanced and unwashed man sneak up on the unsuspecting Smith and pierce his black heart with pure and Holy Crusader's steel. When Smith was dead, the man would remove his Righteous Protection and reveal himself. All this had been revealed to him in a gardening column, a gig review and the commodities report in the Scum, the Guardian and the FT respectively.

Eric listened to all this patiently. He even made a few suggestions along the way. But once the man had finished, Eric had an alternative to suggest. He sympathized with the man's aims but not with him methods or motives. In fact, Eric saw the situation exactly in reverse to the man. Black to his White. Lucifer to his Gabriel. He agreed with the need for Smith to die, but he had different reasons why. If John Smith were killed by this lunatic Angel of Death, then Eric would benefit twice over. The church would be embarrassed and humiliated and the late John 'Now and Then' Smith would become a martyr. A modern secular martyr, an instant and enduring cult figure, whose message was exactly one by which Eric lived his own long, long life.

Eric did not want to found his own religion. What would be the point of that? He would not be around long enough to enjoy the fruits. (He gave himself only about another ten or twenty years at his current pace.) He was not definitely interested in founding a cult. For one thing it would require hard work, the crystallisation of fluid ideas into rigid dogmas and the setting up of a hierarchy to enforce and oversee everything. That could have been fun. But Eric did not like the limelight. He preferred shadows, dark corners and dingy basements. He was a creature of the night. He was doing this because he believed what Smith had said. That life passes most people by. All he wanted was people to wake up and take notice. To see life as it really is.

Granted, Smith would be dead and maybe the man might not survive either. In fact, that might need to be seen to. But as Bomber Harris used to say, you cannot make an omelette without smashing a couple of chicken embryos, beating them together and burning the bodies in hot oil.

Eric removed the pistol from his pocket. It was wrapped in an oil cloth. It was a Luger P-09, standard issue to officers in the Schutzstaffel. Eric had had this one since 1943 when taken this one from the still warm hand of Sturmbannführer Müller. A friend and colleague of his from Hamburg who, for complicated reasons, he had been required to kill. Eric had other guns, of course. But, for some reason, this one was the one he had picked out as his gift to the man. Perhaps he was getting sentimental in his old age. He placed it on the kitchen table.

When the man first saw the evil black gun, he had become frightened and paranoid. But Eric's soothing reassurance convinced him to pick it up. Holding it in his hand, the cold, heavy and slightly oily texture of it brought him completely into the present. He had never completely believed his own plan. He could see there were aspects of it that he had not worked out properly. Which item should he get first; the helmet to evade them? the breastplate to hide? or the sword to cut the other items free from their alarmed glass cases? Holding this gun in hand, he cut the sword from this plans. He could see a new way. He let Eric explain to him how to use the Luger.

But he would still need the helmet and breastplate. Eric had an answer to this too. He explained the man the principles of camouflage. At least as they related to their particular problem. Anything more abstract would be beyond the grasp of the man's crippled mind. Eric showed him how he could put the tin foil on the inside of his trilby. He explained slowly and diplomatically that the best way to become invisible was to look normal. To blend into the crowd. Maybe he could have a bath? And a shave and a haircut? And wear clean clothes, that matched?

Eric was kind, patient and understanding as they plotted the murder of John Smith.

The man had just about followed all these new things that his Guardian Angel had told him. He had to write a lot of it down so he would not forget. The Angel had left and now he must wait for the Angel to arrange the time and the place.

Eric went away, well pleased with his day's work. The whole thing was coming together better than he had ever expected. It was almost too perfect. As if someone had planned it. Which let's face it, I did!

Eric had never broken a bone in his body. At least, never by accident. He had once had two of his fingers broken for him. It was one of those terribly frustrating conversations were the other chap had kept repeating the same thing over and over again. "All we need from you is a name" etc. etc. He had said it a few times in German, and then felt he had to repeat the question in English. Even though Eric had already replied in very good accentless German that "Ja, he understood the question" and "Nein, he did not know the name." After forty minutes of this tedious rigmarole, they had broken one of his fingers. This did not help him remember a name that he had not known in the first place but they persisted. When it started to look like he was in for another forty minutes of the same, Eric had broken a second finger himself to hurry things along. It did the trick, the shocked interrogator quickly came to believe that Eric really did not know the name. Perhaps somewhat foolishly he had also believed many of the other things Eric went on to tell him and shortly after that Eric was working for both 'THEM' and 'US'.

In comparison, pretending to be a Angel had been easy.

INTERMISSION SIX
DEISTS DESIST.

I read about an Eskimo hunter who asked the local missionary priest, 'If I did not know about God and sin, would I go to hell?' 'No,' said the priest, 'not if you did not know.' 'Then why,' asked the Eskimo earnestly, 'did you tell me?'

- Annie Dillard, *Pilgrim at Tinker Creek*, 1974

God knows I pay Don and the boys too much but it is worth it. Every time there is a knock at the door I give a little prayer of thanks to the security team, because I know it will be someone I want to see, not some door-to-door sky-pilot or some God-botherer bothering me. My doormen are in the gatehouse twenty-four hours a day, seven days a week and I pay 'em double on religious holidays! They work tirelessly to keep out the hordes of Mormons, Jehovah's Witnesses and other morons who roam the streets of my parish.

The way I see it, I am being cruel to be kind. It saves time and karma on all sides. I have had enough of the flimsy arguments of the evangelicals, their feeble pleading and beseeching, seeking my membership for their church, chapel or sub-sect thereof, but I do not wish to be unkind. They are happy in their delusion and I have no illusions that rational debate will deprogram them. So I have given up on the confrontation and nowadays politely shake my head and mention 'religious differences' as my reason for not 'sparing a few minutes'. Cease your bleating in my ear, I am not interested; I do not want to hear. I am getting old and not exactly being a candidate for eternal life after death, I feel my time is too precious to waste.

Don't get me wrong; my mind unlike my door remains open. Within reason. As the idiocy of extreme relativists prove, if your mind is too open your brain falls out, spludge to the solid ground beneath your feet, whence the relativist finds its solidity is more than just a preconception of western prejudice. The claims of scientists are more valid than those of your friendly neighbourhood witchdoctor. But I digress.

We will prey for you!

At university earnest members of the Christian Militia often pestered me. (I must have one of those faces.) Always eager for fresh blood engaging in a little innocent chit-chat before somehow or other always bringing the topic round to Jesus (not so difficult: after all he is supposed to be everywhere!) A nod, a grin or anything less than an outright "FUCK OFF!!!!!!!!!!" and they would be off. Telling you about how fantastic Jesus is and all the fun you have when he's your friend.

A helpful aside: I understand how it is when you have such amazing news that you just want to share it with everyone. It was like that when I won the lottery, I wanted to tell every one, (it was a roll-over after all) but I kept it to myself and ultimately that was far more rewarding!

Jesus loves me (but he hates you)

I found their youthful enthusiasm for smiling stupidly, singing songs and CS Lewis highly unappetising. We had nothing in common; their idea of heaven was my idea of hell, and there was always that small point that I did not believe in God. But I egged them on anyway.

I took a childish delight in forcing them to admit to me that they thought I was going to hell. These happy-clappy moon-faced loons who wanted to be my friends were backed into admitting that I was going to burn in hell. Otherwise nice people, who more than anything wanted to share they joy they felt, to love me like they claimed Jesus does, were forced at the same time to concede that he doesn't like me that much after all.

It is easy to do. Butter them up a bit then innocently ask the familiar child's question "If I live a good life but do not believe in God, can I still go to Heaven?"

There are two responses

a. Yes - whence you reply 'Fantastic! No point wasting time in church then!', finish your drink and skip off happily to find your real friends.

or

b. No (it will be b, trust me!) - whereupon you wind them up further. Gleefully wondering aloud if theirs really is a God of Love, and if so it is hardly Infinite Love or Infinite Mercy. Why, if Jesus died for my sins, can I not go on committing them? Why does an eternity of pleasure or pain get allocated on the evidence of the blip of three score years and ten? By the end of your evening they WILL hate you!

Wouldn't you have thought that eternal life is sufficient reward for the faithful? Not happy with the flock you already have, you always want more. For some highly irrational reason there is more joy in heaven over the one repenting sinner than the 99 good Christians. (Look it up, it's in The Book and being so, of course it must be true.)

And what was my sin exactly? It seems I could lead an exemplary life but if my omission is not to be sufficiently grateful by not worshipping God (or not in the appropriate fashion) then, it appears, choosing not to believe is sufficient grounds for Eternal damnation. If those ARE the rules then I would prefer not to keep the company of such a petty deity. (God's love appears to be far from unconditional.)

Besides if Big G. does get more delight from repenting sinners then the more I sin now the greater the delight will be if I ever really repent. (There must have been angels dancing in the ethereal aisles when Jeffrey Dahmer & Robert Mugabe joined the throng. How sad that Hitler & Stalin went unrepentant to their deathbeds.)

As an optimist with nothing to look forward to but the heat death of the universe I am disinclined to preach to anyone. But while we are all sitting here on this small slimy stone spinning through space we might as well try to be polite to one and other. Let us rock and let us roll but if you are going on to the heavenly after party, go it alone. Leave me behind; I would only hold you up. It is the journey that interests me, not the chimerical destination. I would be too inclined to dawdle along the way; pick up rocks, catch bugs, ask questions (& we know how much the evangelists hate that!)

So any evangelists out there: leave me alone, keep your Good News to yourself, restrain your pity; it will only rub vinegar in the wound. Forget about me, I am sure you have enough problems of your own.

CHAPTER FIFTEEN
WEMBLEY

They think it's all over..
– Kenneth Wostenholme, Saturday 30 July 1966, commentating on the FIFA World Cup Final between England and West Germany held at Wembley Stadium

Only forty-five thousand people had seen the event.

But not before they had spent an average of two hours waiting in queues to be told their lives were passing them by. They had paid between twenty and two hundred pounds to be told not to let people tell them what to do and think. It is not known how many of them were aware of this irony. Besides a certain amount of queuing was inevitable. It is impossible to fill an arena as large as Wembley stadium quickly.

And, for someone who until two months before had been a complete unknown, it ought to have been impossible to fill it at all. But all the original thirty thousand tickets to John Smith's one-off show had sold out in less than two hours. A new licence was applied for and another fifteen thousand tickets were sold the next day. But that, it was emphasised would be that. This was a one-off show, never to be repeated. The chance of a lifetime.

Not all those attending were so keen to see John but by some Machiavellian manoeuvre worthy of Colonel Tom Parker, Eric had managed to book DeathStar as support.

DeathStar were a noise-metal band with two lead guitarists, two drummers and a reputation for spectacular pyrotechnic live shows. At that moment, they were the biggest, loudest band in America and as luck would have it none of the band were currently in jail or rehab. They had never played in Europe before. They were due to tour next year, if they could acquire the necessary safety permits and if their lead guitarist lived that long. By fair means or foul, Eric had managed to short-circuit the usually tortuous negotiations and got permission for them to perform. By even more amazing magic, Eric persuaded them to appear second on the bill behind some limey they had never heard of and who was just going to stand there talking.

Before the show, John had been quite nervous but standing back stage watching while DeathStar screamed through their blasphemous and pornographic set had taken his mind off it. It was too hard to think through that level of noise and you needed to keep your wits about you, in case a discarded guitar flew in your direction.

DeathStar went mad. The crowd went mad. DeathStar screamed. The crowd screamed. DeathStar's lead drummer set the rhythm drummer's drum kit on fire and the crowd cheered. DeathStar's rhythm drummer pissed on his drum kit to put the fire out and then threw a tom-tom at the bassist. Half the crowd watched more hesitantly. Half the crowd cheered more wildly.

The next song began with the fight still carrying on. Somehow the musicians were able to play and hurt each other simultaneously. It was one of the things that made DeathStar famous and widely unwelcome. By now, the two guitarists were getting involved and the singer was encouraging the audience to throw things at them. Fortunately for Wembley's insurance there was nothing heavier than plastic bottles within easy reach, although a few enterprising idiots threw their shoes. This seemed to disappoint the singer, who went off to join the fight, singing all the while.

Some of the audience wanted to get involved too and tried to climb on stage in order to dive off it again. But the scowling security staff seemed to be winning that battle.

The violence reached screaming pitch and the music did likewise. The two drummers had abandoned their posts entirely and were wrestling to what seemed like the death. The two guitarists circled each other like cage-fighters, screaming at each other. The bassist was screaming at someone or something that no one else could see, swatting about his head with his guitar. The singer's voice, never melodic at the best of times, now cracked even further, as he collapsed to the ground in spasms. It was impossible to tell if he was laughing or crying.

Then it was over. The speakers went silent and the stage was plunged into darkness. Those at the front could see that the band members barely noticed. The audience applauded. They stamped and screamed to fill the void in the noise. Hoping that the show would go on. But the lights stayed off and dark burly shapes came onto the stage to drag away the band.

The audience weren't sure what had happened but they wanted more. Their loud demands went unanswered and eventually died out in embarrassment and disappointment.

DeathStar didn't do encores. Not when they weren't top of the bill.

The house lights came up and something more recognisably

musical came over the PA.

They were a hard act to follow. The interval dragged on. John waited for as long as he could before stepping out on the stage.

He started simply enough with a recap of his story so far. What it was that had got him here. The audience all knew that already. That's why they were here too wasn't it? They wanted something new. They listened with one ear, waiting to be entertained. John tried to turn up the pace.

"Today we have learnt that it is best to treat this life as if it's the only one you get, because, you never know, it just might be! Fired up with this precious knowledge, we should never squander another moment. Boredom is a crime against existence!"

Though in the minds of 30,000 people it was a crime he was committing right now, John was anything but bored. He was terrified.

"Let us not bother with small talk, never again sit through some dull film, board-meeting or medical procedure. Let's be reckless, remembering that we may be hit by a bus at any moment and that would be it, but take more care crossing roads for the same reason. We should live as Godless heathens because God couldn't really expect us to do otherwise. Besides, I have plenty of time left to be one of those who repents too late and is merely destined for purgatory.

"Wait."

Half a minute passed.

"That was half a minute. How many thoughts did you have in that interval? It would take you a long time to reconstruct all of them and even longer to even attempt to explain them to someone-else. Your own thoughts are an efficient shorthand, you use to negotiate through the sum total of your history.

"And yet, that was only half a minute. There are nearly three thousand of these in every day and each one is just as long. Where have they all gone? What were you thinking?

"At the corner of my road there is a twenty four hour funeral service. Yes, people die at all times of the day and night. But while I can see how you might like an ambulance to get to you quickly, once it is too late for an ambulance, it is too late for anything"

This was going wrong. John was delivering the speech but the audience weren't really enraptured.

"No-one can be in that much of a hurry once they are dead. It is the living wanting to remove the evidence of their own impending demise. But that's wrong. We need to face death every day if we want to get the most out of life."

That's went something really went wrong.

It must have looked great on the big screens on either side of the stage. From the moment the gunman had climbed on stage at its far left hand edge, the cameras had picked him out. A sharp-witted producer had flicked the pictures onto the leftmost screen. The gunman cut a stylish figure in black and white, sporting an eye-catching golden crucifix round his neck and an eye-disguising caricature mask over his own features. This grinning Prime Minister appeared to have climbed out of the audience carrying a silver and black assault rifle that he had inexplicably got past security.

The audience at the front left could see straight away that this man was on stage. It took a little longer for those further away to figure out that this was not some stock shock footage taken at another time. The people at the front left could also see the panic spreading through the crew. They panicked too.

John Smith had not noticed any of this. He was in the flow of his speech. Right in the middle of a really good bit about how people should stop and look around them.

"We are blind to the really interesting things going on in front of our noses and deaf to.. " he was saying just as he heard the gun go off.

Anyone with the wherewithal to make it onto the stage at Wembley armed with a semi-automatic assault rifle would probably have made sure to learn how to use it first. Sure enough, the gunman was putting in a workmanlike performance. He did not shoot from the hip, but had taken the time to bring the gun up to shoulder height and take aim at his target before firing. He had sighted Smith along the barrel and let out three or four sharp bursts of fire in his direction.

He need not have bothered. The first burst was sure to have done the job. It had found its target. Smith's chest exploded with red and he was thrown backwards by the force, his body twisting round and sprawling to the floor. The second and third bursts mostly hit the air where Smith had been before smashing into a bank of unfeasibly large stage monitor speakers that DeathStar's lead guitarist Bloomberg Necessity claimed he needed to create that unmistakable DeathStar's sound. These exploded spectacularly as if this was all in a day work[*]. For the benefit of those in the cheap seats, all three screens now showed this scene.

Perhaps pleased with these theatricals, the gunman turned towards the audience and let out a joyful burst of fire. He was still careful with his aim and no-one was in any danger as he fired out and over their heads at the roof. Nonetheless, it caused a panic. People were screaming and running for the exits. The gunman was not interested. Already, he had turned his back and could be seen walking to centre stage in his workmanlike fashion.

He was lost for a moment as he passed behind an equally large bank of speakers stage left, which DeathStar's other lead-guitarist, Exploding Peter, insisted he have to be able to hear himself feedback over the din of Bloomberg Necessity's competing axe-work. The gunman came up to where the body was lying. Again he raised his gun and at kicking distance he fired down at what was clearly an already very dead body. Each shot sent up sent up shocks of red blood and caused it to jerk and twitch spasmodically. This was not a residual sign of life but Isaac Newton's Laws of action and reaction coming into what was Smith's life once again.

The reaction of the audience followed more closely the laws of Charles Mackay. The crowd went mad. Some screamed helplessly fixed to the spot, some screamed while trying desperately to get away. Some turned to run, some ran but not wanting to risk taking their eyes off the stage they ran backwards. They tripped over others who had curled up into balls. Many others further back, who felt there was relative safety in numbers, pushed forwards for a better look.

On stage the Prime Minister was waving his shiny assault

---

* And working for DeathStar this was not outside the bounds of possibility.

weapon above his head, Hezbollah style. He made his way to the vacant microphone.

"See what happens if you don't pay attention?" He shouted, clearly a bit over excited.

He fired his gun into the lighting rig causing a light shower of sparks and glass to spread from the South East. It quickly cleared as he finished the last of his ammunition.

"I told you!" He told them.

Gripping his gun by the barrel, he hurled it, Hendrix style, at the nearest available stack of amps. After the recent pyrotechnics, it made disappointingly little noise. It is doubtful whether DeathStar would have approved. Perhaps running out of things to throw or other ways to show his anger the still smiling PM removed his heavy crucifix and threw it after his gun.

"I don't know why I bother!" He shouted, obviously bothered by something.

He cast about himself chaotically for a moment as if unsure what to smash next. Finding nothing he pulled his mask off.

All three screens caught the moment. And the audience became even more confused when they saw the face of the man who had just been gunned down. It was Smith standing up there in front of, smiling and very much alive. The quicker of the crowd realised that they had just been victims of an Extraordinary Unpopular Delusion.

It had been a con trick.

"That was all faked, but perhaps you are now awake! Thank

you and goodnight!" he shouted to them before the stage lights all cut quickly to black.

The house lights came on and the security formed a visible and secure line in front of the stage in case the audience got angry at being tricked. They didn't, they were too relieved, too confused. To help defuse any tension, "Always look on the bright side of life" started playing over the Wembley PA. It seemed to help and the audience shuffled out in a somewhat subdued fashion, some of them still sobbing to themselves.

CHAPTER SIXTEEN
HA HA BONK

XX.
Ah! my Beloved, fill the Cup that clears
TO-DAY of past Regrets and future Fears-
To-morrow?--Why, To-morrow I may be
Myself with Yesterday's Sev'n Thousand Years.
– Edward Fitzgerald, *The Rubaiyat of Omar Khayyam*, 1st Edition

The Sheraton Mayfair was a tall building. A hideously ugly relic of the nineteen seventies ruining the skyline of the otherwise extremely elegant area of town. The fabulously rich and chic residents in its shadow had long ago learnt to pretend it was not there. That there was not some thirty-odd story concrete monstrosity spoiling the Georgian charm of their privileged postcode. Equally rich and chic visitors to London would also like to stay in the heart of marvellous Mayfair but having just arrived on an over-night flight from New York, Los Angeles or Dubai, they had not had time to develop the necessary selective attention. The simple solution for them was to stay in the one place in Mayfair where your view was not ruined by this monstrosity, namely at the Sheraton Mayfair.

John's room wasn't just on the thirty-third floor. It was the thirty-third floor. For some reason, Eric had installed him in the presidential suite. Parnell had turned up at his last hotel mid-morning to evict and upgrade him. As they drove across a couple of very expensive postcodes, Parnell explained that Eric was concerned for John's safety and privacy and didn't want him staying anywhere that the press or anyone else could find him. He was checked into the Sheraton just before noon under an assumed name.

Parnell had accompanied Mr Clive Smith to his room, all 100 acres of it. He had told John that Eric did not want him to leave and then disappeared, taking a tour of the place to see it was safe. Eric, it seemed, was finally taking the death threats seriously. Eventually Parnell was satisfied that there were no assassins and left for good. Leaving John a prisoner until morning. Albeit in an open prison with room service, no guards and as many extra pillows as he desired but a prisoner nonetheless. Not that he wanted to escape. He had no home to go to and there did appear to be someone trying to kill him.

He tried and failed to relax. None of the very many sofas and chairs seemed quite right and he didn't want to mess up any of the beds. Several times he got out his phone to call Natalie to come over and join him but he was too nervous about tomorrow. The show would be on at ten AM and it would be live.

John hated mornings and he hated Sunday mornings even more. But the Sunday Show was always on a Sunday and it was always live. They weren't going to make any special exceptions for him.

No more than they had already made. Eric appeared to have called in quite a few favours to make this happen. The Sunday Show was the country's most respected and highest rated current affairs show. It was broadcast on the BoCorp satellite network but such was the stature of its presenter, Patrick Rodero, that it pulled in a wide audience and regularly set the political agenda for the week to come.

Any politician with big news to break or a reputation to

recover tried to get a spot on Rodero's sofa. He did not give you an easy ride but if you survived that, you generally survived whatever crisis had brought you there in the first place. The opposite was equally true.

Tomorrow, however, Patrick Rodero would not be on his own show. God knows how or why Eric had done it but tomorrow's edition would be hosted by Shona. And it would not be a one-on-one interview but a live three-way debate between John, Hazel and the Right Reverend Donaldson Cake.

John had never been on live TV before and had never had to defend his own ideas to an audience more challenging than the clientele in White's nightclub. He hadn't been in a debate since junior school when he had unsuccessfully tried to stop Stevie Wonder being thrown from a metaphorical balloon.

He spent all afternoon pacing about talking to himself. Trying to work out what exactly it was that he was defending. At about 6pm he had given up trying to do it sober and made himself large rum and coke. There was no ice.

He thought of calling room service but thought better of it. He could not face another obsequious servant scampering around after him. He had called down a couple of times for room service to bring him up a club sandwich or fruit basket or whatever. They never merely did what you asked but would scurry round the place smoothing beds, emptying ashtrays and scooping up as much detritus as they could carry. It was positively tiring to watch, especially when there was absolutely nothing for them to tidy up. Wanting only a couple of ice-cubes for his rum and coke, he did not want to re-roll that whole rigmarole. Instead he decided to take his life in his hands and pop out into the corridor to forage for it himself.

So John left his room on the thirty-third floor, which in the Presidential suite was harder than it sounds. The suite took up almost the entire top floor, and as best as he could tell consisted of five or six interconnecting bedrooms, hallways, living areas and one (or possibly more) kitchenettes. Many movable partitions (some of them electric) increased your disorientation and behind every second or third door was yet another en-suite bathroom or walk-in wardrobe. After a few futile minutes hunting the hallway that lead to the lift, he gave up and made for the fire escape. With his glass in hand, he pushed open the door to the fire escape stairwell and went down to the floor below in search of an ice machine.

Disconcertingly, in the fire escape he could smell smoke. It was only cigarette smoke. Probably one of the valets had ducked in here for a crafty fag. He walked down the lino-covered back stairs, about the only part of the hotel not bedecked with either thick cream carpet or (like the lobby and his many bathrooms) dangerously slippery marble. Clearly guests were not meant to be here, unless the time came that they had to stop being the rich and pampered, who travelled everywhere in private jets, limousines and express elevators and became just another couple of people fleeing a fire. Turning the corner to the second half of the flight down, he saw someone sitting on the final step, a cigarette in one hand, and a small tin ashtray in the other. At the same moment, the grey haired woman turned round to acknowledge him.

"They won't let me smoke in my room. Do you want one?" Doctor Cole said by way of explanation of her presence.

"Thanks, I don't smoke."

"Good for you."

"I am looking for ice." John gestured to his drink. Hazel

shrugged and went back to her cigarette. John stepped past the seated figure and back into the hotel proper on the 32nd floor. He got lucky. Right next to the fire escape was a small utility area with two parked valet's trolleys and a humming ice machine. It was the first thing he'd seen since he'd arrived that looked like it had been there since the 1970's. John reached a hand into the frosting interior and retrieved a handful of cubes.

He took a refreshing swig and, for a moment, he stopped worrying about his problems. Not much more than a moment. His second swig nearly choked him when halfway through it he realised whom it was he had passed on the stairs.

A couple of minutes later he had recovered and stepping bravely into the fire escape saw that she was still there.

"Hazel Cole." She said putting her tin down and rising from the step to offer her hand.

Smith shook her extended hand, somewhat bewildered. "Yes, I know. I'm John Smith. Hello."

"I know. Bit preoccupied?"

"Yes."

"Me too. Hence these," she said indicating her cigarettes.

There was a silence. John tried to think of something to say, Anything... Anything... Nothing.

"I like your approach to the Hard Problem." Hazel said.

"The Hard Problem?"

"It's what the philosophers and neuroscientists call the problem of consciousness. They do not know the answer and yet they know that they are extremely clever so therefore it must be a very hard problem."

"I've no idea what you are saying but I feel ridiculous having this conversation in a hotel stairwell. Would you like to come up to my floor? You can smoke as much as you like up there."

Hazel followed John back up the stairs and soon they were seated in highly luxurious but slightly awkward silence.

"Tell me a joke." Hazel asked

"Okay. Er... Why do the Scot's get cancer?"

Hazel waited.

"Because they deserve it." John delivered the punchline and realised, not for the first time, that he should not have told the joke. Hazel wasn't laughing but, after a moment's pause, a small smile flickered across her face.

"It is a bit sick," she said "But I guess that's the point? Is that what makes it funny?"

"I'm probably not the best person to ask."

"What with being a heavy smoker and, well.. other stuff.. I could have completely failed to see the funny side. But it was obvious that you don't mean it."

"Yes," said John. "You did ask me to tell you a joke. That's my favourite. Not many other people like it though."

"Do you tell that on stage?"

"No, it's not mine. My own are not as good. It is not the done thing as a comedian to tell other people's jokes. Not that I'm a comedian anymore.. or ever was, I guess."

"No."

"Now I'm doing *this*. Whatever this is."

"I can relate to that," said Hazel. There was another awkward silence

"Would you like a drink?" John asked. "I've got most things. Can you believe that instead of a mini-bar, there is an actual bar? Madness. It still has the giant minibar prices though."

"Red wine, thank you."

John selected the dustiest looking bottle he could find, something French from 1971. This would probably cost Eric several hundred pounds but John had got used to spending other peoples money, and feeling like his life could end at any moment he no longer bothered to worry about what would happen when Eric discovered. He filled a glass for Hazel. He had a quick sniff to check that this ancient liquid was still drinkable. It smelled extremely drinkable so John discarded his over-strong Rum and coke and poured another glass for himself. He handed approximately one hundred and fifty pounds of fermented grape juice to the visiting clinical psychologist.

They decided to cost Eric another six hundred quid.

"I am worried about tomorrow. It is television, they set things up for conflict," John said.

"No one can make you say anything you do not want to. And the same goes double for me. I have even wondered if they want me to do what they do not want me to. Shona's producer keeps going on about how different and refreshing I am."

"I know what you mean I spent nearly three years trying to give people what they wanted. Provide a full comedy package. As soon as I start being myself and saying my own thing I am unwarrantedly famous. That, and being Eric's marionette."

"I do not like Eric Hayle," said Hazel.

"Nowhere near as much as he dislikes you. He really, really hates you, though I have no idea why. I can understand why do not like him after what he writes about you."

"It is nothing to do with that. Sticks and stones and so forth. There is just something about him that reminds me of the worst kind of psychopath. I have seen a lot of men like him locked up in Broadmoor, Ashworth and Rampton."

"Oh, he's not that bad. He can be rude and aggressive but he is charming too. And I honestly do not believe that story about him pushing his editor off a tall building."

"I do not know anything about that but most psychopaths are charming. They are manipulative. They are also completely without remorse or consideration for others. They have no empathy. They are impulsive and addicted to risk taking."

"That does sound like Eric," John admitted. "But let us not talk about tomorrow any more. We are still here and now. I am enjoying tonight."

"Me too. Cheers," Hazel said, realising that she was actually having fun.

"Cheers. Tell me about yourself. Are you married?"

This threw Hazel. For forty years almost as soon as anyone found out she was a psychologist, they would wish to lay out their problems for her to pass judgement on or else get defensive and strongly deny that they had any problems whatsoever (which often told her far more than people's self serving confessions ever could). Almost never did they ask about her personal life. Unless they flirting and this charming, disarming young man could not be doing that, could he?

"My husband died in nineteen ninety five. Though his life ended about a year before that. He had a malignant cancer, he was fighting it but it caused him a massive stroke and his last year was spent in a semi-coma in intensive care."

"I am sorry. How did you cope?" John asked leaning closer. He genuinely was interested in talking to her. Her hand went instinctively to her hair, brushing it away from her face.

"It was traumatic. When it had just been the cancer he was still himself, he was positive and enthusiastic and doing everything his doctors recommended. All I had to do was trail along behind him supporting him. After the first stroke he broke up, only fragments of his mind remained. His memory vanished, the world confused him.

"He could understand speech but he could not produce it. It was as if he knew what he wanted to say but could not find the words. He would point and look meaningfully at you but all he could say was "That one, that one." When he was tired he would even forget 'Yes' and 'No'.

"If I had not known him for thirty years I would have been as lost as the doctors and nurses usually were.

"After the second stroke, I do not think there was anything left of him at all. I did my grieving of his still breathing body. At the end when he died, it was just a huge relief."

"So you have been alone since then?"

"I tried dating again but nothing ever felt right. Even the word sounds wrong to me. Colleagues set me up with a few blind dates. Not good. It makes you wonder how other people see you."

"Did you worry?"

"I didn't give myself time. My last few years of work were the busiest of my career. You reach a certain seniority in your field and enough people know your name that you automatically get invited to sit on all sorts of committees and attend tons of conferences. In the year after Andrew's death I threw myself into everything that came my way. Saying yes whenever I was asked. A year or two after that I was involved in all manner of projects."

It may have been a rich complex and exorbitant wine that deserved to be sipped, savoured and favourably compared to freshly cut grass, with praises sung for its camphor high notes and its long, long legs admired. But it had simply tasted so warm and delicious and was so easy to drink that they finished the bottle before it even occurred to them to commence penning odes to its nose.

Unused to the effects of uninhibited drinking Hazel became uninhibited and wanted to drink some more. John offered her the joint that he had inexpertly rolled. She politely declined.

After a lifetime working with people with drug problems and others for whom doctors decided that even more complex drugs were the solution, Hazel had an ambivalent attitude to recreational drug use. Her general feeling was that proscribed drugs were bad but prescribed ones were okay. If you got it from a bloke in a hoodie it was not good but if it was from a white-coated pharmacist then it must be okay. John was neither but she didn't pop pills and she didn't smoke dope. Though maybe it might be better than all these cigarettes.

She had another wine instead. John had one too. Still feeling self-conscious, she changed the subject and started asking him about his life. He was less screwed up than she had been expecting. If pressed for a professional diagnosis, she might have even said he was sane. Though at no point in the conversation did her inner therapist want to intervene. They were just chatting.

She was having to do more of the talking. The drugs were making John somewhat dopey, making it ever more difficult for him to find his words. In the end, he seemed to have given up looking for them altogether and just sat there staring at intently into her eyes. She hadn't been this close to anyone in a long time. It was disconcerting, unfamiliar but not unpleasant.

She was only half surprised when tried to kiss her. She evaded him easily enough. He started laughing. She had to smile herself. And have another large mouthful of wine. She realised she was blushing. She reached instinctively for her handbag. She needed a distraction. She needed a cigarette.

She fished on out and brought it to her lips. John was still watching her. She knew she should probably go. In the back of her own mind, she could hear herself telling herself so. But she was drunk and she was tired of always doing what she told herself to do. She didn't have to go just yet.

A week ago she had been having dinner with the wife of the Prime Minister and she had been bored out of her mind. She hadn't been bored once yet this evening. With a weird detachment, she watched herself put down her cigarettes and pick up the half finished joint instead.

She could answer to herself in the morning. But now she having fun, thank you very much.

Eleven minutes later, they were naked.

INTERMISSION
THE LAST QUESTION

Here we are in the final interruption. I promise.

People waste their time being entertained by cheap and obvious films, by books that are nothing more than a chain of flimsy set pieces, strung out on an ordinary plot and mildly enlivened with forced jokes, puns and similes so bad they would embarrass the manufacturers of Christmas crackers. At least I hope you are being entertained. You've read this far.

How many times can people sit through the same film, the same episode of some nineteen seventies 'classic' sitcom, or worse a season of repeats of an American sitcom where every episode is essentially the same?

People have no sense of occasion. The greatest day of their lives was when their side beat another side in some sporting fixture. It is not difficult to create your own magic moments. To stop waiting for it to be handed to you on a plate by some sportsman, film star, musician or bartender.

Yes, these thrills are tried and tested, and can be shared, but it is a little more difficult than that to obtain some authenticity.

Look at how hard it is for people to turn off their televisions.

You might get carried away by the stories they feed you but what truly do you get out of it?

Not much more than the distraction from the passing of time.

Your life is ticking away and you do not notice.

Maybe I get bored too easily.

Why do we feel that getting through a day of work is an achievement enough? That an evening in front of the television is a well-earned and worthy reward?

Reward for what, for having avoided having to face up to the inevitability of death? Of embracing life's futility and accepting that this is as good as it gets?

There is no rush to reach death but would it matter if it arrived tonight. We have been living by proxy anyway, letting all the really exciting things happen on the screen. Let adventures be nice and clean, life simplified.

Straight off the page we find lives that we have the subtlety to understand and relate to. We are all inside Hamlet's head but we cannot look so clearly at our own internal monologues. They are mostly disjointed daydreaming and self-deceiving self-justification.

We are even worse at reading the minds of others. We think we know the thoughts of others. We pigeonhole our friends according to the simple labels. He is shy, she is judgemental, he is selfish, and you are so thoughtful. We see these 'characters' acted out by a thousand hams, who themselves think they have a handle on how it all goes. But it is another form of language, a vocabulary of personality.

Yes, it comes close but this is not definitive, as soon as you assume that you are in tune, that they are playing only one melody that you will always hear.

The arts are good when they are creative, when they represent things you could not have guessed at yourself, remind you that you did not know everything and suggest new things to know.

There will always have to be a neat ending.

The worst bits are the endings; they never resist the opportunity to tie things up, to tell us how it all should be.

The Bible has a good ending, or the gospels do, Matthew, Mark, Luke and John all end their books in an unsatisfying incomplete way. I like it. They leave a lot hanging, ending on an inverted deus ex machina. The sky comes down to Earth and God vanishes up into Heaven, off the stage, never to be heard from again and leaving nothing explained and everyone wondering. Is He coming back? When can we expect Him? What should we do in the meantime?

What a wonderfully ambiguous way to end an otherwise unremarkable story. Why did it end like that? Why could they not have been more clear?

And for two thousand years, people who know better than you (they must do because they said they do) have offered explanations. They have tried to tied the ends up neatly into a social and political package that involves a lot of unquestioning obedience and a long time on our knees.

The best ending is the one that admits our own stupidity. This takes us back to the story of Socrates. I think the story of Christ ought to be one like that of Socrates but ends up looking more like that of Santa Claus.

Belief in Santa Claus is a 'good thing' for children, it makes them happy and maybe even makes them less naughty and more nice (for a few weeks in December at least). As such, it is a lie adults are happy to perpetuate, but none of them choose it for himself or herself.

I think there is a strong parallel to be found in many of the liberal apologies for religion.. 'it isn't necessarily true but it's good for society', 'my own faith is complex but churches shouldn't confuse people with subtle points of theology' .

Socrates on the other hand was the Clint Eastwood of early thinkers. The first person to say "A man has got to know his limitations."

Socrates was one the first people to come up against this question. Someone went to the Oracle at Delphi, and asked who was the wisest man around. The answer was 'Socrates', and this deeply vexed the great man when he heard of it, for he was well aware of his own shortcomings. But being a simple trusting fellow he did not for a moment consider that the Oracle was mistaken. It was after all the most reliable Oracle around.

So Socrates set himself the task of discovering why he was the undisputed heavyweight thinker of the time. (And this was before Plato's hour in the sun, so there was in our historical opinion some justification in the appellation.) What was more, if he was indeed the wisest of men, then he should, if anyone could, discover why.

After much thought and discussion on the subject, Socrates came round to the Oracle's way of thinking. (That is, if Oracles can think, which, probably being almost omniscient, they have little need to do.) He reasoned thus: "I, Socrates, know nothing. That is I know that I cannot be certain of anything, and this is the only thing I know. It must be this that makes me wise, and what is more other men must be ignorant of their own ignorance, making them, by the judgement of the Oracle, doubly ignorant. The fools. Right that solves that I think I will go off and corrupt the young with these fashionable theories, and with any luck cause a political storm resulting in my own martyrdom to my cause and bestow upon myself certain, if dubious, immortality. "

What happens is you are not paying attention to what is going on, really paying attention. Now that I think about, that is going to be hard work. You have a drunken conversation with someone and if you agree that you will both endeavour to achieve some grand dream. Yet when you wake up the next day so many more drinks later although the idea remains a good one you are not interested. Tipped over into hangover, you skip over that part of the night. You remember it clearly enough but you are embarrassed by your former enthusiasm. You cannot fathom where it came from because right now you could not care less if your entire family was being threatened with death.

Sartre said that Hell is other people. It goes without saying that Heaven is other people too. Life is other people.

Morality is like inertia. A single object alone in an empty universe feels no inertia. There's nothing to compare it to, to be able to tell where it is going or how fast. Add another thing and then there are relationships between them. But it's different every time. It's only when you add a whole universe that inertia becomes a universal property.

Morality is the same. It doesn't exist because of God, It isn't decided by a single expert. It's the emergent property of a whole load of people trying to get along. If you deny morality you are denying humanity. If you invoke God, so be it. But you are just another man.

Or to look at it a different way, is morality absolute or relative? Does it precede the existence of people? Or is it a consequence of who we are and how we live? Let's say it was absolute and one of the rules was that killing is wrong. Would killing be wrong in the world populated entirely by ants? Are the ants sinning? You may say yes. I say, good luck trying to convince the ants.

We think killing another person is wrong because they are another person. Morality derives from understanding that we all share something that

This is a little bit simpler than the Golden Rule which states "Do as *you* would be done by." The trouble with that is that relies on *your* predilections.

This is more like a Crystal Rule, "Do as *someone* would be done by." It has crystal clarity because it is empty of *you*. But it is also like a crystal ball, you have to peer inside and imagine a morality that works for some unspecified person. The Crystal Rule is shot through with uncertainty and ignorance. You have to decide what will be done *before* I tell you who that someone is. In fact, philosopher John Rawls' said we could call this the Veil of Ignorance argument. Imagine yourself reincarnated into a society run by your rules. Would you still feel it was fair? Ideally, it has to be just as fair to a millionaire as to an orphan with AIDS. Not surprisingly, Gandhi was a big fan.

But even if Crystal rule is an abstract starting principle. Morality doesn't involve one rule applied to everything. It's everything your society has ever learned. The Ten Commandments with ten million amendments. It is every bit of advice you have ever received and every bit you've given to yourself or others. There isn't a shorter answer than that.

Remember Gyges? He's still stuck in that room. There's that button on the desk. If he presses it a distant stranger dies but

Gyges gets £10 and is free to go, safe from any punishment. Gyges seems to be taking a long to do the right thing so it's time we helped him out. It's pretty easy, all he has to do is remember that there is a world outside that door. Let him take a step back and ask who has put him in this tricky situation?

If he believes that a God or a Devil has placed him here then his choice about the button ought to be easy enough. In fact, the same goes for any third party. He should do the right thing, knowing that whatever he had done he was sure to have much bigger problems once he goes outside. The real problem here is very little to do with the button. It is about working out what 'they' expect of him and whether they've really given him any real freedom at all.

But, more often than not, we get ourselves to these messes. Gyges most likely put himself in this situation. He is welcome to my advice but ultimately, he has to make a choice for himself. He may find it difficult to discern the 'right' answer. But I will tell him this for nothing acting on my advice only is certainly wrong. If he can't look around him at everything and see that some things are wrong and some things are right, then he must have been living in a box.

CHAPTER SEVENTEEN
SHOWDOWN AT THE TOP OF A TALL BUILDING

Happiness is not a brilliant climax to years of grim struggle and anxiety. It is a long succession of little decisions simply to be happy in the moment.
– J. Donald Walters

• * ¢ Ψ ? †

The BoCorp broadcast headquarters was a very tall building; a large glass and steel skyscraper that had recently won some architectural award as the best tall glass and steel skyscraper constructed since last year. It was a very boring building, fifty storeys tall with a square floor plan. The architects had won the prize because they had the revolutionary idea of rounding off the corners of that square cross section and rotating the panes of glass that formed it's ground to sky curtain-wall through forty-five degrees. Instead of the usual endless sheet of square panels, the BoCorp building was swathed in endless sheet of diamonds. These award winning windows were a tasteful shade of pink.

The obvious phallic appearance of the building was not missed by its many critics.

Eric's sleek black helicopter came into land on the frighteningly small heli-pad that shared the roof with half a dozen satellite dishes, some large cooling units and space age window-cleaning machine. The man saw it from four hundred feet below where he was about to enter the building. The man knew the signs of conspiracy. He knew that Black Helicopters meant that 'THEY' were here; 'THEY' were involved in this situation. It only steeled his nerve. He walked up to the building's reception and was directed past the security guards to the express elevators.

The forty-second floor of a modern office building is the very last place to put a television studio. The ceilings are too low. There is no space for all the cabling and soundproofing. There was no dedicated sub-station for the large power requirements and not enough ventilation for all the heat from the lights. You would never put a television studio on the forty-second floor of anything.

The fact that so many people had told him this was reason enough for Yegevny Swan to insist that this is precisely where he wanted the main studio of Mercury satellite news. As the most powerful man in the Eurasian broadcast market, Yegevny Swan was used to getting his own way. Today Yegevny was in Saint Petersburg but that was only 100 milliseconds away by fibre-optic cable, if anyone needed reminding of that fact. But he wasn't expecting any more protests. His staff were used to agreeing with their leader and doing whatever it took to keep him happy.

Its many critics did not miss that the bland and one-sided reportage of the Mercury News Network was broadcast from a rose-tinted building. The only person with any independence at MMN was Patrick Rodero and the only program with any integrity was the Sunday Show. At least, that is how it had been last week.

If the Mercury News Network staff thought it strange that Eric Hayle was being given control of their flagship program, they kept these thought to themselves. They didn't want any trouble.

Parnell had a philosophy about troublemakers, they would be making it wherever they went and so were easy to identify by challenging them and asking a few simple questions about the purpose of the visit. Your typical troublemaker would often not be able to help himself and answer such an inquiry with a question of his own, already intent on starting a confrontation. More sophisticated nuisances with a degree of self-awareness would be more defensive and attempt to avoid the question. Everyone else generally took it at face value. The man had sailed straight past Parnell. Knowing in this own mind that he was doing 'Right', he had barely registered the professional suspicion Parnell had sent his way. So Parnell had no reason to suspect that the man was carrying a gun. He also had an official audience ticket so Parnell directed him into the guest reception area.

The man was singing as he went,
> *A mighty fortress is our God,*
> *A bulwark never failing;*

He seemed to have not a care in the world.

The floor manager had plenty. The show was due to start in 25 minutes. A show that he was responsible for, though he hoped he wouldn't be held responsible for what was clearly going to be a total disaster. Apart from the floor manager and his team of four cameramen, four runners and assorted technicians, everyone else was a stranger to the studio and everything was being done differently from the normal Sunday Show format.

First there was Shona. She had brought her own producers and her own make-up artists. She had insisted that there was a live studio audience. She had rearranged the set for her and the three guests. Three guests! They never had three guests.

Then there were the guests. Amateurs to a man, woman and priest. Dangerously unpredictable amateurs who apparently all hated each other. He sent his assistant to check that they hadn't started the fireworks too soon.

And finally, Eric Hayle was somewhere around here too. Lest he forget. Hayle had not been much in evidence so far today. But if Yegevny came looking for anyone to blame, the floor-manager would be first to denounce Hayle. Not that he could see that happening. Whatever Hayle had on Yegevny, it had to be huge to be worth all this. Blackmailing Russian oligarchs shouldn't even be possible. Especially not someone like Swan, who had absolutely no shame. The floor-manager couldn't begin to imagine.

If a genie appeared right now granting him three wishes that would be the first thing he'd ask. Then he'd ask to be taken as far from here as possible. He closed his eyes and reopened them. The nightmare continued.

John was alone in his dressing room when the runner popped his head round the door.

"Dr Cole?"

"Last I saw her, she was going to try and meet some of the weathermen," said John.

The morning had been slightly awkward, of course, but he didn't have any regrets. He didn't think Hazel did either. They had both been more worried about all *this* than all *that*. This was the first moment of peace he'd had since waking up. He thought of Natalie. He was glad she wasn't here but as soon as this was over, he wanted to go straight to her. He needed that peace.

"Live in ten, nine, eight, seven, six" If it wasn't his own voice he could hear, the floor manager wouldn't have believe they had made it this far. He wasn't much more than spectator from here onwards. He had got everybody to his or her place; he had got the show rolling. If anything went wrong from here, it was someone-else in the firing line.

The man was clearly mad. Certainly he had no sense of drama. He didn't even wait for Shona to finish introducing herself before he took out his gun and advanced on his target.

Mercifully for John, he was not aware of the man coming towards him with a gun until it was too late. The shot was fired; he did not see it coming and had no chance to move. It may have been this that saved his life.

The man's shot had been wildly inaccurate and if John had moved there was more chance he would have ducked into the path of death by lead. In fact, the bullet had sailed past him and spoiled the scenery instead.

"John!" Hazel had reacted faster, she had seen the man get up and start moving towards the stage. The moment she had seen the gun in his hand, already coming up to aim, she had cried out. Her call came too late to change fate with the first shot but split seconds after it, she called out again.

"John! Drop the gun!" John Smith did not drop the gun but it drooped as he turned to see who was shouting at him and second shot buried itself in the studio floor.

"Oh hello Doctor Cole. How are you?"

"I am good thanks, John." Hazel stalled, looking for clues as to how to handle her former patient. Her mind trying to untangle this man from the dozens of others with similar conditions. Aware too that time would have changed his diagnosis, his demeanour and his demons. "And how are you? I hope you are still taking care of yourself? Still taking your medication? That is very important, you know?"

"No, I couldn't. I stopped" the man said sheepishly. "The troxies were confoxing me. They stopped me being me. I could not see clearly, I was missing what was going off, missing my mission. I needed freedom from dem Demons."

"You are off your dopaminergics?"

"I was confoundulised before but not no-more, nosiree. Gabriel's instructions are touching my mind gland and his beams are guiding my holy hand." At this the gun swung up, aiming again (mainly) at John Smith. John Smith the impostor, the false Smith, prophet of nothing.

The False Smith had overcome his perceptual and volitional blockage. But, perceiving his predicament, had chosen to remain motionless.

He was not alone (though that is how he felt). Around the studio no one else knew what to do. Since this woman appeared to be taking charge and that man was unpredictably firing a gun, most of the other people in the room who had not made a break in the initial confusion, were resigned to waiting to be told what to do either by the woman or the man. They were acting innocuous, trying not to draw attention or draw fire.

Shona was half collapsed on the sofa and Reverend Cake was stuck to the spot. He was not praying. Prayer to him was a public show of faith, and an essential element in the appearance of piety. It was for Sunday best, for standing in front of the congregation, looking out over their heads mouthing the words and checking their faith. Right now, he was trying to remember where it was that he had seen the gunman before.

In the wings Parnell had seen what had happened and though he still had his wits about him, nothing in his 17th Century T'ai Chi training was appropriate for tackling a schizophrenic armed with a World War II pistol. Nevertheless he edged onto the more brightly lit studio floor.

John with the gun was shaking quite badly, though he wasn't in the least bit nervous. Long-term use of dopamine retarding anti-psychotics had given him pronounced muscle shakes.

Eric, also in the wings, had always been a man of action and he was also a World War II veteran He even had medals but 'hero' was too simplistic a label to apply to his case. He had been at both ends of the barrel of a Luger 49 and he knew exactly how many bullets this one ought to contain. He had been keeping a careful count and creeping closer to the action. Mainly to get a better view.

"What are you doing here, John?" Hazel asked the man. It was a risk to draw his attention back to the current moment, but she counted on his habitual need to explain his mania. It was obvious why he had attached his delusions to the image of this other John Smith. But she had only the vaguest of ideas about why he might be trying to decide to act in this way. His brain being the way it was now, he would not have any coherent picture either but he might allude to something that she could make into an escape from his delusion and if nothing else it bought time. (For what she did not know.)

Eric had been right. Being shot at concentrates the mind

wonderfully. Right now John's consciousness was focused in a tight ball, oblivious to everything but the small dark ring of the barrel of the Luger, still smoking slightly and being waved erratically in his approximate direction.

"Camera Four stay on the crazed gunman, Camera Four?"

Camera Four was pointing at the ceiling. The moment he had seen the gun, cameraman four had dropped to the floor and started crawling under the audience seating scaffold.

Camera One had been the first person through the fire escape, his headphone lead bounding along behind him.

Camera Three was getting a good shot, his position was more exposed than One or Four and making a break for it was more dangerous and keeping the camera between him and the gunman was the best way to stay unshot.

Camera Two appeared to have a death wish, he was not watching the man at all, and he was doing his job. Getting reaction shots. There were plenty of those.

"John, why are you doing this?"

"He told me to," the man answered, waving his gun indistinctly.

Always a man with a guilty conscience, Reverend Cake denied it immediately. He was in no position to know that Smith was not gesturing at him but at Eric, who was advancing onto the set.

True enough, Eric had given the Luger to Smith, but he was not about to admit it. In fact, for once Eric wasn't entirely sure what he was going to do. All he knew was that he wanted to be in the middle of it all.

John stood facing John. The former comedian was staring down the barrel of the gun. Here he was facing death in front of an audience. Granted it was a little more serious this time but weirdly it had felt much worse the last time. He froze and then there he was in the moment again. A speech started forming in his mind. He was prepared, he was ready. He had three months to practice it and this time it would save his life. Searching for the first word his eyes flicked around the room.

He wasn't on stage. He wasn't alone versus an anonymous audience. Everyone in this room was in this together. The gun was pointing at him but that did not make him the centre of attention. Maybe he could help himself but he did not have to. Others could help him too. Hazel knew these men, this type of man, this man. He said nothing.

Hazel started again. "John, listen to me."

And he probably would have done too but right then Eric had turned to Hazel and had shouted,

"Oh shut the FUCK UP!"

The man jumped. The gun went off.

Parnell jumped. The man went down.

It all went very quiet.

His breathing was weak now. Less and less oxygen was getting to his brain, the pain ebbed but perception clouded too. His vision narrowed to a long, dark, tunnel, his hearing muffled and his sense of his body left him, space folding up around him. But he could no longer think clearly about it, about anything. It was a fight to remain conscious to make each thought catch the train of the last. In some dim way, he sensed peace beyond the striving. One last thought passed through his brain. "I guess this was my own fault."

With that Eric let go.

EPILOGUE

> Tomorrow, and tomorrow, and tomorrow
> Creeps in this petty pace from day to day
> To the last syllable of recorded time;
> And all our yesterdays have lighted fools
> The way to dusty death.
> Out, out, brief candle!
> Life's but a walking shadow, a poor player
> That struts and frets his hour upon the stage
> And then is heard no more; it is a tale
> Told by an idiot, full of sound and fury
> Signifying nothing.
> -- Shakespeare, Macbeth, Act 5, Scene 5

There was not a lot more to it than that.

They all lived happily ever after.

After the shooting incident, the police were finally able to connect the dots which placed John Smith at the wheel of the rogue Routemaster and at the window of the Other Smith's flat, throwing a four pint milk carton of four star in to start a fire in his living room. Admittedly, the details had been spelled out for them in large tabloid headlines by journalists who were quicker off the mark and who did things for the front page, not by the book. Vernon Associates never mentioned to anyone that they had known all this for several weeks.

The community at large had once again been found wanting in its ability to care for the dangerously mentally ill. John "God's

Gunman" Smith was returned to a secure mental health unit. He was locked away out of harms way for his own safety, but not his well-being. Forced to take his meds again, his more florid symptoms abated and he became the calm, train enthusiast he sometimes was.

Eric miraculously survived the shooting because no first time author can bear to kill off their favourite character. Everyone believed that Eric Hayle had given the gunman the gun. But there was no proof. It was just the word of a single madman with a doctor's certificate versus a multi-millionaire psychopath with criminal lawyers.

John "The Tao of Now" Smith, remembering Hazel's description of classic psychopathic lack of remorse and having seen the ruthless efficiency of his lawyers, did not try to take Eric to court or even to task. John shrugged off the fact that Eric had tried to kill him as just one of his little character quirks. He continued to collect regular royalty payments but moved on with his life.

He shambled into a very predictable career, appearing on the B-list and writing for the Sunday supplements. He didn't mind too much. Natalie listened better than any audience. She appreciated him far more too.

Hazel Cole, reawakened as a sexual and emotional being, and a newly converted fan of recreational drugs, headed off on an extended holiday to India, Thailand and beyond in search of sun, sex and chemical fun. She travelled by train.

APPENDICES

Appendix A – Recommendations to the panel on Reassessment of Risk

Report on John Smith by Dr. Hazel Cole, 17th February 1991

Smith has been in the secure unit for seven years following an aggravated assault motivated by religious mania. At the time he was suffering an attack of acute schizophrenia, manifesting symptoms of paranoia, thought disorder, delusions of persecution and of grandeur.

Currently, Smith has several complex and interacting pathologies and many insecurities carried over from an unhappy childhood. His schizophrenia has been in remission for five years, following successful management with chloropromazine. He has previously suffered episodes of epileptic attacks, linked to a focus in his temporal lobes.

The regime of drugs he takes to control his epilepsy restricts the range and effectiveness of the anti-psychotics he may take. Tricyclics have been effective in the past but following an extensive neurological examination, it was the opinion of the case psychiatrist that this treatment should be stopped.

Appendix B –
Suitability for Special Operations

TOP SECRET - EYES ONLY

+-+-+-+-+-+-+-+-+-+-+-+-+-+

REPORT OF 17-FEBRUARY-1941

TO: GORDON FOWLES, HA-WOCS

FROM: DR. F.P.R.VIONI M.D.

MEMO: PSYCHOLOGICAL ASSESSMENT OF ERIC HAYLE

INTERVIEW WITH E.H. TOOK PLACE 21-FEB AT WAR OFFICE, WHITEHALL.

E.H. WAS ON TIME AND ANSWERED ALL Q.'S FULLY AND SUPERFICIALLY POLITELY THERE WAS A UNDERLYING TONE OF INSOLENCE AND DISRESPECT FOR MY AUTHORITY.

E.H. WAS ARTICULATE AND INTELLIGENT (IQ 147 ON WISC-1) CREATIVE ON PROBLEM SOLVING TESTS BUT UNWILLING TO STAY WITHIN BOUNDS OF MY GIVEN INSTRUCTIONS.

RESILIENT PERSONALITY, LOGICAL IN FACE OF CRITICISM, QUICK TO ADAPT IN ROLE-PLAY TEST BUT LACKED EMPATHY.

LIFESTYLE QUESTIONS REVEALED DUBIOUS AND UNASHAMED PERSONAL CONDUCT. MANY ANSWERS SHOWED HIM TO BE CALLOUS AND UNEMOTIONAL. AT TIMES HE APPEARED TO BE GOADING ME WITH HIS CASUAL CONFESSIONS OF SOCIAL TRANSGRESSION. HE ALSO POKED DISMISSIVELY AT THE RULE OF LAW.

POSSIBLE HOMOSEXUALITY.

CLEAR EVIDENCE OF PSYCHOPATHOLOGY.

UNSUITED FOR MILITARY SERVICE.

Appendix C –
Summer term report

John Smith, Form five – Form teachers report, Summer Term 1993
John continues to drift through school, paying little attention to his work. He is a cheerful member of the class and gets by comfortably enough but he is wasting his potential. I am not confident that he will do as well as could in his GCSE's. While my fingers are crossed, I think he should brace himself to be disappointed with his results. A short, sharp shock might be just what it takes to wake him up and start taking things more seriously.

ACKNOWLEDGEMENTS

This book started very quickly. Most of it was scribbled during National Novel Writing Month (www.nanowrimo.org) in 2004. It has been finished more slowly and painfully, thanks mainly to encouragement from friends and family. Thank you Ishbel Addyman, Jake Black, Jemima Cooper, Ana Milusheva, and Róisín Thérèse. Jemima and Róisín also put in sterling, unpaid service as proofreaders and cheerleaders extra *magna gratias agens* to them.

Thank you also to all the philosophers who replied to my impertinent questions. Your answers increased my confusion and left me with questions than when I started. So I would say you have done your job well.

A huge thank you to my first English teacher, John Painter, for introducing young school children to things that people think they should not know, like Wilfred Owen and the Rubaiyat of Omar Khayyam. And to every other English teacher who ever tried to teach me anything. I did not understand it at the time. I probably still don't but it bothers me less and less.

Firstly and lastly, I must thank my dear friend and occasional dealer Mr White for providing me with some excellent *Psilocybe Cubenis* and the good people at the People's Republic of Disco for providing an amazing environment in which to be confused by them. Under the influence of these mushrooms and those tunes I understood that everything all made sense and that if you could just explain this to anyone who cared to ask then you could all get on with experiencing it. Staring at the vacant stage, I thought of a little story that encapsulated that moment of vision and clarity. I thought I ought to write it down. This is not it, but that's probably for the best.

LEGAL NOTICE

The author could not have completed this book without the support of a vast network of researchers and reference checkers. He relied on the expert opinions of many individuals all over the world; Any factual errors are the fault of the Internet.

All characters contained herein are poorly executed parodies of actual people even more poorly disguised. Any resemblance to any persons living or dead is probably real but hopefully very hard to prove in a court of law. Although all the really depressing and depraved bits are based on my own life.

To confuse things further, since I wrote this my brother Max has become a stand up comedian. But a real one with jokes and everything. matAnd those are real letters from real philosophers!

AFTERWORD

Schizophrenia, psychopathy and all forms of mental illness are very real and can be very destructive to their sufferers. They are painful and confusing for all involved. All the more reason to joke about them. Anyone who thinks that laughter trivialises the serious is trivialising laughter. Either that or they are in serious need of a laugh.

Despite the implications of this work of fiction, schizophrenics are no more violent than anybody else. You might also bear in mind that the delusions and confusions of the disease are, to the sufferer, very real.

The author is proud to support www.madpride.org.uk

ABOUT THE AUTHOR

Caspar Addyman has a Ph.D. in developmental psychology. By day, he is a professional infantologist, studying the growing minds of tiny babies. He is interested in what makes them laugh and tick. By night he runs YourBrainOnDrugs.net; an internet and smartphone based research project about your brain on drugs. At the weekends, he drinks, dances and sometimes even sleeps. He lives in London.

www.onemonkey.org

Made in the USA
Charleston, SC
29 April 2013